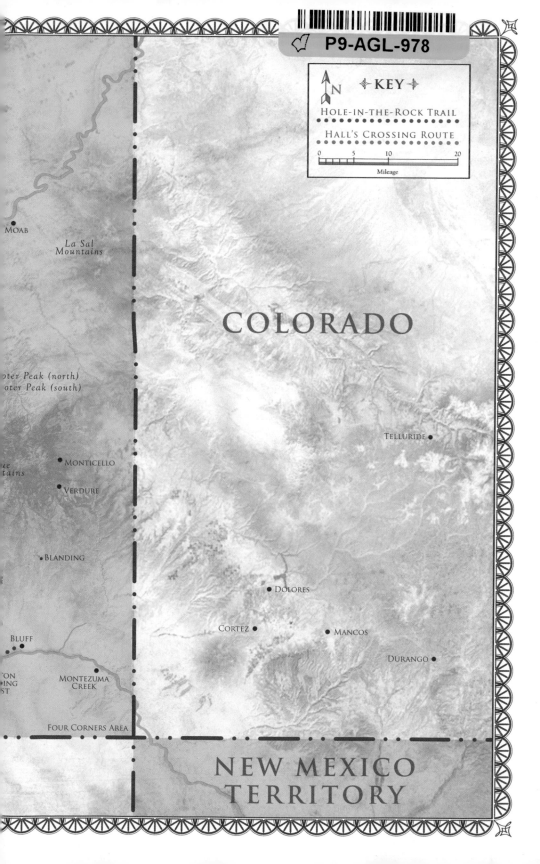

KEY

N

HOLE-IN-THE-ROCK TRAIL

HALL'S CROSSING ROUTE

0   5   10   20

Mileage

MOAB

La Sal Mountains

...oter Peak (north)
...oter Peak (south)

COLORADO

TELLURIDE

MONTICELLO

...ue ...tains

VERDURE

BLANDING

DOLORES

CORTEZ   MANCOS

BLUFF

DURANGO

...TON
...ING
...ST

MONTEZUMA CREEK

FOUR CORNERS AREA

NEW MEXICO
TERRITORY

ONLY
THE BRAVE

ONLY
THE BRAVE

THE CONTINUING SAGA OF THE SAN JUAN PIONEERS

GERALD N. LUND

DESERET
BOOK

SALT LAKE CITY, UTAH

© 2014 GNL Enterprises, LP

Library of Congress Cataloging-in-Publication Data

Lund, Gerald N., author.
   Only the brave : the continuing saga of the San Juan pioneers / Gerald N. Lund.
     pages cm
   Includes bibliographical references.
   Summary: The story of the Mormon pioneers who settled in the San Juan Region in Utah.
   ISBN 978-1-62972-026-5 (hardbound : alk. paper)
   1. Mormon pioneers—Fiction. 2. Frontier and pioneer life—Fiction. 3. San Juan County (Utah)—History—Fiction. 4. San Juan County (Utah), setting. I. Title.
   PS3562.U485O55 2014
   813'.54—dc23   2014036885

Printed in the United States of America
Lake Book Manufacturing, Inc., Melrose Park, IL

10 9 8 7 6 5 4 3 2 1

PREFACE

A Change of Characters

I feel like I need to clarify something for you, the reader, before you begin this book. While you will find the same *historical* characters in this sequel that you met in *The Undaunted*, you will not find any of the *fictional* characters from that book here. I am sure many readers will wonder why. It is a valid question, so let me explain.

The Undaunted: The Miracle of the Hole-in-the-Rock Pioneers was published in 2009. It is the story of the men, women, and children who were called to leave their homes in established settlements throughout Utah to go the Four Corners area of southern Utah. Their purpose was to build stable communities there. Theirs is a story of fortitude, valiance, sheer grit, and undaunted determination. What they did is an inspiration to us all.

To help tell that story, I created two fictional families. The first was the family of John Draper, a coal miner from Yorkshire, England. The other was the family of Patrick J. McKenna, a prosperous businessman in Cedar City, Utah, who immigrated to America from Ireland as a young boy. David Draper and Abby and Molly McKenna, children from those two families, are the lead characters in *The Undaunted*. The book closes with the marriage of two of those characters shortly after their arrival in Bluff, Utah, in the spring of 1880.

In *Only the Brave,* I introduce two new families—the Westlands from Beaver, Utah, and the Zimmers from Richfield, Utah. Both families are longtime members of the Church; both are called to join the San Juan Mission in southern Utah several years after the pioneer company first arrived. The Westlands arrive in the early summer of 1884, four years after the founding of Bluff. The Zimmers come a few months later.

But why? some will ask. If this is a sequel to the Hole-in-the-Rock story, why not just continue with the characters we know and love? There are a couple of answers to that.

One of the things I most enjoy in writing fiction, particularly historical fiction, is the creation of characters who become like actual people to me. Over the years, as I have told their stories and followed them through various circumstances, they have taken on lives of their own. Then, as have I listened to readers tell me which characters they particularly like, I have come to learn that the characters *should*—perhaps even *must*—take on lives of their own if they are to be worth caring about.

What I mean by that is this: as I develop my characters, I find that they often surprise me with what they do. I'll start them going one way, and suddenly, it's as if they're saying, "Wait. I would never do that. Stop trying to push me in a direction I don't want to go."

I know, I know. They are the creation of my imagination, so I should be able to make them do whatever I want, right? But it doesn't work that way for me. They become so real that I feel I have to be true to who they are and not who I originally planned for them to be. And I've learned that when I let the characters play out their own stories this way, they become more real for readers as well.

I'm not alone in that feeling. One novelist said, "When my characters are out of control, I know that everything is fine. In many ways, the novel is smarter than the writer if you're working at it right" (James Crumley, in *Deseret News*, June 18, 1995, E-6).

So while I came to love working with John and David Draper and Patrick, Sarah, Abby, Molly, and Billy Joe McKenna, I decided to leave them to their own lives and introduce new lead characters to you in this book. The historical characters that figured so prominently in *The Undaunted* are still here— Jens Nielson, Ben and Hyrum Perkins, Kumen Jones, Platte D. Lyman, and the incredibly brave women who came with them, but the Westlands and the Zimmers will take over the role of carrying the story forward in *Only the Brave*.

I came to this approach with *The Work and the Glory*, my first attempt at historical fiction. We followed the Steed family through nine volumes, beginning in Palmyra shortly after Joseph Smith's First Vision and ending when the pioneers finally arrived in the Salt Lake Valley. My originally intent was to carry their story all the way forward to modern times. In fact, I even publicly stated on several occasions that I planned to write a volume ten to do just that.

That proved to be a mistake. When I started to write a final volume, it was as if I hit a brick wall. I couldn't make it work. For a while, I couldn't figure out why. But the more I thought about it, the more I came to realize that the arrival of the Latter-day Saints in the Salt Lake Valley in 1847 really ended what we might call the Restoration period of the Church's history. The fundamental doctrines, organization, and policies of the Church had been established by this time. By 1847, the Church had a new prophet, a new home, and new challenges. And as I thought about taking the Steed family into that next stage of Church history, I felt as though the Steeds were saying to me, "Look, you've told our story. Thank you. Now, go tell someone else's story and leave us alone." So that's what I did.

I didn't stop telling the story of the Church's history—I just didn't do it with the Steed family. In *Fire of the Covenant*, I wrote about the handcart Saints, especially those who came in the Willie and Martin companies in 1856. Maggie McKensie and Eric Pederson took over as the lead fictional characters in that work. Then the McKennas and the Drapers took over when I decided to tell the story of the Hole-in-the-Rock pioneers in *The Undaunted*. I say all of this only to show that a change of characters is not new to this volume.

A Different Story

A second reason I decided to use new characters in *Only the Brave* relates to something that happened after *The Undaunted* was published. To be honest, I'd had no plans to write a follow-up volume to the story of the San Juan Mission. In my mind, the "real" story of the San Juan Mission was the incredible journey those pioneers made, which was so unfamiliar even to people like me who were born and raised in Utah. When those Saints finally reached Bluff in April of 1880 and said, "This is where we will stay," that was the end of the story in my mind.

But then the third- and fourth- and fifth-generation descendants of those early Saints started challenging that decision. They were thrilled, they said, that someone had finally told the story of their grandparents and great-grandparents. "But," they would say, with considerable passion, "that was *not* the end of it. What happened as they stayed on to fulfill their mission is equally fascinating, equally compelling, and equally inspiring. You have to let people know the rest of the story."

By that time I was on to other projects and pushed those thoughts aside, though the idea intrigued me. But it didn't let up. More people kept asking about another volume. So I started doing some research. I went back to Bluff several times, but I also started looking into the stories of other settlements in the region: Monticello, Blanding, White Mesa, and so on. It didn't take long for me to see that these descendants were exactly right. April of 1880 did end one aspect of the San Juan story, but what ensued in the years that followed is equally, if not more, incredible. It required tremendous faith, unwavering courage, and unrelenting determination to carry out their calling.

That is the genesis of *Only the Brave*—which explains why you now have a sequel to *The Undaunted* but doesn't really explain why I excluded my previous fictional characters. Normally, sequels carry on with the same main characters. But the more I thought about it, the more I saw that while the settlement of San Juan County is a continuation of the Hole-in-the-Rock story, it is, by its very nature, a very different story, and would require very different characters.

In *The Undaunted*, we emphasized that these early Saints had been warned of the challenges they would face when they got to the region of the San Juan, which was filled with lawless white men, hostile Indians, and vast isolation. Three metaphors were used by Church leaders in describing the role of the Saints going south:

- They were to become a *buffer* between the white man and the Indian.
- They were to be like the *shock absorbers* on a wagon, which soften the blows for those riding in the wagon, or in this case, those in the other settlements.
- They were to be like a *lightning rod*, which draws down the fires of heaven upon itself so they do not consume others.

And that's when I saw it: as difficult as that six-month journey across the desolate red rock country of southeastern Utah was, those who made it never once faced any of those three metaphoric challenges during the actual trip.

But once they got to Bluff, they learned in rapid order that the metaphors represented reality. They faced new challenges, new trials, new adversities—many of which were even tougher than anything the actual journey had thrown at them. And that's when I decided I wanted to start with new characters. I wanted this story to begin with those who followed, those who crossed a road already blazed across the wilderness. I wanted them to be people who came to an established fort and a settled community but almost instantly were smacked in the face with what they were called to be—buffers, shock absorbers, lightning rods—as well as with what they were called to do.

And there was something else, too. I began to sense what a profound influence these hardy pioneers had on their children, grandchildren, and great-grandchildren. In other words, I realized that their story continues on through the rising generations. I began thinking about continuing that story as well. But if I was going to do that, I decided, I needed new characters that I could develop through the decades that were ahead of them. So I decided to start with new lead characters.

My apologies to the Drapers and the McKennas. It's not that they couldn't have done it. It was just that I wanted to introduce new elements early in this story that would explain how the San Juan pioneers became who they became. It would have seemed contrived and forced to put these elements into the Drapers' and the McKennas' lives. So I bid them farewell and started anew. My only hope is that you will quickly fall in love with our two new families as they carry the story forward.

Some Practical Matters

In writing historical fiction, it becomes necessary to have fictional characters interact with actual historical people. That creates several dilemmas. I am committed to being as true to the historical sources as possible. However, a novel requires a lot of details that are rarely found in historical sources. I have tried to resolve those dilemmas in appropriate ways.

In describing the day-to-day lives and events of my fictional characters, I sometimes included names of people who would likely have been present but are not named specifically in the historical records.

I sometimes wanted to share dramatic or amusing stories that were experienced by known people, but I wanted to place them in the context of the novel. In those cases, I have the fictional characters experience the events and then indicate in the notes whose account it really was.

In many cases the fictional characters interact with promi-nent men and women in day-to-day activities. In those interac-tions, I strive to be true to the realities we do know about real people. For example, Bishop Jens Nielson, who served as bishop in Bluff for over twenty years, gives a priesthood blessing to one of the novel's fictional characters. Obviously, that is not "true history," but I believe it is "true to history" because we know he gave blessings on a regular basis.

Many dates are as given in the sources, but many of the personal stories and insights into daily life are not dated. I have tried to put them in the story close to the time they actually occurred, but they may sometimes be off by a year or two.

I have sought diligently to be true to the times, events, and known character of those wonderful pioneers of the San Juan Mission. I am astonished at who they were and what they did, and I seek only to honor them and their accomplishments. If I have erred in that effort, the fault is mine and not theirs.

Indian Matters

The indigenous peoples of North America were called "Indians" for centuries because Christopher Columbus and other early explorers thought they had reached India. From earliest colonial times, they were also commonly referred to as "savages" or "primitive peoples." Some early colonists who were more sympathetic to the natives referred to them as the "noble savage," which is only slightly less demeaning. Those terms have obviously come to be considered offensive, and to-day even the name "Indians" is often deemed incorrect, with some people preferring instead "Native Americans," "American Indians," or "indigenous peoples."

Members of the The Church of Jesus Christ of Latter-day Saints are taught that all people are children of God, and there-fore the pioneers viewed Native Americans as their brothers and sisters. Brigham Young taught his people that it was better to feed the Indians than to fight them and called on the pioneers to befriend and serve them. They lived among three major tribes: the Navajo, the Utes, and the Piutes. While there were renegade Indians who fought the Mormons and all other whites, most of these tribal peoples had a good relationship with the Mormons.

The pioneers used the cultural terms and language of their day. They most often referred to the native peoples as "Indians." They called their women "squaws" and their young children "papooses," and these terms carried no offense. In a similar manner, when they later described interactions with the Indians, they quoted what seems to be the simple pidgin English that many of the Indians had learned to speak.

Many of the Indians named in the novel have anglicized names, such as Mike, Jack, or Toby. Undoubtedly, these were names given to them by pioneers who found their real names difficult to pronounce and remember. But that is how they are identified in the historical records, and so that is how I refer to them.

All of this created a dilemma. A historical novel should reflect the language of its own time and culture, but much of the terminology used in the 1880s would be offensive today. To resolve that dilemma, when I as the author talk about the native peoples in narrative or descriptive sections, I try to avoid anything that might give offense. However, when the pioneers are speaking or when readers are given insights into the pioneers' thoughts, I use language that reflects how they spoke and thought.

PROLOGUE

The San Juan

The people who came to explore and live in what is now southern Utah, where vast blocks of earth were thrust upward to form great rifts, immense plateaus, and scattered mountain ranges, gave it many names. The Navajo called the area *Dee-nay-tah,* "the land of the people." John Wesley Powell named it the Colorado Plateau. Then, when invisible lines were drawn on maps to define states and territories, it took on yet another title—the Four Corners region.

On July 24, 1847, Brigham Young arrived in the Great Salt Lake Valley with the first company of members of The Church of Jesus Christ of Latter-day Saints, or Mormons. Tens of thousands followed. The new arrivals were sent out in every direction to establish settlements.

The Mormons decided that the one lasting solution to make a successful life in this highly volatile area was stability. Stability meant families, homes, towns, farms, ranches, businesses, law, civil order, religion, and faith.

And thus it was that in April 1880, about 250 Mormon settlers, who had left their homes in the more settled parts of the territory, arrived as families to the region of the San Juan in southern Utah. They came to build, not to destroy. They came to befriend the natives and live side by side with them.

No one was naive enough to think that this would be an easy thing. None of them expected to be welcomed with open arms. In fact, when they called these families, their leaders used three metaphors to describe what their role was to be:

They were to act as a *buffer* between the whites and the Native Americans.

They were to be like the *shock absorbers* on a carriage.

They were to serve as a *lightning rod.*

It was spring when their wagons rolled into the flatlands along the banks of the San Juan River. Sheltered by bluffs on both sides of the river, the settlers let their wagons roll to a stop. Their first task was to build a fort, and then they built cabins around it. They called it Bluff Fort. Soon another metaphor was used to describe it. They called it "The Fort on the Firing Line."

CHAPTER 1

As he sat looking down at the river below and the ferry on the far side, Joseph A. Lyman, known to everyone as Jody, saw the cloud of dust a short distance downstream and knew instantly what it was. The dust mostly hid the men, but there was no question whose horses those were. Once again Lyman's party had caught up with the men they were after, and once again they were too late.

⁂

When the call came for families to go to the San Juan, Jody and Nellie Roper Lyman, his bride of just nine months, decided to go. Their leaders had specifically asked for young couples to add their strength to the company. They were sobered by the challenges but excited to be part of something larger than themselves.

Jody removed his hat and wiped away the sweat from his forehead with the sleeve of his shirt. Now he wasn't so sure this had been a good idea. He glanced at his two companions. Lemuel H. Redd Jr.'s family had run cattle out west of Cedar City. Now he ran cattle in the land of the San Juan. Like Jody, Hyrum Perkins, who had been a coal miner in Wales, was now a farmer. Jody pulled a face and corrected himself. Normally they were farmers. At the moment, they were a posse.

About a week ago, two cowboys had come into Bluff. Like so many of the cowmen in the area, they had a look about them that caused women to step back into their houses and hiss at their children to come quickly. The larger and older of the two men was named Bob Paxman. The younger called himself Dickson. First name or last? It didn't seem to matter. They claimed to be looking to purchase horses from the Mormons, but their questions about where the herds were kept and how many horses there were raised suspicions. Two days later, a rider came racing into town from Butler Wash, a deep and wide gully that served as pasture for their horses. Ten horses were missing. The tracks led west toward Escalante, the next established settlement, which was 125 miles away.

This was a serious blow. Horses were the settlement's lifeblood. The loss of even one animal was a serious matter. Jens Nielson, the bishop of Bluff, had called Lyman, Redd, and Perkins in and charged them to go after the two outlaws and get their horses back.

Now in his sixties, this patriarch of the group was much beloved and much honored, so there was no question about answering his call.

Two hours later, their saddlebags were packed and their bedrolls tucked in behind them.

Lem Redd ran his cattle in this wild, red rock country, so Lyman and Perkins deferred to his judgment and experience.

"If we hurry, we can catch them before dark," Hy observed.

Lem shook his head. "That's the last thing we want to do. They know we're back here, and they'll lay an ambush in the canyon for us if we push them too hard. We'll sit awhile with the Hall brothers. Give them a couple of hours head start. Maybe have some grub."

Jody replaced his hat and grinned. "I could live with that."

When the three men from Bluff told Charles Hall and his brother, who ran the ferry together, that they had just helped across two horse thieves and about ten head of stolen horses, they were furious. But there was nothing to be done for it, so the three riders sat for a spell in the deep shade of the gorge and rested themselves and their mounts.

·⁂·

It was about four o'clock and the three Bluff riders were probably three miles up the canyon from the ferry when Jody, who was in the lead, pulled up. He half turned and waved the other two forward. As they joined him, he inclined his head to the left. Here another road forked off from the main one. It wasn't as wide or well-traveled as what they were on, but it was wide enough to take a small herd of horses. "This must be that new shortcut Charles told us about," he said. He looked at Lem. "Which way do you want to go?"

Redd dismounted and walked slowly forward, examining the ground. There was plenty of evidence of horse and wagon traffic in the main canyon, but with so much sand, it was hard to say which of the tracks were the most recent.

Lem finally looked up and pointed up the main canyon. "I'm pretty sure they went this way. If Hall's right and we hurry, we can maybe get ahead of them and lay a little ambush of our own."

Lem got back on his horse. "Let's go slowly and as quietly as we can," he said grimly. "We can't assume they didn't see this, so we could be walking straight into an ambush."

At the moment, the two thieves, Paxman and Dickson, were both thinking one thing. Twice in the last two days they had seen three riders trailing them in the far distance. They had to either shake them or get rid of them before they reached Escalante. Otherwise, this whole deal might fall apart. Paxman suddenly spoke. "I'm tired of it," he exclaimed.

"Tired of what?" his partner asked.

He stood up in his saddle and looked ahead, and then pointed. "See that spot under them cottonwood trees? Let's stop the horses there. Won't take that much to loop a rope around them and secure them for a while."

"What fer?" Dickson asked.

Paxman growled in disgust. He had already determined that the minute they sold the horses, he was dropping the kid. He swore. "Dickson, you are dumber than a rock stuck in six inches of mud. Ain't you tired of having them three dogging our tails? I say, let's end it. Now."

Dickson, for once, was in full agreement. As they tied up the horses and started back down the canyon, had they looked up the road about forty or fifty rods, they would have seen where the shortcut road rejoined the main route. But they weren't looking that way.

It took Lyman, Perkins, and Redd only about twenty minutes to traverse the shortcut. As they approached the junction with the main road, they slowed to a cautious pace. All three had their pistols out. Suddenly Lem pulled up, holding up a hand to stop the others. He put a finger to his lips and slid out of his saddle. The other two then heard what Lem had heard—the soft whinny of a horse. Then another. Using hand signals to communicate, the three dismounted and crept forward. When they saw the horses tied in the trees, they suspected a trap. They crouched down, searching the willows and bushes for any sign of their two enemies. Hyrum Perkins, moving like a cat, circled around and came up from behind the horses. After a minute, he gave a low whistle. "They're not here. Their own horses are tied up behind me and there are boot tracks headed back down the wash. I'm guessing they've gone to set up an ambush."

"That's gotta be it," Jody agreed. He didn't add that if they hadn't decided to take the shortcut they might be dead by now. "So?"

Lem grinned. "Well, we got our horses back. I'd love to take these two back to face the law, but I don't relish that idea much. I say we take the horses and make a run for home. Take their mounts, too, so they can't follow us. Leave these two rattlesnakes for the buzzards."

They moved the horses slowly until they were about fifty rods from where the side canyon rejoined the main one. Lem, still in the lead, held up his hand, turning in the saddle. "It's most likely they've set up their ambush site above the turnoff, since we didn't see them. But we can't be sure. So, Jody, Hy, I'll take the lead. You drive 'em hard. And stay low in the saddle. Don't give those two bushwhackers a chance for a clean shot."

"You say when," Hyrum called.

"I say now." And he spurred his horse forward. Shouting and waving their lariats, Hyrum and Jody drove their horses up behind the herd. Snorting and whinnying, the ten horses leaped forward into a hard run.

In the desert, where about the only things that make any noise are the wind, the jackrabbits, and the lizards, the sound of more than fifty iron-shod hooves clattering on gravel was right up there alongside summer thunderstorms for getting someone's attention.

In the rocks, Paxman and Dickson were both half asleep. They had been there for nearly an hour, and the afternoon heat was still stifling. Paxman leaped to his feet, instantly alert.

Dickson snapped up, eyes wild. "What? What's that?"

Paxman cocked his head to one side. Then he started to curse even as he grabbed his rifle. "Horses! A lot of them! And coming fast." He spun around to look up the canyon. But immediately he realized that the noise was coming from downstream, not from behind them. He whirled back in time to see a man on horseback bust out from the undergrowth about two hundred yards down the wash. He turned down the canyon, and the herd wheeled and followed him.

Paxman jerked his rifle up and almost snapped off a shot, but by then, the narrow canyon was filled with horses and clouds of dust. He swore again when he saw two horses with empty saddles flash by. "They got our mounts!" he shouted over his shoulder.

Dickson's eyes were wide and confused. Moments later, two more men appeared with the herd, half obscured in the clouds of dust. They were riding hard and bent low over their saddles. Paxman fired a shot, knowing there was not a chance of hitting them. Moments later they were gone, disappearing around the next bend.

"Let's go," Paxman yelled, levering a new shell into the

chamber of his rifle. He leaped down and started after the horses.

"Wait," Dickson shouted, turning to look up the canyon. "What about our horses?"

"They've got our horses, you stupid idiot. They've got our bedrolls. They've got our food. And if they get across the river before we catch them, we're buzzard bait."

Lem Redd turned the herd upstream toward the ferry as they came out of the canyon, but then he pulled his horse aside and stopped. When Hyrum and Jody came up, he was shouting before they even reached him. "I saw them," he cried. "They're coming. Hy, you go and help the Halls get the horses across the river as fast as possible. Jody and I will wait for these guys here. Slow them down a little."

With a wave, Hyrum spurred forward. Lem swung down and led his horse into the willows. Jody was right behind him. Grabbing their rifles, they separated so they had a view of the canyon from two different angles. "We'll not be killing 'em if we can help it," Lem called softly. "Just slow them down long enough for us to get across."

Jody waved back. For all his anger and frustration at these outlaws, he was of the same mind as Lem. They had come here to make peace. If word got out they had killed two cowboys, every cowboy within fifty miles would be coming for revenge.

"Here they come," Jody hissed about ten minutes later.

Lem saw them immediately. The bigger one—Paxman— was in the lead, scuttling from bush to bush, headed for a large cottonwood tree. Lem jerked up his rifle, steadied the barrel against the trunk of a cottonwood, and waited for the man to make his move. Paxman was only about forty yards away now, an easy shot for a marksman like Lem Redd. But as his finger tightened on the trigger, he moved the barrel slightly to the right. Paxman appeared and dove behind the tree. BLAM! Even in the deep shadow, he saw the sudden white blossom appear in the bark of the cottonwood tree. The younger man yelled and jumped behind a large rock.

BLAM! BLAM! Jody fired off two shots in quick succession at Dickson. There was a sharp ricochet as the bullets whined away.

BLAM! The answering shot was probably from Paxman, but he was shooting blindly. Then Lem saw movement again, only this time the two outlaws were scrambling backward deeper into underbrush. Lem put another round in the dirt a few feet ahead of them to let them know that they were clearly visible. Scuttling like crabs on a beach, they tumbled backward and disappeared.

Glancing upriver to where the Halls and Hyrum were loading the horses on the ferry, Lem called softly, "They need another five minutes. As soon as they're loaded, we'll make a run for it."

But even as he spoke the sound of hooves could be heard. Both men jerked around. To their surprise and dismay, four of the horses were trotting toward them, evidently spooked by the rifle fire.

"Change of plans," Lem called. "You get those four head to the ferry. I'll stand guard until you're ready."

Jody was off and running before he finished. The horses were skittish, but Jody got them turned around. As they came up to the ferry, Hy shook his head. "Sorry," he murmured. "They got away from us when you started shooting."

"No room for them," Charles Hall cried. "We're already loaded."

"Tie them to the back," the other Hall cried. "They'll have to swim across."

Jody had already turned away. He shouted, waving his arms back and forth. "We're ready, Lem! Let's go! Let's go!"

Redd pumped a shot into the underbrush as a final warning and then came on a hard run, leading his horse. "No sign of them. Let's get out of here."

As Lem tied his mount on the back of the ferry, Charles and his brother untied the flat-bottom boat, and the five men pushed it away from the bank and then jumped aboard.

For a moment it looked like they wouldn't even get off the shoreline. The five horses tied at the back were snorting in fear and dug in their hooves. Seeing that, Lem grabbed the ropes and yanked on them hard. The moment the horses surrendered and leaped into the water, the ferry moved forward and they were launched.

"Jody," Lem called. "You watch the canyon. I'll watch the cliffs. If they show their heads, do whatever it takes to pin 'em down."

No one spoke then. Charles Hall was leaning hard on the rudder, trying to keep the nose of the boat angled toward the opposite side. His brother was on one of the long oars; Hy was on the other. Lem Redd and Jody Lyman paced back and forth, watching for any sign of movement on the shore or cliffs.

"Those last horses are holding us back," Charles called. Then he shrugged, sorry he had said it. "But nothing to be done for it."

BLAM! BLAM! The two rifle shots came nearly as one.

Hyrum yelled and fell back as a bullet ploughed into the wooden seat he was on, missing his leg by inches.

BLAM! BLAM! BLAM! The barrel of Lem's rifle was smoking. "They're on the cliff!" he cried.

Jody had seen the two silhouetted figures a hundred or so feet above them just before they fired. Now they had dropped out of sight. He took careful aim. When he saw a head come up he pulled the trigger. The bullet ricocheted off the rock face with a sharp buzzing whine. The head disappeared again.

A moment later, two silhouettes appeared. They were running hard in the same direction the ferry was going. Three more shots rang out. Charles jerked down and felt a soft puff of wind brush his cheek. The other two shots kicked up water.

Jody and Lem fired simultaneously, but again their two assailants had dropped out of sight. "Keep rowing! Keep rowing!" Hall bellowed. With bullets zinging all around them and horses snorting and jerking their heads wildly, it was hard to keep the boat angling toward the shore. This time Lem didn't wait for their assailants to reappear. He fired twice more. Jody had dropped to one knee to steady himself. At the sign of the slightest movement, he fired off another round.

For the next minute or two—which seemed like forever to the five men on the boat—the firefight continued. But Lem's and Jody's answering fire was so fierce and so consistent that their enemies had no time to aim. One bullet hit the prow of the boat, but the rest splashed harmlessly in the water.

"We're almost there," Hall shouted. "And we're gonna need every hand to get the boat beached and the horses off."

Lyman was reloading his rifle and merely grunted. When he was done, he took two quick steps and leaped off the prow of the boat. He landed in two feet of water and almost went down. Scrambling wildly, he was up on the shore in a moment. Again he dropped to one knee and began firing, slowly, methodically, and with deadly aim.

Lem darted forward to the front of the boat and slid back the pole that kept the horses enclosed. With no more need to steer the boat, Charles Hall let the rudder go and jumped forward. He slapped the nearest horse hard on the rump. "Heeyaw! Git!" Eager to be off the unsteady ferry, the horses lunged forward and jumped off, one after the other. Hall's brother quickly loosed the five horses tied at the back, and they struck out immediately for the shore.

They were still under fire from the cliff top, but Jody was keeping them pinned down enough that nothing was coming very close. Then suddenly, Charles Hall was hollering. He was behind the boat, waist-deep in water, leaning into the ferry. "The current's taking it," he yelled. "Help! I need help!"

The four men leaped to the task. Hy and Lem jumped into the water to join Charles. His brother leaped onto shore and started heaving on the rope. The boat slowed, but not enough. The back was still swinging around.

"Jody," Hy yelled. "Give us a hand."

Jody fired off one last shot and then raced to help on the rope. Heaving and pulling, yelling at one another and puffing like winded buffalos, they finally got the blunt nose of the boat up on shore enough that it halted the back end from swinging around. With the exception of Jody, the men collapsed. Remembering the other danger, Jody ran toward where he had dropped his rifle.

It had taken less than thirty seconds to beach the boat, but that was enough. When Bob Paxman popped up for another shot, he was surprised that there was no answering fire. He stood and saw one figure clearly running away from the boat. This time he took careful aim and fired. BLAM!

The bullet hit Jody in the femur just above the knee, shattering the bone. His leg was knocked out from under him, and he went down hard. Clutching his leg, rolling over and over, he screamed in agony. Lem Redd had his pistols out and was firing blindly at the cliffs, but it was too late. A man was down.

***

The five of them waited in the willows until it was dark. They cushioned Jody's leg as much as possible and bathed his face with a wet cloth. Hy hovered over him and covered his mouth if he started to moan too loudly. The two horse thieves had come down from the cliffs and were across the river from them. Their voices floated to them in the night. They called across that they were willing to make a deal. The five men knew that was a ploy and said nothing. Eventually everything was quiet.

There would be a sliver of a moon in a couple of hours, but for now all they had was starlight. Lem Redd finally called them in close together and told them they could wait no longer. They had to get Jody back to Bluff or he would die. Grimly, the four men gave him a priesthood blessing and then prepared to leave.

Moving stealthily, they rounded up the horses. They wrapped Jody's leg as tightly as they dared and then lifted him onto his horse. He gave one piercing scream of agony and fainted. They all ducked down, expecting to draw fire from across the river, but nothing came. There was no way that Jody could stay on a horse, so Lem climbed up behind him. They bade soft farewells to the Hall brothers and then started out. Again, there was no response from the two rustlers.

By the time they had gone eight miles, Jody could bear no more. As gently as they could, they lowered him off the saddle and laid him on a bedroll. As soon as Jody was somewhat comfortable, Hy took two of their three canteens and headed east, taking Paxman's horse as an extra mount. His task was to cover the almost hundred miles to Bluff and return with help to take Jody home. Or to take his body, which was a very real possibility.

As he watched Hyrum disappear into the darkness, Lem Redd had little hope. Even with two horses, it would take two days for Hyrum to reach Bluff and then another two at the least to make it back. The leg was starting to swell, and Lem sensed that the unbearable pain was sapping Jody's strength with frightening rapidity.

Shortly after sunup, Lem knelt beside Jody's still form and checked for a pulse. He didn't notice when Jody's eyes flickered open. "Am I dead?" he croaked. Then, before Lem could respond, he shook his head. "Can't be. You're too ugly to be an angel."

Lem hooted. "I surely ain't no angel!" Then he sobered. "The leg's bad, Jody. Maybe swollen to twice what it ought to be. Had to slit your pant leg open to give it room."

"My wife won't like that." He managed a wan grin.

"We're nearly out of water," Lem went on. "I'll get you comfortable, and then I'm going to have to walk down to Lake Gulch. There's water there. But it's seven or eight miles round-trip. You be all right for that long?"

There was another effort to smile. "I got a longing to dance some, but I reckon I can resist it." Jody closed his eyes. Even that much effort was too much for him.

Taking the bedroll from Dickson's horse, Lem stretched a blanket between two of the bushes to create some shade for Jody. Then, using the last of their water to dampen a cloth, he laid it over the ghastly wound to keep off the flies. Satisfied that this was the best he could do, he murmured a farewell—which Jody did not hear—and set off at a rapid walk.

It took him over four hours to make the seven-mile trip. Cowboy boots made for a miserable walk, and he had blisters by the time he returned. Jody was conscious, but barely. Lem bathed the wound, which was now a bright, angry red around the torn flesh. The pain was so excruciating that Jody passed out again before he finished. Lem covered the wound again and settled down to wait. And again he bowed his head and prayed for his friend.

By morning, the leg was three times its normal size. Jody's face was a ghastly gray-green, and his forehead was hot to the touch. When Lem removed the cloth from the wound to wet it again, he gasped and rocked back. Two thirds of the leg was a fiery red now. But that wasn't the worst of it. The shattered flesh was crawling with a dozen or more maggots. Breathing through his mouth in quick, shallow breaths, Lem picked the maggots out as best he could and ground them underfoot. Then he forced some water into Jody's mouth and bathed his face, trying not to look at the bucket, which was nearly empty again. When he finished, he bowed his head. The prayer was simple and short. "O God, do not let this good man die."

It was about noon of the third day when a sound brought Lem Redd out of a fitful sleep. Jerking up, he looked around wildly, not sure what had awakened him. For one brief moment, his heart swelled with hope. Had Hy somehow made it back already? But that hope was dashed when he saw who it was. He dropped back down, clawing for his rifle. Utes, Piutes, or Navajo? That was the first question that flashed into his mind. It made a big difference. For the most part the Mormons had established good relations with the Navajo. The Utes could be more troublesome but were not in very close proximity to Bluff. If it was Piutes, that could spell real trouble. They were much more unpredictable and so desperately poor that they stole from the Mormons at every opportunity. Normally they were not violent, but there were exceptions to that.

But as the Indians came slowly toward him, Lem let out a long sigh and laid aside the rifle. They were Navajo. And even better, he recognized their leader. It was Pahlilly, a wise, old clan leader who often came to Bluff and who had been treated well by the settlers. Lem got to his feet, raised a hand, and called out, "*Yah-ah-tay.*" Pahlilly's hand came up and called back the same greeting.

There were nine of them. The men rode horses, and the women and children walked beside them.

After listening to Lem's rapid explanation, Pahlilly knelt beside the wounded man, carefully examining the wound. Jody groaned once or twice, but he was too far gone to come back to full consciousness.

The old Navajo grunted as he sat back on his heels. "He very bad. What you do for him?"

"I'm trying to keep the wound clean. Keep the flies off. And the maggots. I don't know what else to do."

"Not good," the old Indian said. He stood up and spoke in rapid Navajo to the nearest brave. Lem knew a little Navajo but didn't recognize anything he had said except for the final command to hurry. The young man leaped on his horse and kicked it into a gallop, heading back the way they had come.

"He go find prickly pear," Pahlilly explained. "We make . . ." The wrinkles on his leathery face deepened. He held up both hands and moved them back and forth in a curving motion, as if he were stroking a large ball between them. "For the leg. Help make better."

"Poultice?"

A wide smile broke out. "Yah. Poultice." He looked down at the bucket. "Need more water. Where you get?"

Turning and pointing to the south, Lem answered. "Lake Gulch. There's a small spring there. It's a long ways, but I can go and—"

He stopped. Pahlilly was shaking his head and clucking his tongue. "*Bilagáana,*" he said, half in amusement, half in disgust. It was the Navajo word for white men. It wasn't a compliment. Pahlilly turned to the other brave and spoke rapidly. The man grabbed the bucket, dumped what little water was left in it, and took off at an easy run in the opposite direction of Lake Gulch.

Lem turned to Pahlilly in dismay. "The spring in Lake Gulch is closer than the Colorado River."

Pahlilly's grin widened. "You wait. You see. Pahlilly teach *bilagáana.*"

To Lem's amazement, ten minutes later the man reappeared, walking this time and loaded down with a full bucket of water. The old Navajo laughed aloud at Lem's expression. "Red rocks not so far as Lake Gulch." He pointed.

Lem had noticed the long but low outcropping of red sandstone about half a mile away on their first morning, but those were very common out here and he had given them no further thought. For a moment he was puzzled. Then he understood and groaned in disgust. "Water pots."

Water pots were a common thing in the desert southwest. The same wind and rain that sculpted the soft sandstone into all kinds of fantastic shapes often carved out depressions in the base rock. Some of these were small depressions of various sizes that trapped and held the rain. Some reached four or five feet across and several feet deep. One could find water in these larger ones even in midsummer. Lem felt like kicking himself.

Pahlilly flashed him a grin, shook his head, and said again, with much satisfaction, "*Bilagáana*."

As the man brought the water, the other brave returned at a full gallop. Dragging behind him on a rope was a prickly pear plant about the size of a bushel basket. Immediately the women surrounded the plant and went to work. They pulled out the needle-sharp spines with their teeth and then cut the flat, round leaves down the middle so they opened like a book.

Lem was amazed to see the skill with which they worked. When they finished, they brought the leaves to Pahlilly, who carefully laid them across the wound. In a minute or two, he had the whole upper half of Jody's leg packed in the sticky cactus. The women secured it with strips of rawhide. Jody twitched once or twice during the procedure but did not awaken.

When Pahlilly straightened and stepped back, surveying his work with satisfaction, Lem turned to face him. "Thank you, my friend," he said with great solemnity. "The Great Spirit sent you to save my companion's life. You are a true friend to my people."

Though his expression did not change, the old man's jet black eyes gleamed with pleasure. "And the people of the Mormons are true friends to the *Diné*." He looked down. "He better now. His leg crooked, and he have much pain for many winters. But he not die."

Lem nodded. "When you return to Bluff Fort, my family would be honored to have you sit in our hogan to break bread together."

There was another curt nod, but the pleasure in Pahlilly's eyes deepened even more. "It shall be so," he said.

And then, just like that, the old Navajo returned to his horse and threw himself onto it. He spoke to his entourage in his native language. Then to Lem he said two words: "We go."

Lem watched them until they disappeared into a small wash about half a mile away. Then, with a lump in his throat, he bowed his head and dropped to his knees.

Sometime in the middle of the night Lem awoke with a start. He sat up, not sure what had awakened him. A sliver of a moon was up, providing some light. He turned and looked at his patient. To his amazement, Jody Lyman was up on one elbow. "Lem?"

"I'm right here, Jody," he said, half in shock. "Are you all right?"

Lying back down again, Jody let out a long breath. "My leg. I can't feel it. Did you have to cut . . . ?" He couldn't finish the sentence.

"No. A band of Navajo came by. They put a poultice on it. It's drawing out the poison. The swelling has gone down." Lem had readjusted the rawhide strips three times now because the swelling was receding so fast. It was astonishing. "But if you can't feel it, that's not good."

In the near darkness, Lem saw Jody reach down and

carefully probe his leg with his fingertips. There was a soft gasp, then, "Uh . . . yeah. I can feel it."

"You're going to live, Jody. And thanks be to God for that."

"Where's Hy?"

"Gone to Bluff for help. He should be back in a couple more days."

"Sorry to be so much trouble."

Reaching out, Lem put a hand on his shoulder. "You done good, Jody. And now you're gonna be all right. Try to sleep."

There was a long sigh. "Yeah, I think I will."

They were quiet for quite a long time, but then Jody spoke again. "Lem?"

"Yeah?"

"Do you remember what they told us when they called us to come out here?"

"They said a lot. What in particular?"

"The part about us needing to be a buffer between the Indians and the white man."

"Yeah."

"And like shock absorbers on a carriage."

"Yes, I remember. What of it?"

Jody actually managed a soft laugh. "I think I believe them now."

Lem laughed right out aloud. To have the man he expected to be dead right now joking about their situation was like a breath of spring in the middle of winter.

Then the wounded man sobered. "How long do you think it will take? To make it all work, I mean. It is gonna all work out, right?"

Lemuel Redd sat back and then finally shook his head.

"Dunno. Maybe not in our generation. But maybe our kids will live to see it."

"Will they be strong enough to stick it out that long?"

"We keep having days like this and I guess they'll have to be, won't they?"

Notes

In the historical novel *The Undaunted: The Miracle of the Hole-in-the-Rock Pioneers,* the full story of the background, calling, and trek to San Juan is told in detail. For those interested in a brief but excellent historical account of the mission, see David E. Miller's *Hole in the Rock: An Epic in the Colonization of the Great American West.*

Others came to the area in search of more worldly things. Southwest Colorado territory experienced a massive mining boom with the discovery of lead, silver, and gold. Cattlemen followed, lured by seemingly endless grasslands. The lawless came to escape the law.

It was inevitable that these elements would clash with the Native Americans. The white men stole their land, rustled their horses and cattle, raped their women, ridiculed their culture, and destroyed their range land. The Navajo, Utes, and Piutes, who had long warred with each other, now had a common enemy. By the late 1870s, the right spark could have ignited the Four Corners region area into open war.

The experience of Lemuel H. Redd Jr., Hyrum Perkins, and Joseph A. Lyman comes from an account by Albert R. Lyman (see *Indians and Outlaws,* 45–51). Albert R. Lyman was the son of Platte D. Lyman and Adelia Robinson. Platte D. Lyman was the leader of the pioneer company that crossed the Hole-in-the-Rock trail and established the town of Bluff. Albert R. was born on the trail and came to the San Juan as a baby. Albert and Jody Lyman were cousins.

Though Albert R. Lyman was an excellent writer in terms of both detail and drama, not all of the details here come from him; for example, the dialogue is fictionalized, and the name of the second cowboy was not known, so the name Dickson is a fabrication.

But the events are not fictional, and the story mostly comes from Lyman's vivid account. Albert R. Lyman concludes his story of this event with these words:

"That prickly pear poultice worked like magic. When a wagon came, 'Jody' was able to ride, although with much discomfort, to Bluff.

He lived and hobbled through forty years with a crooked leg on which one troublesome operation after another had to be performed. When death came it was due in a great measure to his experience at Hall's Crossing with the human rattlesnake" (ibid., 51).

He also adds this terse note about the two outlaws: "In the days that followed, Paxman and his ally found and calked up an old boat in which they went down the river, and one of them reached Lee's ferry with the guns and belongings of the other" (ibid., 48).

Joseph and Nellie Lyman eventually took part in the settling of other communities in San Juan County, including Blanding and Grayson, Colorado. Jody died on December 18, 1925, at the age of six-ty-nine, having lived long enough to see the Mormons fulfill their call to be the buffer, lightning rod, and shock absorbers for the region (see http://trekholeintherock.blogspot.com/2010/on/lyman-joseph-alvin-and -nellie-grayson.html).

CHAPTER 2

June 20, 1884—Just outside Bluff City, Utah Territory

Mitch Westland stood up in the stirrups, squinting against the afternoon sunlight. "Pa," he called back over his shoulder, "you'd better come look."

His mother's face appeared in the opening of the canvas wagon cover as his father reined in the team. "What is it, Mitch?" He could hear the strain in her voice even from here.

Dropping back into his saddle, Mitch cursed himself for speaking without thinking. He half turned so he was facing the wagon. His mouth opened and then shut again. Telling his mother it was nothing wasn't going to do much good. She would see it for herself soon enough. So he just shook his head. "Just come on up, Pa."

Mitchell Arthur Westland had celebrated his sixteenth birthday just five months earlier, but he was maturing early. Lean as a buggy whip, he already topped six feet in cowboy boots and would likely add another inch or two to that. Beneath his hat, his hair was thick and dark brown. His eyes were wide-set and blue-green—like his mother's—and set beneath thick, dark eyebrows. His nose had originally been straight and well-formed but now had a little crook in it about halfway down. That was a gift from his older brother, who had thrown him a baseball when he wasn't looking. Around his mouth and along his jawline he was starting to show the first fuzz of whiskers. He took great pride in the fact that his father had given him his own straight razor for his last birthday, and he was now shaving once a week—whether he needed it or not.

On this day—the twenty-third of their 200-mile journey—the Westland wagon was the lead of the other twelve wagons. As they topped a low rise, the other wagons were strung out as far as a quarter mile behind it. Mitch's father handed the reins to his wife, motioning for her to come out from the back of the wagon. "Gwen, hold the team. I'll be right back."

"What is it, Arthur?" But she climbed out onto the wagon seat and took the reins without waiting for an answer.

Her husband shrugged as he swung down, waving to the other wagons to pull up. "Not sure. I'll be right back." As he started forward, another head poked out through the opening in the canvas. "What is it, Mama?" Martha, who was ten, tugged on her mother's sleeve. A moment later, a second face poked out beside the first. It was Johnny, Mitch's youngest sibling. He would be seven in another month. "Can I go with Papa?"

"No!" Gwendolyn Westland said. It came out more sharply than she had intended. She softened her voice. "Hush, children. Mitch just wants your father to see something."

Mitch called back. "You stay with Mama, Johnny. There's no danger."

He turned forward, standing again in his stirrups. Before him was a narrow valley between low walls of red and white sandstone cliffs. Not hard to see why the first settlers had named the town Bluff. But what should have been a valley dotted with green fields and young trees, perhaps even an occasional flower garden, was instead a flat expanse of dark, brown, chocolaty mud. And through the middle of it snaked a wide river of almost-black, roiling water.

This was hardly the docile, sluggish stream they had been told to expect. It was a living thing, an angry torrent, roaring softly in the still, morning air. The water churned and boiled like a witch's cauldron. The roiling surface was speckled with debris of all sorts, including full-grown trees. Mitch drew a sharp breath and jerked forward. Three white splotches had caught his eye. Now he could see they were the carcasses of sheep, rolling slowly over and over in the current. Behind them came what was left of a wagon box, it too turning over and over as it if were a child's toy. The sight of it made him shudder. It also filled him with an immense gratitude that they did not have to cross it.

"What is it, son?"

Mitch swung down off his horse and faced his father. Behind him, other men had gotten off their wagons and were coming forward to see what the matter was. There was no need to explain. Mitch stepped back without speaking.

"Ohhhh." It came out in a long, drawn-out sigh.

Pointing, Mitch squinted. "Are those cabins in the river? Or what's left of them? Why would they build cabins in the riverbed?"

His father took off his hat, holding it up to block the sun. Then he shook his head and replaced it. "Not cabins, son. Those must be the cribs they built to channel the river into what they call the Big Ditch. They build a foundation of logs, much like they do for a cabin, but then they fill it with rock and dirt to hold their sluices in place. Remember, that is one of the reasons for our call. We're here to help them build the Big

Ditch. If we can't irrigate the valley floor, we can't turn it into farmland."

"I'm not sure that's true anymore."

They turned as footsteps came up behind them. It was Isaiah Thompson, from Fillmore. He was the oldest man in their group and the one designated as the leader of their little company. He too drew in a sharp breath when he saw what was before them. "Well," he drawled a moment later, "we've had torrential rain about every other day since we left our homes. From the look of things, I guess they've had it too."

Caleb Burr, a father of five from Gunnison, joined them and gave a low whistle. "Whoo-ee!" he said softly. "The whole town's gone."

Mitch's father shook his head. "No. Look there." He raised his hand and pointed. "Just to the left of the cottonwood trees, up closer to the bluffs. I think that square rock building is the fort."

"Yeah," Mitch said. "And aren't those cabins around it?"

Thompson grunted. "Yup. And judging from the ground around them, I'm betting that every one of them's got a foot or two of mud inside."

Finally Isaiah Thompson grunted. "Standing here isn't going to help them much. Let's get on down there and go to work."

As they turned and started back toward the line of wagons, Mitch grabbed his father's arm. "How's Mother going to take this, Pa?" he asked in a low voice.

There was a quick flash of anger in his father's eyes. "Your mother is a strong woman, Mitch. She'll take it just fine." Then, as he started away, he swung back. "No sense taking the cows down into that mess just yet. Get some of the other boys and take the herd back to that last wash we crossed. Leave a couple of the younger boys to watch them. Tell 'em we'll be back for them 'fore dark."

"Yes, Pa," Mitch said as he swung back up in his saddle.

June 21, 1884—Bluff Fort

The meeting was to begin at seven o'clock that night. With the help of the Bluff settlers, who were ecstatic about the company's arrival, the newcomers had spent the afternoon and evening of their first day getting their wagons parked and the teams turned out to pasture. This morning, the new arrivals returned the favor and pitched in to help in the cleanup effort. Somewhere around ten that morning, during a break for water, bread, and slabs of cheese, Jens Nielson, bishop of the Bluff Ward, announced that there would be an official welcome party for the latest additions to their community at the log schoolhouse next to the fort.

The schoolhouse—which was also the church house and community hall—was a long, low building made of twisted cottonwood logs and topped with a sod roof. Mitch was surprised by how crooked the logs were, but his father explained that cottonwood trunks grew that way, and that if there were no other alternatives, you made do with what you had. The cabins surrounding the fort and schoolhouse were built of the same timber, with the same crooked result.

Inside the schoolhouse they had built a raised platform. Here wooden chairs and a small pulpit had been placed. As the Westlands entered the room, the smell of mold and mildew assaulted their nostrils. Mitch pulled a face but said nothing.

This was a smell that now filled the entire valley and probably would for weeks to come.

Glancing up, he saw that there were two large holes in the roof where the sod had collapsed from the incessant rain. Dark mud stains were visible on the floor planking and a couple of the benches. That wasn't a surprise. There were not many houses in Bluff right now that weren't open to the sky to some degree or another.

Mitch noticed three men talking quietly together on the stand as his family found a place on the benches. One he recognized—it was Bishop Nielson. The other two he guessed were his counselors.

He sat back, completely content. Bluff had just suffered a severe flood. Mud and rot were everywhere. The task of cleanup was overwhelming, but there was nowhere else he would rather be. They were here at last. The grand adventure had finally begun, and he was happy to be a part of it.

"Brodders and sisters?"

Every eye turned toward the stand. Bishop Nielson was now at the pulpit. The other two men had taken the chairs. The room quickly quieted.

"Vee vould like to start vit an opening prayer. I haf asked my counselor, Lemuel Redd, to offer that prayer."

The older of the two men behind the bishop got to his feet and came forward. As everyone bowed their heads and closed their eyes, Mitch peeked at his mother to make sure her eyes were closed too, and then he turned to study the bishop.

Jens Nielson was his mid-sixties and had a deeply tanned face and deep wrinkles lining deep blue eyes. His hair was almost pure white, as were his eyebrows and the funny little beard that grew from beneath his chin. Taller than Mitch and broad enough across the shoulders to strain the material of his suit coat, he was an imposing figure, but with a kindly face and a quick smile.

Bishop Nielson's beard was one of the most unusual Mitch had seen. The bishop's upper lip and the front of his chin were clean shaven, but growing straight down out of the bottom of his chin was a rectangular tuft of hair that looked as though it had been stuck on with bookbinder's glue. In a way it seemed almost comical, but then Mitch changed his mind. The bishop was very dignified in his manner, and his beard somehow seemed to add to that.

Brother Redd's prayer was brief but heartfelt. As soon as he sat down, the bishop was up again. He cleared his throat. "Brodders and sisters, vee velcome you tonight to our meeting." His eyes twinkled for a moment. "For you who are new to us, I thought it might be good to explain vhy everyvhere you look there is so much mud. Vell, the problem is that vee haf so much sand in Bluff. Vhen the vind blows, it gets into everything—our shoes, our beds, our food. So vee decided to order in some mud to hold the sand down."

He smiled as the people burst out laughing. Still dead sober he went on. "Now, vee haf another problem. Vee haf too much mud. So vee are thinking of bringing in some sand to help dry out the mud."

Everyone was laughing now. A couple of people even clapped their hands in delight. Mitch glanced at his mother and saw that she was laughing too.

The bishop continued, more serious now. "Vee vant to vel-come all of the new families who haf joined our little mission here along the banks of the San Juan. Vee are so grateful for your faith and your sacrifice. As you can see, you have come at a time vhen vee need your help so much. So, in behalf of all our people, vee thank you. God bless you for your faith."

Mitch glanced sideways, wondering what his mother was thinking.

Gwendolyn Greene Westland had not wanted to come here. Not in any way. The thought of leaving her home, uprooting her family, and leaving Mitch's two older brothers and their wives and children had been almost more than she could bear. Almost. When the stake president told them the call had come from John Taylor, President of the Church, she agreed to go. Not joyfully. She told Mitch's father that as far as she knew, the call didn't require joy. Only willingness.

To find a sea of mud upon arrival must have raised some misgivings within her. But if she was having those feelings now, it did not show on her face.

Bishop Nielson then read the names of the new families and asked each father to introduce his wife and children to the congregation. As that went on, Mitch turned his focus back to the man he had heard so much about but never met.

Bishop Jens Nielson was famous among the settlers in southern Utah. He and his wife, Elsie, had joined the Church when Mormon missionaries came to Denmark with a message of a new prophet, a new bible, and a new church. When they received the call to come to America several years later, they sold their farm in Denmark and caught a steamer from Copenhagen to Liverpool. There, in 1856, they joined a company of Saints from various countries in Europe. That year, for the first time, the companies of pioneers headed for Utah would not be in wagon trains. They would go by handcart. James Willie, who had been in England serving as a missionary for the previous four years, had been called to lead their hand-cart company from Iowa City to the Valley.

The Willie Handcart Company had been the first to be caught in the raging winter blizzards that roared across the high plains of Wyoming. Their handcarts ground to a stop while they were still 300 miles from Salt Lake. Before they reached the Valley, the Nielsons buried their only son and a young girl they were bringing with them for another family. When Jens's feet were so badly frostbitten that he couldn't go on, his wife, Elsie, barely five feet tall and weighing less than a hundred pounds, put him in their handcart and pulled him on to camp.

They both survived, but the frostbite twisted one leg so badly that Jens walked with a noticeable limp for the rest of his life. One night, as their group faced almost certain death, Jens had told the Lord that if He would spare their lives and let them reach the Valley, he would spend the rest of his life answering whatever call his priesthood leaders gave to him. When the call came in 1878 to open a mission around the San Juan River, Jens was nearly sixty. He was not one of those called, but he volunteered to accompany some of his family members anyway.

At the point where it looked like the Hole-in-the-Rock pioneers could go no farther due to impassable terrain, Jens Nielson had made two statements that changed everything. He said that what the people needed was more stick-to-it-ive-ness. In his rough Danish accent it came out as "stick-a-ty-tootie." Then he added with great solemnity, "We *must* go on, whether we can or not." And they did.

"Arthur Vestland." Bishop Nielson's voice brought Mitch back to the present. His father got to his feet, turning to look back at the congregation as he motioned for the rest of the family to stand beside him. The smiles from the congregation were warm, genuine, and welcoming. Mitch smiled back at them, resisting the temptation to give a little cheer when his father finished.

"Thank you, my brodders and sisters," Bishop Nielson said when the last family finished. "Vee cannot fully express how grateful vee are that you haf answered a call from the Lord and joined us in this important effort."

His shoulders lifted and fell as he searched the faces of the new arrivals. Then he sighed. "It saddens me deeply that vee cannot celebrate your arrival vit a dance and potluck dinner. That vould be a luxury for all of us. Instead, not only must you join us in cleaning up after a devastating flood, but in addition, I fear that vee haf some other news that vee must share vit you.

"As you haf seen vit your own eyes, this has not been a goot year for us. Vee haf seen more rain this spring than vee haf seen since vee first come to Utah. Vhen it rained and rained and rained, all of our efforts to shore up the riverbanks vere in vain. All of our vurk to protect the town vas for nothing. Vurse, three years of vurk on what vee call the Big Ditch is gone. This vas to be a permanent solution for irrigating our crops. Now, three years of backbreaking labor, three years of using every spare dollar of cash to pay for it, is gone. The great vahter vheel vas vashed avay like a child's toy. Just like that, the monster river svept everything avay.

"And vhat haf vee left? A valley covered in mud. Our houses filled vit mud." He gestured upward. "Roofs collapsed from too much rain. Fields of new corn and vheat and oats, gone. The air filled vit such a stench that vee haf to wear bandannas over our noses."

He turned and gazed out the west windows to where the

last of the evening sun was bathing everything in soft, gold light. When he went on, it was barely a whisper. "Upstream from here is the town of Montezuma Creek. Eight of our families chose to settle there. The flood hit them vit particular fury. All but two homes were completely destroyed. Most of their livestock vere lost."

The image of the sheep floating in the brown water flashed into Mitch's mind.

"Three of those families are here vit us tonight. The rest decided they vere too veary, too tired to carry on any longer. They packed vhat few belongings they had left and vent looking for new homes in a gentler land."

He turned back to face the congregation. "The first night after all of this hit, vee here in Bluff gathered together. Vee too were terribly discouraged and vanted to escape from this terrible country. Vee asked ourselves, 'Does the Lord really expect us to stay here now? Or is it time to finally admit that vee cannot make it any longer? Is it time to give up?'"

He stopped, letting his gaze move from face to face among those who had just arrived the day before. There wasn't a sound in the hall now. Mitch felt a deepening sickness in the pit of his stomach. *No. Don't say it. You can't tell us to leave now.*

Then Bishop Nielson's head moved back and forth slowly. "Vee finally decided that it vould not be right to release ourselves from a call that came from our prophet. So vee wrote a letter to President John Taylor, which vas signed by almost all here. Vee set forth plainly the obstacles vee are facing, and vee asked for a release from our callings unless suitable help vas forthcoming."

"But what about us?" someone right behind Mitch cried out.

"Yes," a woman's voice chimed in. "Did we come all this way only to turn around now and go back?"

Mitch turned. Sister Lavina Livingstone was on her feet. Her face was strained, her voice anguished. As Mitch watched, her husband reached out to take her hand. His face was flushed with embarrassment, but he didn't try to pull her down or quiet her. They had brought five children with them, the oldest a girl about Mitch's age. The Westlands and the Livingstones had become good friends in the last three weeks. Sister Livingstone was only voicing what all the rest were feeling.

Mitch stole a quick glance at his own mother, again wondering what was going through her mind. But her head was partially averted and he could not see her face.

"Ya, ya," Bishop Nielson said softly. "Your qvestions are goot ones. Vee knew, of course, dear sister, that more families had been called and vere planning to come this summer, but vee had not heard any more about vhen you vere coming."

She sat down again as he went on. "The letter to Salt Lake will take weeks to reach there. And it vill be veeks after they get it before a letter finds its vay back here."

He straightened, squaring his shoulders. With great resolve, he finished his thought. "But vee vill stay until vee hear from them."

Bishop Nielson continued. "So here is vhat vee vould recommend to you; then each of you vill haf to decide for yourselves vhat you vish to do. You haf just arrived. Your teams and your livestock are tired and vorn out. To turn around now and go back vould be very difficult. If you choose to do so, vee vill do vhatever we can to help you on your way. But vee ask that you give careful thought to staying at least until vee hear from Salt Lake. Vee so badly need your help."

He stopped to give them a chance to let his words sink in, and then in a quieter voice, he went on. "But you do not haf to decide anything tonight. Go back to your wagons and your tents and talk about it as families. Think about it. Pray about it. Then decide."

"Amen," a deep male voice boomed out. Other murmurs of assent followed. It was a reasonable plan and one that avoided the awkward question of whether they were abandoning their calls rather than waiting to be released from them. Mitch looked sideways at his mother, but her eyes were fixed on the bishop. She was as still as a stone statue—which did not bode well.

Mitch squared his shoulders now. He knew what he was going to say when they got back to their wagon. His vote was to stay. Period. End of discussion.

Bishop Nielson raised his hands, and the room quickly quieted. Once again his shoulders lifted and fell. Once again he sighed a great sigh. "My dear brodders and sisters," he said apologetically, "I know that you all are exhausted and are eager to fall into your beds. But vee haf one more problem vee must deal vit that cannot vait. I have asked my other counselor, Brodder Kumen Jones, to explain."

He stepped back as the man sitting next to Lemuel Redd got to his feet and came forward. Tugging at his mother's sleeve, Mitch leaned in and whispered, "That's Kumen Jones?"

She shrugged. "How would I know?"

Everyone watched the man who came to the podium. He was the youngest of the three men. Probably a third the age of Jens Nielson, and maybe half the age of Lemuel Redd. He was a handsome man, with a full head of dark hair and a neatly trimmed beard of the same color. He wasn't in Sunday dress, but it was obvious that he had changed from his work clothes and taken off the muddy boots he had worn earlier as he worked among them.

"He's Bishop Nielson's son-in-law. He was the one who drove the first wagon down the Hole in the Rock," he added in awe. "And they say he's amazing with the Indians."

She put a finger to her lips, but nodded.

Mitch was euphoric. *I am in the same room with Jens Nielson and Kumen Jones.* Here was one more reason to stay. Who wouldn't want to rub shoulders with men like these?

Kumen jumped in without preamble. "As a bishopric, we fully understand how stretched our resources are at the moment. And we also realize that our new arrivals have barely had time to unpack. So what I ask for now, I do with great reluctance. But we have a problem almost as urgent as cleaning up the flood damage and replanting our fields. The full heat of summer will soon be upon us. What grass there is left in the valley and in the washes will soon wither away. We have to take our cattle into the mountains and find them a summer range.

"We have a range in mind," Kumen went on with a nod. "It's up on Elk Mountain, northwest of here. You followed right along its base. From below, Elk Mountain looks like a high mesa with steep red cliffs that stretch for miles."

There were nods all around. Mitch remembered them clearly.

"Last spring, three of our brethren set out to find a way to drive cattle up through those cliffs. Unfortunately, it is a favorite hunting ground for the Utes and Piutes, and they are not eager to share with us. When they met a group of the natives, these three brethren tried to negotiate an arrangement but were met with only stony silence.

"So they rode on for miles with no success. Finally, they left their horses and scrambled up the impossibly steep hillsides. Once on top, they found what they were looking for. Here was a region with an abundance of good timber, grass tall enough to tickle a horse's belly, and wild flowers everywhere. When they came back, they were both elated and discouraged. We had found the place, but we had no way to get our cattle up to it."

He stopped, letting his eyes sweep across the group. "Brethren, as you know, our cattle are critical to our survival. So we are ready to try again. Brother Redd is taking a party back to Elk Mountain. Brother Hyrum Perkins and I will be going with him. Our purpose will be to find that trail. We know there is one, for the natives take their stock up there. This must happen."

Lemuel Redd leaned forward. "We have no choice."

Kumen nodded and then went on. "We hope to avoid any confrontation with the Indians, but we must also show that we are strong when we negotiate with them. So we feel that it is important for a fourth and possibly a fifth man to accompany us."

That caused a stir, and he gave it a minute to roll out.

"The problem is, every man is needed down here as well. So, as your bishopric, we have decided to select one or two brethren who could leave their families for a week, maybe a little longer. We would leave at first light Monday morning."

Mitch's hand was up before Kumen had even stopped speaking. "I'll go," he sang out.

He heard his mother gasp and saw his father's head snap around. Then, to his surprise, his father raised his hand too.

"No!" his mother cried. She grabbed Mitch's arm and yanked it downward. Then she gave his father a look that made him drop his arm too. She turned back to Brother Jones. "He's just a foolish boy."

Kumen was trying not to smile, but he did manage to respond with appropriate gravity. "How old are you, son?" he asked.

"I'm sixteen."

Bishop Nielson stood and joined Kumen at the pulpit. "Brother Vestland, I belief you brought cattle vit you. Is that correct?"

Arthur Westland got to his feet, hat in hand. "Yes, Bishop. We have about a dozen head. So this is of particular interest to us."

"And your son has helped vit the cattle, no?"

"Yes." He turned as Mitch's mother cried out and grabbed his hand. "No!" she hissed. But he went on anyway. "He's very good on a horse. He's a good boy. Very mature for his age."

Gwendolyn Westland dropped back down on the bench and stared at her hands, which were clenching and unclenching in her lap. Bishop Nielson and Kumen Jones moved closer together and conferred briefly.

"Thank you for volunteering, young Brother Westland," Kumen said. "We appreciate your willingness to serve and will take the matter under advisement with your parents."

Mitch fell back. His mother reached out to take his hand, but he jerked it away angrily. Then he felt his father's hand reach past her and find his shoulder. His fingers found the cord of muscles that run along the top of the shoulder and dug in hard. Mitch writhed in pain, but his father didn't let go until Mitch apologized to his mother and put his hand in hers.

Kumen was sitting again, but Mitch saw that he had watched that whole interchange.

The bishopric came to the Westlands' wagon about forty-five minutes after the meeting had ended. They invited Mitch's mother and father to step outside to talk. Mitch shot his father an imploring look, but he ignored it as he climbed down and then helped his wife. Just as the wagon flap was closing again, Mitch was thrilled to hear Bishop Nielson ask, "Vould you haf any objections, Brodder Vestland, if your son vas vit us vhile vee talk?"

"No."

Mitch shot up to a sitting position, craning to hear. His hopes were instantly dashed when the bishop spoke again. "Sister Vestland? How vould you feel about that?"

But then came the soft reply. "I have no objection." And everything was all right again. He was out of the wagon in an instant and hugging his mother fiercely. She kissed him on his forehead. "Don't jump to conclusions," she whispered.

They moved a few yards away to where a young cottonwood tree had been uprooted by the flood. Bishop Nielson invited the Westlands to sit on the trunk while the three of them stood. "If it is all right vit you," he began, "my counselors vould like to ask you and your son some questions."

Lemuel Redd looked at the bishop, who nodded for him to continue. "Let us begin by assuring you, Sister Westland, that we will honor your wishes, whatever they turn out to be."

The fact that he had spoken directly to her seemed to please her.

"Thank you."

"Under normal circumstances, we would not consider taking a lad as young as your son into a situation where there might be danger." As she started at that, he rushed on. "We are being straight with you. We do not expect trouble, but our native brothers can sometimes be quite unpredictable, especially some of the young, hotheaded braves. So we don't want to mislead you. There is some risk here."

Kumen Jones jumped in. "However, you should know that because of some remarkable experiences we have had with the Indians, they believe that if they kill a Mormon, they will bring down a curse upon their entire tribe. So we don't want you to think that we are marching into the jaws of death, either."

"I understand." Then she turned to her husband and searched his face as she asked her next question. "My husband raised his hand too. Why is it that you are only interested in my son?"

"Oh, but vee are not," Bishop Nielson said. "Vee haf another brodder from your company who vee decided vould be our first choice, but it turns out that his wife is vit child and—no one knows that yet, so please do not try to guess who it is. But anyvay, the other two volunteers are farmers, not ranchers, and vee think it is best if they stay and help here. So vee haf decided that vhat vee need is a Vestland. Whether that be your husband or your son, that is vhat vee are here to decide."

Mitch swung on her. "Oh, Mama, please let me go. I'll be all right. Really."

She ignored him. "But you are determined to take one or the other?"

"Vee haf no other good alternative, Sister Vestland. We are sorry for that, for vee know you haf your own family to care for."

"But the need is critical, both here and there," Kumen

added. "We are sorry to present you with such a difficult choice."

Mitch was sitting beside his father. Now he leaned forward so he could watch his face. The decision was tearing at his insides; he could tell that for sure. Mitch sensed that his father wanted to go. It was really *his* duty, not his son's. And if there was anything Arthur Westland felt deeply about, it was duty. But then, as Mitch watched, his father's face relaxed and a quiet calm settled into his eyes. He half turned and took his wife's hands in his. "Gwendolyn, my dearest, this is not a happy circumstance, but because it impacts you and the children directly, what would you have us do? Would you rather have me go and Mitch stay to help you, or the other way around?"

If she was surprised by that, it didn't show on her face. She studied him closely for several seconds before nodding thoughtfully. Looking up, she spoke to Bishop Nielson. "Does it really make no difference to you whether it is my husband or my son?"

"Vee vould rather take your son," he answered without hesitation. One hand came up to cut off her protest. "Your son is large for his age, so he can do the vurk of a man. So he vill be of help either here or with them. But if your husband goes, then you haf no father to help you with the smaller children. For that reason alone, vee think it vould be more helpful to haf young Mitch go vit my brethren."

Lem Redd and Kumen Jones were nodding their agreement. Finally, Mitch's mother got to her feet. She reached down and pulled Mitch up to face her. She was only about five feet, three inches tall, so he towered over her. "And you really believe that a sixteen-year-old can do what you need done?" she asked, her eyes locking into his, even though she spoke to the two men.

Kumen Jones chose to answer. "If you stay very long in Bluff, Sister Westland, you'll find that we judge a man more on his performance than on his age."

She went up on tiptoes and kissed Mitch softly on the cheek. "Promise me, Mitch. Promise me that you will listen to these men and do whatever they tell you to do."

"I promise," he said. His voice was suddenly catching, but that was probably as much from excitement as any other emotion. He bent down and swept her up in his arms. "Thank you, Mama. Thank you."

When they stepped apart, Lem Redd was there in her place. He stuck out a hand and gripped Mitch's. "We leave at first light on Monday. If you need anything, let me know."

Kumen's grip was even stronger than Redd's. "Glad to have you riding with us, son," he said. And as if that wasn't thrill enough, Mitch could see in his eyes that he really meant it.

Notes

Additional families were called to join the San Juan Mission from time to time after the original company arrived. The wagon company in this chapter, of which the Westlands were members, is a fictional group. But it is very typical of those who were called later.

Other than the fort itself, the old log schoolhouse and community center was the first public building in Bluff. The Hole-in-the-Rock Foundation and numerous family organizations of descendants of the original pioneers have led a marvelous effort to restore Bluff as it was in pioneer times. The old log schoolhouse was one of the first buildings reconstructed. One of the more recent completions is a replica of the co-op store and dance hall, a two-story stone building (see www.hirf .org).

Most accounts of the early history of San Juan County talk about the floods that came in May and June of 1884. One source says that the highest water occurred on the 18th of June. That same source says that only one house at Montezuma Creek survived and that many of the settlers there barely escaped with their lives (see *History of San Juan*

County, 44–45). The description of what the Westland family found on their arrival comes from those accounts. Of those from Montezuma Creek, some moved to Bluff, but the majority returned to settlements in Utah or went to other places to start over again (ibid., 48).

The Saints in Bluff were so discouraged after the flooding that they too debated leaving. However, they decided to write to Church leadership in Salt Lake City to outline all of the challenges they were having and ask if they might be released. That letter was signed by almost all of those in the mission. As we shall see in future chapters, Church headquarters responded by sending prominent Church leaders down to Bluff to meet with the Saints (see *Indians and Outlaws*, 63–64; *Portrait*, 40; and *Saga*, 66).

Bishop Jens Nielson was not the first bishop of Bluff, but he was called about six months after their arrival. Lemuel H. Redd Sr. and Kumen Jones, who was a son-in-law of Bishop Nielson, were his counselors at this time. Bishop Nielson served in that position for twenty-six years. He died on April 24, 1906, at the age of 85. He is buried in the hilltop cemetery overlooking Bluff.

The search for a trail that would give the Saints access to the Elk Mountain summer range actually took place a year earlier than shown here, but the details of that initial search are as found in *Indians and Outlaws*, 56.

CHAPTER 3

June 24, 1884—Second Valley, San Juan County, Utah Territory

"Hey! Westland!"

Mitch's head jerked up in alarm. Then he grabbed at the reins and yanked hard, pulling his horse to a stop just before it crashed into the rear end of Hyrum Perkins's horse. Hy was turned in his saddle, watching him with a sardonic grin.

"Getting a little beauty rest, are we?" he asked dryly. His Welsh accent seemed especially heavy at the moment.

"Uh . . ." Confused, Mitch looked around. "Where are Lem and Kumen?"

"They rode ahead to find us a place to camp."

"How long have I been . . . uh . . ." He shook his head, trying to knock loose the cobwebs in his mind. "What time is it?"

Hy turned back to the front and fished in his vest pocket. He came up with a silver pocket watch and flipped open the cover. "It's nearly half seven."

Mitch didn't have to ask what that meant. Both of his parents were from the British Isles too, and "half seven" meant half past seven, or seven thirty. "Or at least, that's what time it is here in Utah. Now, if we were back in New York, it would be half nine. In California, it's only half six."

Mitch stared at him. "Are you funning me?"

"I am that," Hy said with a laugh. "You make kind of an

easy target." He kicked his horse into motion and started forward. Mitch moved in alongside him. "But on the subject of time, I'm serious. Haven't you heard? We have what they call official 'time zones' in America now."

"Time zones?"

"Yeah. The railroads are the ones who pushed for it."

Mitch gave him a sidelong glance, still not sure whether Hy was pulling his leg. He was learning that this Welshman had a quick, wry humor and loved to tease, especially Mitch.

"I'm not kidding you, Mitch. We got word of it just a few weeks ago. Look, here's how it always worked before: Time is determined by the sun. When it reaches its zenith, no matter where you are, that's noon. Now in a country as small as Wales, or even all of the British Isles, it's not a problem because there's not that much difference from east to west. But in America, the country is so huge that when the sun is at its zenith in New York City, it's only halfway up the sky in Utah. Since clocks were set by the sun, noon here and noon in New York were not happening at the same time. Clear?"

"Yes, that makes sense."

"When we traveled from one city to another by horse and wagon or on foot, no one really noticed the difference, and back then most people didn't have watches. But when the railroads came along, and especially as they got faster and faster, it fouled up their schedules something awful. As a train goes east or west—north and south doesn't affect it—its arrival times could be off by as much as an hour or more. So they created time zones."

Hy gave Mitch a sleepy smile. "Just thought you ought to know that so you could . . . uh . . . keep up with the times."

"Right," Mitch said, keeping a straight face. "Thanks for the . . . *timely* advice."

Hy laughed aloud as he nudged his horse into a trot. "You're welcome. But right now I don't need no clock to tell me that it's dinner *time*."

"Amen to that," Mitch said as he snapped the reins and fell in behind him.

The four men—or, as some might say, the three men and a boy—had left Monday at first light and ridden until it was almost dark. Lem Redd figured they covered about forty miles. But by then they were approaching what was known as First Valley. That put them in the heart of Ute Indian hunting country, and Lem suggested they make camp so they wouldn't be riding after dark.

This morning they were up at dawn and in their saddles half an hour later after a cold breakfast. By nine they were into First Valley. By two they had crossed into Second Valley. Everyone was on alert because they were deep in Ute territory by now.

Mitch finally decided they were following some kind of Indian trail, though he often wasn't sure whether they were following anything at all. He didn't ask. He had decided before they ever left that he wasn't going to be this wide-eyed, greenhorn kid who kept bombarding his three older companions with questions. As much as he wanted to pepper them with questions, he forced himself to listen and to try to learn as much as he could from them.

Often an hour or more would pass with no one saying anything. But Mitch knew that this was the way of the cattleman. Long hours in the saddle. Often alone for days—or even weeks—at a time. It was part of the unwritten code of the cowboy that if you didn't have anything of worth to say, it was better not to open your mouth and prove it. So he rode along, staying close enough to listen when they did talk but generally talking only when he was spoken to.

June 25, 1884—Near Elk Mountain, San Juan County

The next morning, as they rode single file toward the red mesa that now towered over them, Hy, who was in the lead, suddenly pulled up. He raised one hand, signaling the others to come up beside him. As they joined him, Redd grunted softly. He had evidently seen what Perkins was seeing. Without raising either his voice or his arm to point, Lem said, "I count six. No, seven."

"Look to the left of that large clump of cedar trees," Hy said. "There are at least two more there standing in the shadows."

Kumen grunted softly. "Definitely Utes."

By this time, Mitch's heart was pounding like a bass drum and his hands were suddenly clammy. He was about to say, "I don't see them," when a movement caught his eye in the shadow of a large cedar tree about seventy-five yards ahead of them. As he concentrated on the movement, a horse suddenly came into focus. Then another, and another. One by one he began to pick out the men. One was holding the ponies. Another squatted beside a dead cedar tree. The main group by the cluster of cedar trees was now clearly visible to him. "There's one off to the left," he said. "Behind the rocks."

"Got him," Lem said. "Good eye. So ten for sure. Maybe more out of sight."

Mitch felt a cold sweat break out on his forehead. Even as

they watched, the Indians began to move—not toward them, but spreading out in a line. When they stopped, they were nearly shoulder to shoulder and formed a wide half circle.

"What are they doing?" Mitch asked, forgetting his resolve not to ask stupid questions.

Evidently Kumen didn't think it was stupid, because he was shaking his head in disgust. "They're blocking the way. The trail goes right through the middle of them."

"What do you think?" Lem asked. "Hostile?"

"No," Kumen said after a moment. "They're just trying to scare us off. They know why we're here, and they don't like it. So they're seeing if we'll spook."

It's working. I'm pretty darned spooked at the moment, Mitch thought. But he kept his lips clamped shut.

"Okay," Lem said. "We're gonna sit here for five or ten minutes. Let them know that we're not turning tail and running. But we don't want to look like we're trying to push them, either. Be sure to keep your hands away from your weapons, but let them see that we are armed. They have to know that we're not backing down. This range is critical to our survival, and they're gonna have to learn to share."

Kumen looked over at Mitch. "You okay?" he asked.

"Yeah." Then honesty overcame him. "A little nervous, I guess."

"Yeah, me too," he chuckled. "And you can tell by how straight Hy's sitting in the saddle that he's not real comfortable at the moment either. Right, Hy?"

He muttered something that neither of them caught.

This is good. Keep it light. Don't think about what's going to happen when you start forward and reach that line of Indians.

Kumen spoke again. "What you have to remember, Mitch,

is that no matter the provocation, part of our mission out here is to make peace with the Indians. No one said that was going to be easy, but it has to be done. The native peoples of this land have been betrayed and treated like trash by white men for so long that they have a natural distrust of all of us. As someone once said, they are fed hatred for the whites in their mother's milk. But we have to change that. We have to treat them with the utmost integrity. Even when we disagree and can't give in to their every wish, they have to know that we're different. That we will deal with them fairly. That we never lie to them, even in little things. We feed them and help them whenever we can."

"And there's another thing," Lem broke in. "Take this situation we're in now. We can't back down, but under no circumstances can we let it collapse into a gunfight. First of all, we're outnumbered more than two to one. But second, and more important, if we kill one of them, no matter how justified it may be, it will unleash a war of retribution against our people. So we cannot—we must not!—lose control of the situation. We need to stay as cool as a can of milk in the ice house."

Mitch nodded and then couldn't resist commenting, "I didn't think you ever got ice down in this country."

The other three chuckled. He was catching on.

But the calmness in Mitch's voice was a flat-out lie. His mind was whirling, his stomach churning. Finally, he managed a pasty grin and added, "Thanks for not explaining all of that to my mother the other night."

"Oh, I think she knows more than you think," Hy said. "Our women are not without awareness of what our situation is. And we men don't have a corner on courage either."

"And your mother is a courageous woman," Lem added.

"I know." Then Mitch had a thought. "Is it true what you said to my mother about the Indians being afraid to kill Mormons?"

"It is generally," Kumen replied, "but there are a few bad ones in all three tribes, and there's no predicting what they'll do."

"Tell him about Navajo Frank," Lem suggested. "We're not in any hurry here."

"Ah, yes," Kumen said. "Navajo Frank. He was an interesting one. He was in his mid to late twenties, I guess. He was taller than most Navajo and was a handsome, robust man who was quite happy and pleasant by nature. And very smart. In addition to Navajo, he spoke Ute, Piute, Moki, or Hopi as we call them, Mexican, and a pretty good smattering of English. But, like many others of these native peoples, he had this way of thinking that if you saw something you liked, you just took it.

"Well, one day me and Thales Haskell caught him redhanded with some of our horses."

"You haven't met Thales Haskell yet, have you?" Lem cut in.

Mitch shook his head. "No, but I've heard of him."

"Thales Haskell spent years among the Indians as a missionary," Lem explained. "He and Jacob Hamblin are probably the two best Indian men we have in the Church."

"That's right," Kumen said. "So, when Thales and me finally caught up with Navajo Frank, he was riding one of our lost animals. When we challenged him, he gave this lame excuse about finding him and being on his way to bring him to us. So Thales looked Frank in the eye and said with great solemnity, 'Frank, if you continue to steal from the Mormons, you are going to take sick and die.'"

"Really?" Mitch exclaimed. "And how did he take that?"

"Oh, he gave us this big horselaugh and brushed it off, but he gave us back our horse. When he walked away he was still laughing at Haskell's threat.

"After that we didn't see him for several months. Then one day he came into town. At first we barely recognized him. Instead of the rugged warrior we had known before, he was thin and haggard. His chest was all caved in and sunken. When he talked it was in a wheezing gasp."

"Whoa!" Mitch said. "No kidding!"

"Oh," Hy said. "He looked awful."

"He was looking for Thales," Kumen went on. "Wanted him to write a letter to God and tell God that Frank would never steal again from the Mormons if God would save his life. But Thales, in that same solemn tone, told Frank he wasn't sure he could do that because the Lord had warned him before and he'd had no ears for it. Frank begged him to intervene. Finally, Thales told him that if he would cease all of his stealing from that day on and use whatever influence he had over other Navajo to stop them from stealing from the Mormons, maybe the Lord might change His mind."

"And did he?"

"He did," Lem said. "He became a great friend to our people and regained much of his strength and good health."

"Wow," Mitch murmured. "That's incredible."

Suddenly, Kumen leaned forward in his saddle. "Uh, Lem?"

"Yeah?"

"Look at that brave in the center of the line. Does he look familiar to you?"

Going up in his stirrups, Lem peered forward and then

released his breath in a long sigh. "Is that Moenkopi Mike?" he asked with a grim nod.

"Yeah, I think it is." Kumen turned to Mitch. "He gets his name from Moenkopi, a settlement on the reservation down near Tuba City. That's Hopi and Navajo country, so no one knows how a Ute got that name. But he's a bad one. Word is that he's killed several men in cold blood."

"Then let's not waste any more time." Lem flicked the reins. "All right, here we go. Everybody stay easy now. Silent prayers might be in order too."

As the four men approached the half circle of stone-faced Utes, Mitch could count only two rifles and three or four pistols in the group. The others carried bows and arrows and hunting knives at their belts. Though he studied all of the Indians waiting for them, Mitch's eyes kept going back to the man who was directly ahead of them.

He was a savage-looking man, short in stature but with solid muscle in every part of his body. He had a massive jaw, which gave him an oversized mouth and made his head, which sat on a neck as thick as a bulldog's, seem out of proportion to his short body. Throw in the long-barreled six-shooter he wore on his hip and the overall effect was chilling.

The four of them were riding abreast now, their stirrups nearly touching one another's. Instinctively, they inched even closer together. They reined up about twenty feet in front of the Indians, keeping their hands on their saddle horns in clear view of the warriors. Lem raised an arm in greeting, palm to the front.

"Greetings, my brothers," Lem said quietly and with perfect calm.

Every eye was on him, but no one moved or spoke. The expression on the faces of these natives was not encouraging.

The lower lips were pushed out, which Mitch knew was a sign that they were angry.

"And greetings to you, Mike," Lem went on, not bothered at all by their silence. "We've not seen you for a while. Is all well with you?"

Not the tiniest flicker that Mike had even heard him.

"Has the hunting been good?" Lem went on, as if he weren't carrying on a one-sided conversation.

Nothing.

Lem smiled, then shrugged and raised his hand in farewell. "Well, good hunting." Then, moving very deliberately, he wheeled his horse to the right and walked it around the end of the half circle of braves before turning back and returning to the trail.

The next minute and a half was the longest of Mitch's life. He didn't look at the Indians as he rode past them, but he could feel their gaze burning into his back. He fought back the temptation to hunker down in the saddle in case one of them tried to put a bullet or an arrow in his back.

No one moved. No one spoke. Mitch wasn't even sure if they blinked. They remained as silent and stoic as before. As the Mormons passed around them and started down the trail further into Second Valley, the braves turned and watched them go, but that was all.

A minute or so later, Mitch risked a glance over his shoulder. Nothing. They had vanished into the cedar forest as silently as ghosts.

⁂

They rode steadily for several hours, passing through Second Valley. Lem, the only one who had been with the scouting party the previous year, seemed to know where he was going, so he led the way.

Though they had climbed considerably, the rugged escarpment of the vast plateau still loomed high over their heads. There were unshod pony tracks everywhere, which confirmed that the country was heavily used by the Utes, but the tracks were so random that they gave the group no clue as to a trail. Kumen speculated that this was done deliberately to throw the white men off.

By three o'clock they found themselves in broken country, moving into a veritable maze of canyons, cliffs, and ledges. It was not looking good, and their spirits were flagging.

"Hey!"

Mitch's low cry brought the others up short. They were scattered now, looking for some way up the steep canyon walls. If they could get high enough, Lem kept saying, maybe they could spot some distant landmarks and locate where they were. When the group turned to look at him, Mitch was pointing and gaping at the same time. About fifty yards ahead of them, an Indian astride a horse with no saddle and only a rope for a bridle had suddenly appeared from a stand of cedar trees. He sat there, staring at the four men, not moving.

Mitch's hand started edging down to touch his pistol before he remembered Kumen's advice and jerked it away. He waited for his three companions to join him. "What do we do?" he asked.

Before anyone could answer, the Indian raised a hand and called out to them. To their surprise, he was waving at them to come forward.

"It's a young lad," Hy said, squinting against the afternoon sunlight. "'Bout your age, Mitch, I'm guessing."

Kumen was standing in his stirrups peering at the solitary figure. "Ute. No question about that."

And without waiting for a response, he nudged his horse forward. Instantly, the boy kicked his heels into his horse's flanks and disappeared into the trees again. But as he did so, he again waved them forward with a sweep of his arm.

"What is he doing?" Mitch asked.

"Looks like he wants us to follow him," Lem answered. He said it like he didn't find that thought a particularly happy one.

"Think it's a trap?" Hy asked.

After a moment, Kumen shook his head. "Don't think so. Let's follow him and find out."

They didn't see him again until they had become hopelessly lost once more in the tangle of boulders, cedar trees, escarpments, blind canyons, and narrow washes. There were still horse tracks everywhere, so they had no way of determining which set was his. Finally they pulled up, trying to decide which way to go.

It was Kumen who saw him first. "There he is." He had come out of the trees again, this time only twenty or so yards ahead of them. His arm came up as he waved them on and then rode back into the trees.

And so it went. If they got lost, their guide would appear for a moment or two to make sure they were still following, and then he would slip away again. The fourth time it happened, Kumen nodded his head. "I think he's showing us the way up to the top."

"Or leading us into a trap," Lem observed. "If he's helping us, why so secretive?"

"I'm going to find out," Kumen said. "Stay here." He

cupped one hand to his mouth, shouted something unintelligible, and then spurred his horse forward.

For a moment the boy looked startled, but then he stopped and turned back to face Kumen.

As Kumen rode away, Mitch had a sudden thought. "Does he speak Ute, too?" Mitch had heard he was fluent in Navajo.

"Enough to get by," Lem replied. "Kumen doesn't talk much about it, but he was tutored in the ways of the Indian by Thales Haskell himself."

They watched Kumen slow his horse to a walk as he approached the boy. One hand came up, and they could hear him say something to the Indian. The young brave visibly relaxed and raised his hand in the same gesture. A moment later their horses were side by side and they were launched in a vigorous conversation. Once the boy waved his hand around in a big circle. Twice he motioned toward a ridge ahead of them, pointing out a narrow canyon in the steep slope.

Two minutes later, Kumen was on his way back to the others and the boy was gone again.

"All right," Kumen said as he rejoined them. "Here's the situation. He is just a boy. His name is Henry. When I asked him how old he was, he wasn't sure, but he thought that this winter would be his thirteenth."

"Is he Ute, then?" Mitch wondered.

"Oh, yes. He's part of that hunting party that confronted us back there."

"I don't understand, then," Hy said. "What's he doing?"

Kumen grinned at them. "Helping the Lord answer our prayers, that's what. He wants to show us the way up Elk Mountain."

"Why?" Lem and Mitch asked at the same time.

"Because he's a good boy. He likes the Mormons. I guess he knew Thales Haskell and developed a great love of the Mormons from him. He says that the other braves were out ahead of us until about half an hour ago. Now they want us to pass through so they're behind us."

And have us trapped, Mitch thought.

Kumen went on. "They've split up and are riding separately so we can't use their tracks to find the trail. So this boy is pretending to do the same, only when he's sure none of the others are close by, he pops out to help us."

"Well, I'll be," Hy breathed in wonder.

"He says we go up that little backbone there and then the trail is easier to see. But he'll stay ahead of us and make sure we reach Kigaly Springs. Then he's going to have to rejoin the band or they'll wonder where he is."

"Kigaly Springs?" Lem chortled. "Get me there and we're not lost anymore. We camped there last year. It's a beautiful place with lots of water and feed for our mounts."

"Henry says that Moenkopi Mike will be watching us now, so don't search the trees too carefully for the next hour or so."

Kigaly Springs was set in a narrow draw with thick timber on the north-facing slope above them. It wasn't a large spring, but the water was ice cold and a welcome reprieve from the tepid water in their canteens. They made camp quickly and settled down to wait.

They didn't have to wait long. The first sign came when their horses pricked up their ears and turned their heads to look up the draw. Then Kumen's horse whinnied softly. A moment later another horse answered.

"Well," Mitch said, "they know where we are now."

"Oh, I think they've known that for some time," Lem grunted.

Two or three minutes later, they heard the sound of something coming through the brush. "Calm and unruffled," Kumen whispered. "Let them make the first move."

But there was no such move. When several figures appeared, it was as if the white men were not there. Mike was in the lead, with the rest of them in single file behind them. Henry was in the rear. One by one they passed by. They looked down their noses at the white men, and their lips were pushed out even more than before. Moenkopi Mike glared at them but didn't speak. Neither did any of the others. When Henry passed them, he kept his eyes straight ahead.

Little prickles of fear were doing a dance up and down Mitch's spine. What was Ugly Mike's intention? That was Mitch's name for him. Here they were, four men against eleven. They were forty or fifty miles from the nearest settlement. Up here, the Indians could massacre the lot of them and perhaps no one would ever find them. How would his mother take that?

But then came another thought. *We're here because of Henry. Henry's here because of the hand of the Lord. So have a little faith in what the Lord is doing, Mitch Boy.*

They sat quietly, waiting for the Indians to come back, but the forest was still except for the sound of the wind in the pines. Finally, Lem stood up. "Let's start supper."

They ate slowly and talked quietly, but their focus was not on their conversation. They jumped when they heard a twig snap behind them. They jerked around in time to see Moenkopi Mike step out of the trees and stride boldly right up to them. He didn't speak a word as he loomed over them, but he moved his hand to rest on the butt of his pistol. Kumen looked up and nodded pleasantly and then went back to eating. Mitch kept his head down, afraid that Mike would see the naked fear in his eyes. Up close, Mike was even more frightening.

The four of them continued to eat, speaking occasionally but being very careful of what they said. They ignored Mike as much as possible as he bent over and glared at them. Finally he burst out, "You come our land. Bring cows. We mad."

The four white men looked at each other in feigned surprise. "Oh?" Kumen asked after a moment, seemingly puzzled by the accusation. Then he did something that nearly knocked Mitch over. He turned to him. "Mitch, which saddlebags have those loaves of bread our wives cooked for us?"

"Uh . . . mine do." *Bread? He was thinking about bread?* "Want me to get one?"

"If you would. And that bottle of molasses in my saddlebag, left side. Mind getting that, too?"

He did so, turning his back on Mike for a few moments. When he came back and handed the loaf and the bottle to Kumen, he saw that Mike was watching them closely. And curiosity had replaced some of the anger.

Moving very slowly now, Kumen took his hunting knife out of its scabbard. Then he put the loaf between his knees. Ignoring Mike completely, he cut off a thick slice, opened the molasses jar, and used the knife to cover the bread with about a quarter-inch of the thick, aromatic liquid. Satisfied, he licked the leftover molasses from the blade of his knife, making sounds of pleasure and looking like he was in ecstasy.

He set down the knife and lifted the slice to his mouth. Moenkopi Mike was watching his every move hungrily. Then, just as he was about to bite down, Kumen stopped, as if a sudden idea had just hit him. He looked up at Mike and held out the bread. "You hungry? You want bread?"

There wasn't so much as a grunt, but the Indian reached out and took the bread from him. "Mmm," he said, with obvious relish. Three or four bites later, the bread was gone.

Kumen had avoided looking at him during all of that. Instead, he had sawed off another thick slice and spread it with molasses again. Again he set the knife down and lifted the slice to his mouth. Again, Mike's eyes never left the bread. Again, Kumen paused just before biting into it.

Mike suddenly grinned down at him. "Only little mad now."

Mitch nearly choked to stop himself from laughing, but Kumen soberly nodded and handed the second slice to him. They watched as he consumed that with equal relish and then licked his lips. "No mad," he declared. He waved in the direction from which he had come. "Others they mad, but me *toitch tikaboo*."

"Good, good," Lem said. He went to the saddlebags and got two more loaves. "Would your brothers like some bread too?"

That was the right question. Moenkopi Mike whirled around and clapped his hands. Suddenly there was movement in the trees, and dark shapes started appearing. Henry again was the last one out.

Mitch leaned in to Kumen. "What does *toitch tikaboo* mean?"

"*Toitch* means very. *Tikaboo* means friendly, like, 'everything's good between us.'"

"I can't believe it. Just like that, everything's good now."

"That's another thing to remember about the natives. They are very honest and open in their feelings. When you treat them with respect and show courage at the same time, it makes a big difference to them."

On impulse, Mitch asked one last question. "Looks like we're going to mingle a little now. Is it all right if I introduce myself to Henry?"

"Sure. Just be sure he's not the only one. And make it look like you're meeting him for the first time."

"Got it. Thanks."

As he started to get up, Mitch whispered down to Kumen. "*Toitch tikaboo*, I like it."

Kumen just gave him a lazy smile, as if this kind of thing happened every day.

When the natives finally left, well after dark, Lem Redd waited until they were out of earshot and then grinned at the others. "Did you hear what me and Moenkopi Mike agreed to?"

Hy Perkins shook his head. "I thought I saw some money change hands."

"Yep. We now have grazing rights. I paid him fifty dollars. That and twenty-five pounds of flour and some other small items from the store to be paid the next time they're in Bluff. So what say you? Instead of exploring up here any farther, I say we head back to Bluff. Take a bath. Kiss our wives and—" He looked at Mitch and grinned. "Not you, kid. And next week we start bringing the herd up here."

Mitch feigned a most forlorn look, though the relief had made him weak in the knees. "Isn't there anyone I could kiss?"

Notes

Time zones in North America were officially introduced through the combined efforts of the US and Canadian railroads on November 18, 1883 (*People's Chronology*, 564).

The story about Navajo Frank comes from a written account by Kumen Jones (see *Saga,* 70–71; see also *Portrait,* 49).

Albert R. Lyman describes the search for a way up onto Elk Mountain, including meeting a band of Piute Indians led by Moenkopi Mike along with the young boy who provided critical help to the Mormons. The details about the bread and molasses and the treaty that followed come from his account as well (see *Indian and Outlaws,* 55–59). In his *History of San Juan County,* chapter 18, Lyman tells this same story with slightly different details. In that account, he says the Indians were Utes rather than Piutes, but he doesn't change the story or its outcome (*History of San Juan County,* 40).

In Bluff, almost all references to interaction with the natives involved the Navajo. But once they were away from the Navajo Nation, most accounts of native encounters were with the Utes. Because of that, I decided to make this hunting party Ute rather than Piute.

Albert R. Lyman's account of the expedition to Elk Mountain states that the men were camped at Kigaly Springs when Moenkopi Mike and the other natives confronted them. On modern maps of the area, there is no place identified as Kigaly Springs. However, on Elk Mountain there is a Kigalia Canyon and a Kigalia Point. Nearby is what is now called Twin Springs. Since names of isolated places often change over time, it is likely that Twin Springs is where the men camped.

CHAPTER 4

June 27, 1884—Bluff City, Utah Territory

The four trail-weary men passed through Butler Wash, five miles west of Bluff, in the early afternoon of the second day after leaving the springs. There was great rejoicing when they came across a group guarding the herd outside town and Lem reported what had transpired on Elk Mountain.

One of the young men guarding the cattle, eager to be the bearer of good news, mounted his horse and took off at a lope to let the town know the scouts were back. So it was no surprise that when they came plodding into town at about four o'clock, most of the townspeople were gathered to applaud and call out their appreciation to the triumphant explorers. Everybody started shouting questions at them before they even dismounted. Mitch ignored the crowd as he swung down from his horse just in time to sweep his mother up in his arms and swing her around and around.

Bishop Nielson finally raised his hands and called for quiet. "Brodders and sisters," he chided. "These brethren are tired and hungry."

"And dirty," Hy Perkins added.

"Let them go to their homes to rest and clean up. Vee vill meet in the schoolhouse at 7:30 this evening, vhere vee can all hear their full report."

There was some good-natured grumbling about that, but the people moved back and let the explorers through, though they continued calling out their thanks and congratulations.

Gwendolyn Westland didn't wait for Mitch to rest or clean up or eat. As they started for their campsite, she took him by the hand. "I know you're hungry, and I know we're going to hear it all tonight, but I can't wait. I want to know everything."

His father was nodding. Little Johnny was literally dancing with excitement. Filled with pride that her brother had been part of the expedition, Martha took Mitch's other hand and wouldn't let go.

"Okay, okay," he laughed as Johnny kept peppering him with questions. "Just let me sit down in the shade. My backside feels like it's still got my saddle attached to it."

"Get Mitch a blanket," his father told Martha. "Spread it out on the log over there beneath the tree."

As they got settled, Mitch's mother reached out and took her son's hand. "Now, Mitch, I agreed to let you go, even though it was against my better judgment. But I don't want you leaving anything out just because you think it will upset me. I deserve that much, all right?"

Mitch glanced at his father, who nodded. "She has a right to ask that, son."

Actually, Mitch was glad. He wanted to share the whole experience, including the times he was too scared to spit. He also wanted to try to describe the enormous sense of relief that came when it was all over. "Okay, Mama. But I'd like to tell it all first, and then you can ask questions afterward."

"Fair enough," his mother said. She looked to the younger children. "No questions until your brother is done."

And so he began. He talked briefly about his three

companions and how much he had learned from them. He watched Martha's and Johnny's eyes grow larger and larger as he described Moenkopi Mike and the line of Indian braves that blocked their way. At one point, Johnny's hand shot up, but his father pulled it back down again and told him to wait.

His mother sat quietly as Mitch spoke, her eyes never leaving his face. Her expression was inscrutable, and Mitch wondered what was going on behind those pale, blue-green eyes. He also wondered if maybe he should have softened his account just a bit, in spite of her counsel. Then he decided that she did have a right to know the full truth.

As soon as he finished, both Martha's and Johnny's hands were in the air, waving wildly. "No, children," Arthur said. "Your mother first, please."

Gwen gazed at him for what seemed like a full minute but was probably only about fifteen seconds. Then she cocked her head slightly to one side. "And what is the most important thing you learned from all this, Mitchell?"

He reared back. *Now, there was a question.* And it wasn't one he had expected. He shifted his weight a little as he gave it careful consideration. "A lot of things, I guess, Mama," he began. "It was a wonderful thing to be with those men. I didn't ask a lot of questions of them. I just listened to them and watched."

"Good," his father said.

"But . . ." He let out a breath. "I guess the most important thing I learned is that Heavenly Father was with us. We were all praying furiously the whole time, but two things stand out in my mind. First, Henry showing up out of nowhere. I mean, think about it. Here was this band of Indians out trying to protect their hunting grounds, led by one really mean and dangerous man. I mean to tell you, just looking at Ugly Mike—that's what I started calling him—gave me the chills. But to have in that band a young boy who just happened to have known Thales Haskell and—"

"Who's that?" Johnny cut in.

"Later, Johnny," his father murmured.

"—and whose family had been helped by Brother Haskell? And who because of that actually liked the Mormons? I mean, what are the chances of that?"

"Slim to none," his father murmured.

"Exactly! Henry actually put his own life at risk to help us. If Big Mike had known that he was showing us the way up to Elk Mountain, I'm sure he would have killed him on the spot. What Henry did is really quite amazing when you think about it."

"More than amazing," his mother said softly. "It was a miracle."

"Yes! And then the other thing that stands out was when Kumen had the idea to offer Big Mike that piece of bread and molasses. That was brilliant. It changed the whole situation in a matter of minutes. Up to that point, I thought there was a chance Mike would pull out that huge pistol he had and start blasting away at us. We asked Kumen later how he came up with that idea, and he said, 'I don't know. It just came to me.'"

Mitch's mother's eyes were glistening, and to his surprise, he suddenly found it hard to talk himself. He reached out and took her hand. "And I'm sure your and Pa's prayers were part of that too."

"The whole town has been praying for you, son," Arthur Westland said in a husky voice.

At that, the tears spilled over and trickled down Gwendolyn's cheeks. Mitch stood and pulled her up so he could hug her tightly to him. "When Brother Redd told us that we couldn't shoot anyone or we'd bring down retribution on the whole town, I felt this great sense of hopelessness. How were we ever going to get out of it alive? And then, just like that, everything worked out. It *was* a miracle, Mama. And I've never had my own miracle before."

Her lips brushed his cheek, and then she looked directly into his eyes. "Then you going was the right thing to do."

Summer, 1884—Bluff City

As it turned out, the people of Bluff didn't take their stock up to Elk Mountain that summer, for two reasons. First, the people fully expected the mission to be closed by President John Taylor and so, in addition to their cleanup efforts, they began to pack their things, thinking they would be leaving before winter set in. Second, the spring rains had brought an abundance of grass to the desert country, and so the need for Elk Mountain turned out not to be as critical as they had expected.

A flutter of excitement swept through the community in midsummer when it looked like the whole of Bluff might pick up and move to a place called Yellow Jacket, which was farther upriver in Colorado. It was not as prone to floods and had more farmable land. But when the owners asked $30,000 for the property, their hopes were dashed.

When Bishop Nielson finally received a letter from Salt Lake on July 23rd, the day before they were to celebrate Pioneer Day, another flurry of excitement swept the town. The letter said that leaders from the Church would come down to personally assess the situation and would be arriving just one month later.

This was wonderful news. The people were confident that once Church leaders saw how desperate their circumstances were, there would be no question whether the mission would be dissolved. Their enthusiasm was dampened, but not extin-guished, when another letter arrived saying the Church leaders had been delayed and would not arrive until late in September.

Sadly, at least in Mitch's mind, some found their patience had run out. Like those families from Montezuma Creek who had left after the floods, they decided they could endure no more. In mid-August, eleven men and their families returned to the established settlements in the West. That included three families from the group that had come earlier in the summer with the Westlands.

Tearful farewells were made, and some, like Mitch's mother, watched with envy as those departing rolled out.

As the last wagon disappeared over a small rise, Mitch shook his head. "Sure glad we're not turning tail and running," he said.

His mother whipped around. "What did you say?"

"I . . . uh . . . I was just saying that—"

"Don't you dare criticize their faith, Mitch Westland."

Even Mitch's father was shocked by the ferocity of her out-burst. "Gwen—"

She lifted a finger and shook it about two inches from his nose. "Don't, Arthur." Then back to Mitch. "You don't know what's in the heart of a person. And it isn't your place to judge what they are or are not doing."

Sixteen years of age is often a time when young people, es-pecially young men, develop an absolute surety that they know more than their parents, so Mitch ignored the warning flags and fired back. "Say what you want, Mama, but we're a lot worse off than some of them, and we're not going. All right, so their cabins were flooded and their gardens washed away and their wells were polluted. But at least they had cabins. At least they had gardens. They had wells. They had stoves. They didn't have five people living out of a wagon box and cooking over an open fire and carrying water from the river every day."

"You want to go," she snapped. "Then go."

"No, Mama. I *don't* want to go. That's the point. We were called here by President Taylor, and—"

"That's enough, Mitch," his father cut in. "Let it go."

"No, Pa. Mama's got as much reason to give up and go back as anyone in this settlement. But she didn't go. She's staying. And I'm proud of her for it."

She stepped squarely in front of him and looked up at his face. Gwendolyn Westland was a few inches over five feet tall. Mitch had now passed six feet, so she had to tip her head back to look up into his eyes. To Mitch's surprise, the anger was gone and there was only sorrow there. "You are right," she said. "But I chose not to go only because we were called here by a prophet. And until a prophet says we can go home, then we'll be staying in that wagon box, and we'll be cooking over an open fire, and we'll be drawing our water from the river."

She started to turn away but then stopped. Her voice was trembling with emotion now. "But know this, Mitch. If our leaders say that we are released, we *are* going. And there'll be no talk about 'turning tail and running.' Do you understand me?"

"Yes, Mama." He had to turn away from the intensity of her eyes. "I'm sorry, Mama."

Only about an hour later, Mitch saw Lemuel Redd coming down the street. Since their wagon was the last place of occupancy on the west edge of town, Mitch wondered if Brother Redd was coming to see them. When he saw Mitch, Lem raised an arm and waved. Waving back, Mitch turned his head. "Pa? I think we've got company."

His father was sitting on the wagon tongue, mending some broken harnessing. When he saw who it was, he got to his feet. "Mother?" he called softly. A moment later she poked her head out of the wagon. "Lem Redd's coming. Looks like he may be coming to see us."

Mitch had learned on that trip to Elk Mountain that Lemuel Redd was a man of few words, so it didn't surprise him that the preliminaries were cordial but brief. After inquiring how things were with the family, he got right to it. "I'm here on assignment from Bishop Nielson. The bishopric has decided to occupy the cabins that were left empty today. Those still living out of wagons or tents get first priority. If you have a mind to, you can move into the Johnson cabin."

"Really?" Martha blurted. "We get to live in a cabin?"

"You do," Lem drawled. "And you can move in as soon as it's convenient for you. Today, if you wish."

One hand flew to Gwen's mouth. "Thank you," she whispered.

He smiled. "You're welcome, but I'm just the messenger." He replaced his hat. "Well, I've got to tell the others, so I'll be off." He took about three steps and then turned back. "You'll find that the Johnsons left a hand-hewn table with two chairs and a couple of stools. There's a small dish box in the corner for storing things and some slats that made up their bed." He looked at Arthur. "It's going to need some repairs."

"We can do that."

"Oh, and they left their stove as well. It's all yours."

Gwen was overcome. "Thank you, Brother Redd. And thank Bishop Nielson."

He smiled and lifted a hand. "I will." He turned and walked away.

Gwen turned and clapped her hands, blinking hard to hide the tears. "Well, come on, children. What are you standing around for? We've got a home now."

CHAPTER 5

Fall, 1884—Bluff City, Utah Territory

The best thing about being in a cabin, tiny as it was, was that it gave some peace to Mitch's mother. The cabin was still drying out, so they had to leave the door open during the day or the smell of mold and mildew became overpowering. That brought the flies, in thick, black swarms. Mitch's father finally told Johnny and Martha that he would pay them a nickel each for every quart bottle of dead flies they could produce. But as much as Gwendolyn hated the smell and the flies, she never once complained. Mitch decided that was a trait he needed to learn from her. He found that he could feel deep gratitude for something, such as what had happened up on Elk Mountain, but all too soon the feeling faded and he found himself griping about trivial things again.

For those in Bluff, the informal treaty Lem Redd had worked out with the Utes for grazing rights on Elk Mountain brought some relief. Both the Navajo and the Utes were showing signs of becoming more cooperative with the Mormons.

This led Bishop Nielson to declare that the settlers no longer needed to confine themselves to living in the one large block that constituted Fort Bluff. They decided not to spread out into new settlements until they heard from Salt Lake, but Bishop Nielson did say that they could leave the fort and begin to settle anywhere in the narrow valley that ran along the north banks of the San Juan River. This announcement was met with much rejoicing.

Mitch never heard anyone else in the community condemn those who left. Those who had come through the Hole in the Rock with that first company often talked about the remarkable sense of harmony and cooperation they had experienced during that very difficult six-month trek. So when some of them left, the attitude of those staying seemed to be, "They came, didn't they? And they stayed for four years. It's not our place to judge."

Gradually, Mitch came to understand. He apologized again to his mother and vowed to himself that he would not judge what others did. But in his heart, he grew more and more determined that he would not be one who left, even if his own family decided to go. Even if the Brethren from Salt Lake said it was all right to go. If they closed Bluff, then he would find another settlement. If his parents refused to let him go, then he would return with them to Beaver, but as soon as he could choose his own path, he would be back. He had been here only a few months, but San Juan felt more like home to him than Beaver ever had. Here he would make something of himself. Of that he was sure.

Very soon after the announcement about leaving the fort, new homes started to spring up all around. Mitch rejoiced in that. He welcomed any sign that Bluff was not going to be abandoned. He was thinking about that one day when he and his father went out to Butler Wash to check on their cattle.

"Pa?"

"Yes, son?"

"Are you and Mama thinking about starting a new home?"

It clearly caught his father by surprise, which Mitch assumed was his answer. But after giving his son a long look, Arthur shook his head. "Not at this time."

"What do you mean, not at this time?"

"I mean, not at this time."

And then Mitch got it. "You mean not until we know whether or not—"

"I mean," he said tartly, "not at this time."

Mitch was wise enough to drop the subject and not bring it up again. Nor did he ever share his thoughts about staying in Bluff with his parents, or anyone else for that matter. He was afraid if he did that word would get back to his mother.

Mitch had watched his mother through the summer with growing concern. The cabin was a great blessing, but life was still hard. She put on a brave face and forced herself to smile, but that couldn't hide the strain that was slowly wearing her down. Without being asked, Mitch suggested that he and John continue to sleep in the wagon until the weather turned cold. It was parked right next to the cabin and could serve as a temporary bedroom.

Each night he would take his two siblings outside as soon as the supper dishes were done. They would play games, or he would read to them, or they would go down to the Swing Tree and gather with the other young people of the town. Sometimes the three of them would just lie in the wagon and talk until Martha got sleepy and went inside.

Martha and Johnny seemed to understand why they were doing this and never complained. His mother never openly acknowledged that she recognized what he was doing, but he could see the gratitude in her eyes, and that was enough for him.

If anyone had asked Gwen how she felt about being in a cabin, she would have been very warm in expressing her gratitude, but in her own mind, the cabin only marginally simplified their lives. Life along the San Juan was just plain hard, and there was nothing to be done for it. Their closest neighbor had a well and allowed them to draw drinking water from it, but it still tasted like the river smelled. So once a week, Mitch and his father took the wagon to Cow Wash and filled a barrel with water from the spring there. But that took nearly a full day, and they had to carefully ration each week's water until the next trip.

For cooking purposes they brought water from the river in buckets. But it was so muddy and hard with minerals that they had to put the hot ashes from the stove in each bucket and let it stand overnight before the ashes would be strained out and the water could be used. Mitch was certain that for as long as he lived, he would have the taste of ashes in his mouth.

His mother went down to the river with the other women once a week to do the laundry. By summer, the river was no longer muddy brown as it had been in the spring, but there was still so much silt in it that even when you put on "clean" clothes, you could feel the grit against your skin. If you perspired a lot, which everyone did in the heat, the sand in your armpits turned into a thin, gritty paste that rubbed you like sandpaper and left a red rash.

Gwen hated the sand almost more than the flies. It was everywhere, in everything, and impossible to avoid. Sandstorms were a common and constant plague. When the winds began to blow, even the most conscientious homemaker accepted that the fine sand would be everywhere, in and on everything.

It came in underneath the doors, through cracks in the logs, through loosely fitted windows.

The stove proved to be a mixed blessing for Gwen. It was much easier to prepare their meals than it had been. There even was a small oven in which she could bake biscuits or a loaf of bread once or twice a week. But this was midsummer, when daytime temperatures often hovered as high as 110 degrees. In the confines of a one-room cabin, the heat became stifling. So, on many mornings, she didn't build a fire. She would soak their cracked wheat in water, put a little sugar or molasses on it, and let that do for breakfast.

One day, while his mother was baking bread, Mitch was working in the small garden alongside the cabin. He heard a noise and looked up in alarm as his mother burst out of the cabin, staggering outside. Her face was beet red. Her hair was plastered to her forehead, and there were large, wet stains beneath her arms and around her neck. She was swaying dangerously and looked like she was going to faint. Sending Martha off to find their father, Mitch took his mother to the wagon, made her lie down, and laid wet compresses on her face, neck, and arms until Martha and Johnny returned with their father.

Thereafter, they only fired up the stove two or three times a week. Instead they built a fire out back to cook on each morning.

For all the hardships, life was good, too. After the spring rains, the full heat of summer brought out the stinkweed in grand profusion. It grew as high as ten feet and formed walls on both sides of the sandy streets that ran through town. Loaded with rich, purple blooms, it filled the air with a heavy scent and attracted swarms of bees. The plants grew so tall that they provided a welcome shade in which the children often played.

For Martha and Johnny, the whole summer was a grand adventure. The pioneer company that had arrived in the spring of
1880 had been almost one-quarter children, so they had lots of
friends. The children had plenty of chores to do, but there was
plenty of time for fun, too, especially in the evenings. And this
wasn't limited to just the younger children.

The favorite gathering place for the pioneers of all ages
in Bluff was the old "Swing Tree." On the riverbank just to
the south of town was a huge cottonwood tree with a canopy
of overhanging branches that provided a deep and welcome
shade. Someone had the idea to hang a rope to one of the
upper limbs and tie a swing to it. Because it was so high, the
swing made a long, lazy arc back and forth. Children and adults
would line up to take turns on it.

For all of the hardships and challenges, there was a great
sense of community in that valley of the San Juan. And children being what they are, there were the usual pranks and mis-
chief as well.

Mitch looked up from cutting firewood one day when he
heard his mother calling him. He dropped the ax and went
around to the front of the cabin. "Yes, Mama?"

"Have you seen Johnny lately? I sent him to the river for
water half an hour ago."

"No. But I'll go find him."

Before he even reached the river, Mitch could see that no
one was there. He spun on his heel and started for the home
of Ben and Mary Ann Perkins. They had two boys: Dan, who
was two years younger than Johnny, and one Johnny's age,
who was also named John. These three had become like peas
in the same pod. You could always find them with their heads

together, giggling or playing cowboys and Indians with stick guns or makeshift bows and arrows.

Mitch stuck his head in the front door of the Perkinses' house and called in to Sister Perkins, "Know where the boys are?"

"They were out back. Check behind the barn," she called back.

"Thanks."

"Tell Dan I need him to check the wash and see if it's dry. Tell them to bring it in if it is."

"I'll tell him."

The Perkinses had five children, so Mitch was not surprised to see freshly laundered bedding, towels, and clothes hanging on three separate clotheslines behind their cabin. However, the boys weren't out by the clotheslines, nor were they behind the barn. Mitch went around to the corral. Not there, either. There was a single calf in the corral and several cows out in the pasture behind the house, but no little boys.

Not sure where to look next, he started back for the street. That's when he heard a giggle. He stopped and turned around, looking for the source of the sound.

"Make sure it's real tight, Dan." That was Johnny's voice, and it sounded like it was coming from the corral. Mitch turned around and retraced his steps.

"You hold the head, John," Dan whispered. "And don't let go 'til I say."

Mitch lifted his head to call to them, but something in that sentence made him suspicious. Moving quietly, he started toward the corral. And then he saw John. He was facing the calf, holding on to a rope tied to its halter. But where were the other two boys?

As he moved closer, he saw a movement behind the calf. Curious now, and careful not to make a sound, he started to circle around to get a better look.

What he saw made him stop dead. Dan and Johnny were behind the calf, bent over.

"Tie a square knot," Dan said.

"I did," Johnny shot right back.

"Then let's go."

Mitch took a step closer, still not sure what was going on. To his surprise, his brother and Dan sat down on the ground directly beneath the calf's tail. He chuckled. That was a recipe for disaster. If that calf suddenly did his business, they would be in the direct line of fire.

Then Mitch did a double take. They weren't sitting on the ground; they were sitting on the lid of one of Mary Ann's large laundry kettles, which had a rope tied to one of its double handles, and to which Johnny and Dan were clinging with both hands.

Mitch gave a low cry. *And the rope was tied to the calf's tail!*

Two things happened simultaneously then. Mitch shouted, "No!" just as Dan shouted, "Let her go, John!"

With a loud bawl, the calf lunged forward, nearly knocking John down. The rope snapped taut. The pan lid, which was now serving as a makeshift sled, shot forward. Dan and Johnny whooped with joy as their heads jerked back.

Mitch stopped, utterly dumbfounded. In a wild panic now, the calf darted to the left, which snapped their sled sharply to the right. Johnny lost his grip with one hand and nearly rolled off, but he recovered quickly. "Yahoo!"

The panicked calf bucked and snorted and kicked back at

the rope as it dashed wildly around the corral, which only tightened the knot all the more.

Mitch couldn't help himself. He exploded with laughter. This was a sight to behold. "Ride 'em, cowboys!" he yelled.

The corral was not a large one, so the running room for the calf was limited. It darted to the right, whipping the sled in the opposite direction. This time it was Dan who lost his grip. The lid bounced a foot in the air as it hit a dried cow pie, and he went flying.

The laughter died in Mitch's throat. Dan rolled over and over like a tumbleweed in a windstorm and bowled into his brother, mowing him down like a giant scythe. John screamed, then started to howl.

Mitch whirled around and cupped his hands. "Johnny. Let go! Let go!" Whether he heard that or finally saw the danger, Mitch wasn't sure, but as the calf headed straight for the fence, his brother let go and went bouncing across the ground.

In three leaps, Mitch was yanking open the corral gate. Out of the corner of his eye he saw the lid bounce upward. There was a loud WHANG! as it hit one of the rails and left a two-inch gash in the wood. He darted into the corral, waving his arms and shouting. Seeing an escape, the calf burst through the gate at full speed, the lid bouncing wildly behind it.

"Are you all right?" Mitch yelled as he came up to Dan and John. John was still crying. Dan's face was white, and he had an abrasion over one eye. But both were okay. He turned toward Johnny, but just then he heard something. It sounded like the twang of a bow.

He spun around just in time to see the terrified calf plow straight into the bedsheet hanging on the first line. One horn hooked on the fabric. The clothesline bowed sharply, and then, as the calf jerked free, it snapped back. The calf whirled and plowed into the line filled with women's and girls' dresses. This time the rope did not hold. It snapped in two, and the whole line went down onto the sandy ground.

Hearing the noise, Mary Ann came bursting out of the house just in time to see the calf get tangled in the second line. Trussed up like a pig, the poor animal went down, taking two clotheslines and all the freshly laundered clothes down with it, eyes wild, bawling like its very life had been taken.

Mitch got to his feet, gaping at the havoc. Mary Ann Perkins came forward, her hands to her mouth. Then she whirled around. "Daniel!" she screeched. "John!"

Hearing a sound behind him, Mitch swung around in time to see three little boys running as hard and fast as they could as they ducked around the barn and disappeared.

Mitch turned back as Sister Perkins came slowly across the yard, clearly in shock. And then, Mitch couldn't help himself. He began to laugh. In moments, he was doubled over, holding his stomach to stop it from hurting.

And then, after a moment of dazed bewilderment, Mary Ann Perkins sat down and did the same.

Note

The descriptions of Bluff and daily life in that small, isolated community come from several sources (see *History of San Juan County*, 72–73; *Saga*, 66–67; *Lariats*, 50, 64). The account of the boys who caught a ride on a dishpan lid tied behind a half-grown calf was shared by Mary Ann Perkins (*Lariats*, 54). Obviously, Johnny Westland is a fictional character and was not part of the original story. Also, the calf did not pull down the wash on that day, but that happened in an account of another child's prank. The two are combined here to show another dimension of life on the frontier.

CHAPTER 6

September 12, 1884—Bluff City, Utah Territory

When Mitch stopped at the front of the cabin, it was no surprise that the door was open. The summer heat was finally softening, but it was still in the low nineties even though it wasn't yet noon.

He stopped, wondering if his mother was asleep. But then, as his eyes adjusted to the dark interior, he saw that she was at the table preparing the bowl of string beans the Bartons had sent over. Moving very carefully, he stepped over the doorsill and onto the hardpacked dirt floor. His feet didn't make a sound. His mother was humming softly to herself as she worked.

He took another step, half holding his breath. But she heard that one. With a low cry, she leaped up, sending the pan of beans flying. She whirled around, her hands coming up to defend herself.

"Mama, it's just me," Mitch cried. She stared at him, eyes wide and frightened, and he realized that he was silhouetted against the light from the door. He went to her and took her in his arms. "It's me, Mama. It's Mitch."

Sagging against him, her body trembled violently.

"I'm sorry, Mama." Mitch felt awful. "I didn't mean to

frighten you." Actually, that was exactly what he had planned
to do—give her just a little scare.

She backed away, brushing quickly at her dress. "You gave
me such a start." Then she smacked him on the arm. "Don't
do that to me, Mitch. You knock or say something before you
come sneaking up on me. My heart's pounding like a blacksmith's hammer. You scared the daylights out of me."

"Sorry." Then he took her by the hands. "Can I make it up
to you?"

"I'm not sure. It would have to be something pretty good."

He let her go and strode back to the door. "Oh, I think this
will do. Wait here." A minute later he appeared with a sack of
flour over his shoulder and a tin of lard under one arm.

"Flour?" she squealed. "Where did you get that?"

Setting the haul down on the table, he held up a finger
for her to hold that question and disappeared again. A moment later he came back with a smaller sack, this one made of
a looser fabric.

"What is that?"

He held it up so she could see the label. For a moment,
she couldn't make it out, and then she clapped her hands in
delight. "Apples! Are those really apples? Where in the world
did you get them?"

Setting them on the table, he gave her another hug. "So am
I forgiven for startling you?"

"Four times over," she cried. "Where did you get them?"

"Ben Perkins just got back from Durango. There's a
Mexican grower over there. They're right in the middle of the
apple harvest now."

She bent over and inhaled deeply, then sighed. "Oh, Mitch,

how much did you have to pay for these? Not that I care. They're wonderful."

"The better question is how many people did I have to fight off in order to get a bag?"

"I can only imagine," she said. "How many?"

"Actually, when I told them that my mama baked the best apple pies in all of Utah Territory, they let me have first pick."

"Oh, this is wonderful. We'll have apple pie for dinner tonight."

"That's why I bought the flour and the lard, too."

She blew him a kiss. "And I don't care what your father says, you're getting the biggest piece."

"I'll hold you to that, Mama." He started backing away. "Well, I promised Ben I'd help him unload the wagons for giving me first pick, so I'd better run."

"Tell Johnny and Martha to go get some water from the Bartons' well. I'm not going to put river water in the pie crust."

"Okay." As he reached the door, he stopped. "Oh. Guess what else? There are several Indians in town, and Henry was with them. Do you remember Henry? The boy up on Elk Mountain who helped us?"

She had gone very still. "Indians? How many?"

He shrugged. "I don't know. Four men and their squaws, two or three papooses. They call their leader Old Toby, though don't ask me why. But Henry is with them. And he remembered me."

It was like she had barely heard him. She was staring out the window, her mind far away. He went over and kissed her on the cheek. "Remember," he teased. "I get the biggest piece."

She finally smiled. "After me, of course."

Laughing, he went out the door. "I'll be back before sundown."

"Mitch?"

He stopped and turned back. "Yes?"

"Will you shut the door, please?"

"But it's so hot in here, Mama."

She nodded. "I know, but I don't want the flies going after our apples."

He shrugged and pulled it shut after him.

She waited until Mitch was half a block away, and then she moved a chair over and propped it up against the door. Only then did she get out pans, knives, and dishes to start working on the apples.

Gwendolyn Greene Westland did not like Indians. Or, put more accurately, she had a deep and abiding fear of Indians. All Indians. The tribe didn't matter. This had nothing to do with their race or color. It had everything to do with their fearsome reputation as warriors and their known hatred for white people.

The Greenes and the Westlands had not known each other in England, even though they were both from Staffordshire. Not until they reached Liverpool and were assigned to the same ship going to America did they meet each other. And only when they reached Iowa City and were assigned to the same handcart company, captained by Edmund Ellsworth, did a friendship form that would last the rest of their lives.

Gwendolyn was fourteen at the time. Arthur was four years older and barely paid any attention to her while crossing the plains. But their parents had a little more vision and a great deal of patience and began to make plans. Upon their arrival in

Salt Lake City, both families were assigned to a group called to open up a new settlement on the Beaver River in central Utah. That and their parents' quiet determination to bring them together made it almost inevitable that sooner or later, Gwen and Arthur would marry. They were married in the Endowment House in Salt Lake City in November of 1863. By that time, Gwen was twenty and Arthur was twenty-four.

Her fear of Indians began before they ever left England. As the missionaries from America began baptizing people by the thousands, the vicars of the Church of England united in an effort to stop them. The Church of England petitioned Parliament to declare The Church of Jesus Christ of Latter-day Saints to be a false church and to banish it from the British Isles. Fortunately, Parliament stood by the laws protecting religious freedom and told the vicars that if they treated their flocks better maybe they wouldn't lose so many members to the Mormons.

Furious at that, ministers and other public figures took up another strategy: they started a smear campaign. Newspapers published all kinds of lies about the Church, including that their missionaries were here to seduce young girls and take them as plural wives. Preachers thundered out against them from the pulpits.

Soon employers started firing Mormon employees if they refused to denounce the Church. Children of Latter-day Saints were taunted by their teachers in school and hounded by other children. Gwendolyn's teacher had somehow learned that her family had been baptized and began mercilessly attacking her and the other two members in their class. When the teacher learned they were going to America, he devoted an entire school day to Indian atrocities in the American West.

He had done his research well and regaled the class with stories of Indian battles, Indian massacres, and Indian torture. Just before class ended, he went to his desk and opened a drawer. By this time, England had developed a morbid curiosity about the American Indian. Native Americans were brought over on ships to be paraded before the people. That curiosity also fueled a brisk trade in human scalps, most of which had been taken by white men from their so-called savage enemies.

Somehow, the teacher had obtained one of those scalps. He pinned it to the end of a ruler and waved it right in front of Gwendolyn's face. The other children shrieked with delight when she fainted. When they revived her, the teacher leaned down and told her that she and the other two Mormons were being expelled.

Her nightmares started a few days later.

Somewhere between Chimney Rock and Fort Laramie, the Ellsworth handcart company saw a large band of Indians coming toward them. This was not an uncommon sight, but the fact that all the men were wearing war paint was. And it was a fearsome sight. When the leader came into their camp and angrily demanded food from Captain Ellsworth, Gwendolyn had nearly fainted again. The pioneers were already short of food and were still several days away from meeting the relief wagons from Salt Lake. They had no food to spare. When Ellsworth started out to meet the chief, he looked over his shoulder and called back, "Pray for me." Gwen did, more fervently than she had ever prayed before, but she did so from beneath the cover of their handcart. She buried her face into a blanket, too frightened to peek out and watch what was happening.

As it turned out, Ellsworth convinced the Indians that they didn't have food and offered them some beads instead. The offer was accepted, and the group moved on. That evening, Gwen's nightmares returned.

By the time Gwendolyn married Arthur, her childhood fears had mostly disappeared. There were Indian skirmishes around the territory from time to time, but they rarely impacted her or her family. Then a few months after their marriage, a local Ute chief by the name of Antonga Black Hawk formed an alliance with the Piutes, Apaches, and Navajo and unleashed war on the whites. Arthur was part of the local militia and was called up to fight in the Black Hawk War.

It was a horrible time for Gwen. Arthur would be gone for weeks at a time, leaving her alone with the children. Even when he was home, her fear was only made worse because he wanted to—needed to—talk about what was happening out there. She would lie by his side in silent horror as he recounted some of the things he had seen and experienced. Then, long after he was asleep, she would relive his words over and over in her mind.

Did Arthur know any of this? She wasn't sure. She didn't think so, for she had determined long ago that this was her own private battle. Yet more than once he had taken her in his arms when she woke in the middle of the night screaming and wet with sweat. But he never asked her about her nightmares. He just held her in his arms until she fell asleep again.

The nightmares hadn't troubled her for years. Then came the call to go to the San Juan to live among the Indians and make friends with them. She was still fighting that reality when Mitch went to find a way up to the high plateaus of Elk Mountain. Her nightmares were not as frequent or as horrible as before, but they still left her with her heart pounding and her pillow soaked with sweat.

⁂

When the children returned with the water from the well, she made them stay with her. Ostensibly it was to help her with the pies. but even when the pies went in the oven she convinced them to play checkers with her. But that only lasted for so long. Begging leave from the hot cabin, they convinced her to let them go play again. She went to the door, removed the chair, and looked all around. There was no one in sight, not even any of the Bluff settlers. "All right," she agreed. "You can play outside until Mitch and Papa come home. But stay close by. No going down to the river."

"Yes, Mama."

"And . . ." She bit her lip. "And if you see anyone coming other than your brother and your father, you come get me. Understood?"

"Yes, Mama." And they were gone. She watched them go, Martha squealing as Johnny tried to yank on her pigtails. Smiling, Gwen went back inside and started to shut the door. But the heat inside the cabin was suffocating, and she changed her mind. Leaving the door half open, she fell onto the bed and dropped off into an exhausted sleep.

Half an hour later, Gwendolyn awoke with a start. She was lying on her side, facing the cabin wall. Her whole body was damp with sweat, and she could feel her hair plastered against her scalp. Yawning, she stretched mightily and then settled down again, telling herself that it wouldn't hurt to lie there for a few more minutes.

There was a soft scraping sound, and light suddenly flooded

the room. Crying out, she jerked up to a sitting position and whirled to face the door. Chills shot through every part of her body when she saw the dark shape framed in the doorway. She couldn't see a face, but the figure was too short to be either Arthur or Mitch, and too large to be Martha or Johnny. It was a squat, thick figure, with broad shoulders and a squarish head. Outside the door a horse was visible.

Gwen gasped again and fell back against the wall as the door opened wider and the figure stepped into the room. "Squaw no be afraid," a deep, gravelly voice said. "Old Toby not hurt squaw. "

"Get out!" she yelled.

He stopped but made no move to leave. "Old Toby hungry. Squaw have biscuits for Toby?"

Getting a grip on herself, but still trembling violently, she stood up and edged away from him, looking for something she might grab if he attacked her. "No. No biscuits," she stammered. "Go away!"

With more light in the room, she caught a glimpse of his face. It was one she had not seen before. It wasn't a particularly savage face, but it was always hard to tell with the Indians. His cheeks were scarred from the pox. In the dim light, his eyes appeared as two dark spots above his cheeks. His mouth was large and he was smiling at her, revealing teeth yellowed from tobacco. He sniffed the air. "No biscuits? Me hungry."

Strangely enough, what came to Gwendolyn's mind at that moment was the first and most important of Thales Haskell's rules for dealing with Indians: don't show fear.

She heard a little, derisive laugh in her head as she saw the six-shooter in a holster strapped to the Indian's waist. *Don't show fear? Oh, really?*

She took a quick breath and stepped forward.

"Toby, I am Mrs. Westland." She was sure her voice sounded like a little girl's.

"Me Old Toby."

"Yes, I've heard of you, Toby."

"Me hungry. Want biscuits."

"I . . ." *Keep things simple.* "I know you are hungry, Toby. But I don't have any biscuits right now." Then her eye fell on the sack of flour Mitch had brought her earlier. "But you go outside. Chop wood for me and I'll fix you biscuits. But it will take time."

He moved closer, his eyes searching the room. "No chop wood. Want biscuits. Want to eat now."

It took every ounce of her will not to try to bolt past him. His voice had turned hard, and now she saw that he had a riding whip in one hand and was slapping his leg with it. *No fear. No fear.*

"Toby, listen to me. I will cook you biscuits but it will take—"

Totally ignoring her, Toby walked over to the window. He bent over, peering at the two pies there. He sniffed again. "Smell good. Toby like pie." He reached out to pick one up.

"No!" She yelled it loudly enough that he stopped and swung around to face her. In the light from the window, she could see that his mouth was pinched and there was fire dancing in his eyes. He lifted the whip and shook it at her. "Squaw no tell Toby what to do. Toby hungry. Toby want pie."

And as if that settled everything, he turned back around and picked up the pie.

Later, people would ask her what went through her mind at that moment. She had to admit that there was nothing she could remember except a blind fury that he was stealing her apple pies. In three quick steps she reached the stove, above which hung their large frying pan. Going up on tiptoes, she snatched the pan, gripping it in both hands. In another step she was behind Toby, who had set the pie on the table and was preparing to sit down.

WHANG!

The frying pan sounded like a bell being tolled as it connected with the back of Toby's head. He screamed in pain and dropped to his knees.

Horror struck her as she realized what she had just done. As Toby staggered back to his feet, dazed and holding the back of his head, she dropped the frying pan and let it hit the floor. "Squaw cook you biscuits, Toby. But you wait." And then she did another unthinkable thing. She turned her back on him. She picked up the frying pan, hung it back on its hook, and went to the table to put the pie back on the windowsill. All of this without breathing. All of this as she pictured him pulling out his pistol.

Finally, taking a deep breath to steady herself, she turned around. "You chop wood. I make biscuits. You chop wood, you have pie. Do you understand me?"

She held her breath again. His hand was resting on the butt of his pistol. He was staring at her in a murderous rage. "You liar. You no make Toby biscuits. You one angry squaw." His jaw thrust out, and she saw his hand close around the pistol. "Maybe Toby shoot you."

She didn't flinch nor move. As calmly as she could manage, she said, "Squaw no lie. Squaw tell truth. You want food, you work."

Again she turned away, and with every ounce of will she

had, she went to the chest and began taking out dishes and setting them on the table. She heard a sound behind her, and then a shadow passed through the light from the door. A moment later, she heard him yell something. She turned just in time to see the horse leap forward and disappear. She ran to the door in time to watch him go.

When the realization of what she had done hit her, she blindly groped for a chair and sat down, placing both hands under her so they would stop shaking.

When Martha and Johnny returned, she said nothing about her visitor. She only asked where they had gone. It turned out they had found a desert tortoise over by the Bartons' well and had completely forgotten their mother's warning to stay close. They had seen nothing.

�֎

That evening, sensing that something was different, Arthur kept looking at her, questioning her with his eyes. She pretended not to notice. Mitch kept giving her questioning looks too. She ignored them.

They were nearly through with supper when a shadow suddenly appeared in the doorway. Martha yelled out. The rest of them whirled in surprise. It was Old Toby. Arthur shot to his feet, but Gwendolyn grabbed his hand and pulled him down again. "Good evening, Toby," she said, managing a thin smile. "Did you come back for your biscuits?"

"No, Toby want pie." He removed his hat. "Squaw, me not mad now."

"Good, Toby. Squaw not mad now either."

"I chop wood?"

"That would be nice. When Toby is done, Toby will have apple pie."

He grunted and disappeared.

Knowing that her whole family was gaping at her in utter astonishment, she picked up her fork and started eating again. When none of them moved, she turned to them, her eyes wide with feigned innocence. "What?" she demanded

"What in the world was that all about?" Arthur asked.

"What is Old Toby doing here?" Mitch exclaimed.

"Oh, for heaven's sake. He's going to have dessert with us. What is all the fuss about?"

Notes

The Ellsworth Handcart Company did have an encounter with hostile Indians somewhere along the North Platte River, but they were able to defuse the situation without incident (see *Handcarts to Zion*, 71).

Thales Haskell, who had served for years as a missionary among the Indians, was considered by the Saints in the San Juan Mission to be the resident Indian expert. His rules for dealing with Indians were well known to the settlers, and one of the prime ones was to show no fear. Others included always being plain, frank, and straight-talking with them; speaking slowly and clearly and using simple language; not accusing them of wrongdoing unless you were sure they really did it; never lying to them; and letting them do most of the talking (*Saga*, 219).

Gwen's experience with Old Toby is based on two actual incidents. One is credited to Jane M. Walton and the other to Mary Jones, wife of Kumen Jones. Both involved a Ute Indian named Posey. In Jane Walton's case, she was out hoeing in the garden when Posey rode up demanding biscuits. She told him she would get him some as soon as she finished hoeing the row. Angry that she didn't respond, Posey drew his gun on her. She went on hoeing. He got off his horse and followed after her, swearing at her and threatening her. She whirled around and hit him over the head with her hoe. He dropped like a rock. She was afraid she had killed him, but still turned her back on him. A minute or two later, he got up, gave a bloodcurdling yell, and ran for his horse. The dog went after him and took a piece of his trousers before he jumped on his horse and tore away. In this case, he didn't come back for several years. When he did, he cautiously opened the door and told her he wasn't mad anymore. She said she wasn't either and told him she would get his biscuits as soon as she finished what she was doing. He accepted that and went out and chopped her some wood while he waited (see ibid., 225–26).

In the case of Mary Jones, Posey came to the house while she was fixing her husband's lunch and asked for bread. She told him that if he would chop some wood, she would fix him some breakfast. Instead he started poking around looking for bread. Mary had a short, iron stove lifter in her hand. When she saw him looking beneath a cloth where she kept the bread, she told him that if he tried to take the bread, she would hit him with the lifter. That made him so angry he took out his horse whip and started whipping her across the shoulders. She screamed, and her husband ran in, knocked Posey down, and drove him out of the house. In this case, when Posey returned some time later, he went right to the woodpile and chopped some wood. Then he rode away without asking for food (see *Lariats*, 54–56).

There are enough similarities in the two stories that some have wondered if they are not two different accounts of the same incident. But there are enough significant differences that it's possible both occurred with the same Indian.

CHAPTER 7

September 17, 1884—Bluff City, Utah Territory

The word elixir comes from a Greek word meaning a "medical powder," or a "powder for drying wounds." But in common use, it refers to a sweet-flavored liquid that you drink to cure whatever ills have befallen you.

Joseph F. Smith, Erastus Snow, and others from Salt Lake City arrived unexpectedly a week early. Their coming was met with great excitement and anticipation. For Gwendolyn Westland, that excitement and anticipation quickly turned to pure joy. In their initial meeting with Bishop Nielson and his counselors, these Brethren confirmed that they had come with the permission of President John Taylor to do one of two things if conditions warranted it: They could either disband the mission completely and allow the people to return to their homes, or they could start new settlements somewhere else. Either way, the San Juan pioneers would no longer face the triple threat of lawless cowboys, hostile Indians, and a relentless, untamable river.

To Gwen, that news was like a restorative elixir to both body and spirit. The effect on her was amazing. It was as though she shed ten years overnight. She was reenergized, rejuvenated, reborn. She went about humming softly as she worked, often swaying back and forth to the music in her head. When Mitch's father reminded her that they no longer had a home to return to and that they would have to start over in Beaver or elsewhere, she cried, "I know, I know. Isn't that wonderful?"

Mitch received the news as if he were hit by a runaway hay wagon. The thought of going back to Beaver left him sick to his stomach. But when he saw how his mother took the news, he clamped his mouth shut and put on the best face he could muster.

That night, as the family was preparing for bed, Mitch finally became so frustrated with his mother's euphoria that he dared to suggest that no final decision had yet been made. Gwen was tucking Johnny into bed. She stopped, turned, and gave Mitch an incredulous look. "President Taylor sent Joseph F. Smith down here, Mitch. *Joseph F. Smith!* Son of Hyrum Smith, nephew of the Prophet Joseph Smith."

Mitch saw that as a tremendous leap in logic. "Mother," he exclaimed in exasperation, "I know all that. And while it's a wonderful thing to get to meet him in person, his lineage has nothing to do with him coming here."

"Maybe not," she admitted. "But he is *President* Joseph F. Smith, Mitch. Don't you see that? President Taylor didn't just send Elder Snow or another member of the Twelve to handle this. He sent his counselor in the First Presidency. That means *President* Smith speaks for the First Presidency."

Mitch gave his father an imploring look at that point, but Arthur sided with his wife. "Your mother's right about that, Mitch. President Smith comes on assignment from the First Presidency. Whatever he decides will be final." He gave Mitch a very hard look. "And we will accept it. We *all* will accept it."

"But he hasn't decided for sure," Mitch retorted.

"That's enough, Mitch. Let it be." The tone of his father's

voice told Mitch it was time to stop. So he did. But if the conversation turned in any way to the possibility of them leaving, he would leave the room.

September 19, 1884

For the next couple of days, President Smith and Elder Snow toured the ravaged valley and the surrounding area with Bishop Nielson and his counselors. They saw what few remnants were left of the Big Ditch. They were shown the ruined cribs and the smashed remains of the great water wheel. They walked the mud flats, now dried into something akin to cement. They stepped inside cabins with inside walls stained with mud. They drove the fifteen miles to Montezuma Creek to survey the ruins of what had once been a small community. They rode out to Cottonwood Wash and Butler Wash and saw how limited the feed was for their cattle, even after a wet spring.

But that was not all. In the evenings, the Brethren visited with individual families. They asked some questions, but mostly they just listened as the members described what life in Bluff was like. Mitch was quite irritated when they spoke with his mother and father and never once asked him how he felt about it. Yet through all the frustration, he held his tongue. Incurring the wrath of his father would only make things worse.

When all of the touring and interviewing was done, President Smith and Elder Snow retired to the home of Bishop Nielson and spent several hours conferring together in private. They came out at about four o'clock in the afternoon and asked Bishop Nielson to convene a meeting for all settlers at seven o'clock that evening in the log schoolhouse.

Hope filled the air like a breath of spring as the Westlands left their cabin and joined the throngs making their way toward the schoolhouse. People spoke in hushed but excited whispers. The pall of discouragement that had hung over the settlement for so long was gone. Adults laughed like children as they greeted one another. It would have been an exaggeration to say that Gwendolyn skipped along as she walked, but there was a lightness to her step that Mitch had not seen for months. Even his father seemed to have had a heavy load lifted from his shoulders.

Not Mitch. He walked behind the others, staring at the ground, his mind working furiously. When his friends called to him in greeting, he barely heard them. He fully expected the visiting General Authorities to close the mission. But now, he had the tiniest glimmer of hope. Just as his family was leaving the cabin for the schoolhouse, an idea had come to him. Now his mind was analyzing it and exploring what it would take to make it work.

The hall was already filled to capacity when they entered. They stopped at the doorway, looking for a place to sit. Two rows down, one bench was filled with the Perkins family. Mary Ann saw them and leaned over to say something to Ben. He nodded and got up, waving for the Westlands to come over. Mary Ann started squeezing her kids together to make room for them.

As Arthur and Gwen walked over, Ben shook their hands. "I'll stand in the back," he said. "Make a little more room here. I think we're going to have a crowd tonight."

Arthur motioned for Gwen to move in. "I'll be in back with Ben," he said. Gwen nodded. Men were already standing along the back wall to leave more room for the women and children in the seats.

"Thank you, Brother Perkins," Gwen said, touching his arm.

"I'll go back there too," Mitch said. But his father shook his head. "No, you sit here with your mother."

"An exciting day," Mary Ann Perkins said as Gwen got settled beside her.

"Indeed," Gwendolyn replied.

Mitch looked around. The room was buzzing with conversation. Everyone was sitting as families except for the men in the back. All of the windows were open, and Mitch was glad to note that the room wasn't unbearably hot and stuffy, as it had been all summer.

The small stage up front was filled with chairs, and all of them were occupied. Mitch was impressed as he let his eyes move from face to face. What a collection of faith was represented here. It filled him with awe and gratitude. *Someday*, he thought, *I'll tell my grandchildren that I knew these people.*

Precisely at seven o'clock, Platte D. Lyman, president of the stake, stood up and opened the meeting. He warmly welcomed the visitors from Salt Lake City and expressed the gratitude of all those present for their willingness to come so far in their behalf. There were several chuckles when he then announced that the opening hymn would be "Let Us All Press On." Bishop Nielson offered the opening prayer. Then, after a few brief remarks, President Lyman turned the podium over to President Joseph F. Smith.

President Smith had a few sheets of paper in his hand, which he set on the podium before taking his spectacles from his pocket and slipping them on. Mitch watched him, feeling a sense of awe. His mother was right. There was something about *who* he was, in addition to *what* he was, that was pretty impressive.

His countenance was pleasant. He had a full head of hair and a full beard, which was jet black. Some of the old-timers who had lived while the Prophet Joseph was still alive said that he bore a strong resemblance to both Joseph and Hyrum, his father.

Finally President Smith looked up. "Brothers and sisters, welcome. Thank you for coming. Thank you for the warm hospitality you have shown us since our arrival. There is much to do, so I shall be brief.

"My brethren and I have been shocked and saddened as we have seen the evidence of what you have endured and the conditions under which you have lived. The story of the San Juan pioneers is known now throughout the Church and serves as an example of faith, courage, and endurance. We commend you for who you are and what you have done. We do not condemn those who have chosen to leave. They answered the call and served faithfully, and we wish them well. But we especially commend you for your willingness to obey counsel and stay on under the most trying of circumstances until you could receive counsel from your priesthood leaders."

He stopped and looked around. Absentmindedly he removed his eyeglasses and took out a handkerchief to polish them. When he finished, he replaced the glasses, put away his handkerchief, and picked up the papers before him. He studied the first page for a moment, his thoughts clearly far away. Every eye was locked on him. Not a whisper of sound came from the congregation.

At last he laid the papers down again and looked up. "My dear brothers and sisters, as you know, Elder Snow and I came down with authorization from President Taylor to release you honorably from your calls to the San Juan Mission. Our expectation when we came was that we would do so. And after seeing your circumstances these past two days, those feelings were confirmed again and again. The challenges here are too extensive, too difficult. Your sacrifice is inspiring."

Mitch's head dropped. This was it. Everyone else sensed it too. This was the moment they had all been waiting for. Well, most of them. He frowned. Maybe all of them but one.

"But . . ." President Smith stopped and stared out over their heads for several moments.

Mitch's head snapped up. *But? But what?*

Beside him, his mother had obviously sensed the significance of that word too. All around them people were leaning forward, hardly daring to breathe. That single word hung in the air like an aerial bomb about to explode.

"But, as Elder Snow and I have counseled together and prayed earnestly for the Spirit's guidance in this matter, our feelings have changed."

"No!" came a soft whisper from somewhere behind Mitch.

Yes! Mitch instantly responded. He didn't say it aloud, but in that short moment, his heart leaped with exultation.

"We believe that the Lord feels that the mission you have undertaken here is of such great importance and has so many implications for the whole territory that we should not—indeed, we *cannot*—disband it at this time."

It was clear that he had anticipated the reaction this would bring, for he stopped and let the noise explode all around him. And explode it did, and not just in whispers. There were cries of dismay. Cries of disappointment. Cries of bewilderment. Some of the women were weeping. The younger children looked at one another in confusion, not sure what had just happened.

After a moment, Bishop Nielson leaned over to Elder Snow and said something. He nodded, and the bishop got to his feet and stood beside President Smith. The sound died away quickly. "Brodders and sisters, please. Let us hear President Smith out. Then there vill be time for qvestions."

"Of course there will," President Smith said. "Thank you, Bishop."

He let things settle down for a moment before he went on. His expression was sorrowful but resolute. "We fully understand what we are asking of you. And we want it to be clearly understood that anyone who chooses not to stay will be released without question, without criticism, and without condemnation. And you will go with our warmest expressions of gratitude for your service and your faith."

He stopped, letting his eyes sweep across the room. The whispers had broken out again, and this time a sense the relief could be felt in the room. There was an out—an honorable out. Mitch's euphoria evaporated instantly. He knew exactly what his mother was going to say. "He's *President* Joseph F. Smith, Mitch. He speaks for the First Presidency."

"But!" President Smith raised one finger, pointing it in the air.

There was that word again. Mitch had never realized how powerful a single word could be.

"But, if you choose to stay, as we are asking you to do, then I feel impressed to promise you, in the name of the Lord, that you shall be doubly blessed as you face the difficult situation that lies before you."

Then, as if another thought had just come to him, he turned and looked at Bishop Nielson. "Bishop?"

Jens Nielson got to his feet. "Ya?"

"I'm guessing that you are one of the oldest members of the mission, if not the oldest. Is that correct?"

His eyes began to twinkle. "Vell, President, it sure feels like it vhen I get up in the morning."

That won him a warm burst of laughter.

President Smith smiled, but it faded quickly. "We also understand that in your efforts to establish this settlement, you have incurred considerable personal debt."

The bishop's head fell but he nodded. "Ya, that is true."

"Well, I say to you, Bishop Nielson, that if you choose to stay, I promise that you will see the day when you will prosper to the point that all of those debts will be removed."

The old Dane was startled for a moment, and then tears sprang to his eyes. "Thank you, President. As many here know, I pray that my creditors do not call in my debts, because I haf no way to pay them. But I trust in the blessings of the Lord."

He sat down, wiping at the corners of his eyes.

"As should we all," President Smith said, his own voice touched with emotion. Then he cleared his throat. "To all of you, I say again: if you choose to go, you will be blessed for your faithfulness in staying here for these very difficult four years. But know this: as of this day, we are revoking the counsel that you establish no other settlements than Bluff and Montezuma Creek. You may now feel free to search out other favorable locations and start new settlements, as long as Bluff is not abandoned. And I make this promise to you also: in addition to being doubly blessed, you too will prosper."

His shoulders lifted and fell as if he had shrugged off a burden. "Go back to your homes and your tents and your wagons. Talk together as families. Decide what is best for you and what the Lord would have *you* do. Before we leave tomorrow, I shall ask Elder Snow to record the names of all present and your decisions on this matter so that we can report back to President Taylor and record this important historical moment."

Notes

In response to the letter written to Church leaders in Salt Lake City during the flood season of 1884, John Taylor, President of The Church of Jesus Christ of Latter-day Saints, sent a delegation to Bluff to meet with the settlers and assess the situation. Elder Erastus Snow was a natural choice because he was the priesthood leader over the southern part of Utah Territory. No explanation is given in the records as to why President Joseph F. Smith was chosen to lead the delegation. Certainly, his position in the First Presidency gave added weight to whatever decision he would make.

Sources note that the delegation took time to tour the area and assess the situation before making a recommendation. A meeting was called in which the decision was announced. Unfortunately, a detailed account of that meeting was unavailable. Therefore, much of President Smith's speech was created by the author. However, these additions are based on key elements of the meeting that have been described by those present.

Accounts differ as to how many families left Bluff after this meeting. One source says that all but twelve families left, but that seems questionable in light of how many of the original names are mentioned as being in San Juan County in the following years. There is no question that the population was significantly reduced. However, many of those who left Bluff either started new settlements as noted or moved to existing settlements in Colorado and New Mexico, which were also in the San Juan Mission. Interestingly, the population of Bluff today is about 300, which is what it was at the time depicted in this chapter.

Bishop Jens Nielson was deeply in debt at this time with no idea of how he could pay off those debts if they were called in. While he was at the pulpit, President Smith turned to Bishop Nielson, making the promise of prosperity as described in this chapter. When he died in 1906, Bishop Nielson's estate was valued at about $20,000, an impressive sum for those days.

Finally, there was a record made of those who decided to stay and those who chose to go. The assumption is that this was done to include in the official history of the Church (see *History of San Juan County*, 48–49; *Portrait*, 41; *Indians and Outlaws*, 46; *Saga*, 76–77).

CHAPTER 8

September 19, 1884—Bluff City, Utah Territory

Mitch's parents refused to talk about the meeting on the way back to their cabin. "We'll not be discussing this until we get home," his father said as they exited the log schoolhouse. When Mitch started to object, his father gave him such a withering look that he clamped his jaw shut and said not another word.

"Does this mean we're going back home to Beaver, Papa?" Johnny asked after two or three minutes had passed.

"No talking about it until we get back to the cabin, son," Arthur said gently.

Mitch was watching his mother out of the corner of his eye. If she heard either exchange, she gave no sign. Her expression was unreadable. And she looked neither to the left nor to the right. When they reached their home, Johnny complained of being hungry. Martha said she was too, so their mother got out some bread and molasses. When they were finished eating, she turned to Mitch. "Mitchell, I think your father and I will get the children to bed before we talk. The buckets are almost empty. Why don't you go down and get some water from the river so we can let it stand overnight?"

"Yes, Mama." But as he grabbed the buckets and dumped out what little water was left in them, he muttered, "You just don't want me here while you talk about what we're going to do."

"What did you say?" his father snapped.

"Nothin'."

"Or," came the curt reply, "if you prefer, we can put you to bed too along with the other children." The last word was said with heavy sarcasm.

"I'm sorry."

As he hurried away, his mother called after him. "Mitch, there's no hurry. It will take at least half an hour to get the children to sleep."

"Yeah," he growled under his breath. "That's what I thought."

It was only a three-minute walk to the river, so after the two buckets were filled, Mitch decided to give them their full half an hour without his protests so they could decide they were going back. It was clear that Mitch was not going to have a voice in this anyway.

He turned to the left and followed the river a short distance to the Swing Tree. The sun was down now, but there was enough lingering light for him to see clearly that no one was there. He snorted bitterly. That was easy to explain. All the other families were talking *together* now, just as President Smith had suggested. But, oh no, not his family.

He set the buckets down and then, grumpy as an old setting hen in molt, he swung slowly back and forth in the swing, working out in his mind what he could possibly say that might change his parents' minds. And changing their minds was what needed to happen. Now that President Smith had given his official permission to return home, Mitch had no question about what his mother would do. They were already halfway packed, and her heart had returned to Beaver weeks ago. Now there was nothing stopping them except maybe for Mitch, and he was realistic enough to know that the chances of that happening were probably a hundred to one.

He sat there, staring at the river, barely aware of the time, thinking how totally and completely unfair life was. And he discovered something about feeling sorry for yourself: it had a certain perverse satisfaction to it. If no one else appreciated the injustice of the world, then at least you could. You could wrap your wounded feelings around you like a blanket—even wallow in them if you liked.

How long that went on, he wasn't sure. The mire of self-pity is a deep bog, and he was well lost in it when he remembered the thought he'd had previously. Only now it came to him as a complete idea. He stiffened, letting the swing come to a stop. Hope was shooting through him like a Chinese rocket. The simple brilliance of what had just come to him was stunning. He sat motionless for another minute or two, testing the idea from every angle. Then he jumped off the swing and headed back toward town at a swift walk.

Kumen Jones had two wives. His first wife was named Mary. She was the daughter of Jens and Elsie Nielson. His second wife was named May. She was one of the Lyman girls. Mitch knew who they were, of course—he saw them in church every week—but he couldn't keep straight which one was which. Not that it mattered. He wasn't there to talk to them.

The door swung open, and a woman considerably shorter than Mitch stood there in the lamplight. "Yes?"

"Uh . . . hullo. Is . . . uh . . . Brother Jones here?"

"Hello," she said with a pleasant smile. "You're the Westlands' boy, right?"

"Yes, ma'am. Mitch Westland, ma'am. Is Kumen here?"

He heard footsteps, and then Kumen's voice called out. "I'm here. Be right out." He appeared a moment later. He was in stocking feet and was tucking his white shirt into his trousers. "Evenin', Mitch."

"Good evening, Kumen. Uh . . . could I talk to you?"

A little surprised, Kumen nodded. "Sure. Come on in. I'm just leaving for a meeting with the bishopric. How much time do you need? I'll be back later this evening if we need more time."

"No. This will only take a few minutes. I just had a question." Then he shrugged. "But I guess it can wait till morning."

Kumen looked at his wife. "May, will you get my boots, honey?" Then to Mitch, "If it's only a few minutes, we can do it now."

"Thank you." Mitch stepped back. He didn't want to talk to him with anyone listening. "Uh . . . I'll wait out front, if that's okay."

Kumen shrugged. "Okay. I'll be right out."

When Kumen joined Mitch out on the street, he moved even farther away from the house, sensing Mitch's need for privacy. "What can I do for you, Mitch?"

He let his breath out in a long, low sound of discouragement. "I think my folks are gonna choose to go back to Beaver."

"Okay," Kumen said slowly. "As President Smith said, there's no shame in that. Your folks are good people, Mitch. No shame in that at all."

"I know that. I don't think Pa's as keen on going back. But my mother is. And he'll do it if that's what she wants."

"Your mother is a woman of faith and courage, son. But she's got some real health problems, and those can't be ignored.

Back in the settlements, she can get much better treatment than here."

"I understand that. But *I* don't want to go back. I feel like my place is here. Especially now that President Smith said that we'd get double the blessings for staying."

"I see." Kumen's eyes narrowed as he studied him. "How old are you again, Mitch?"

"I'll be seventeen in January."

"But you're big for your age." There was a twinkle of amusement in his eyes as he said it.

Mitch winced. That was his standard answer when adults asked him how old he was. But it was a good answer. "Yes, I am. You saw that when we went up to Elk Mountain. I can hold my own."

"Yes, you can. And I'll tell you straight out, Mitch. You earned your spurs out there. I'd be happy to have you ride with me any time. So would several others."

"What if I worked for you for a year?" he blurted. "Until I'm eighteen. Then I can go out on my own. I'm determined to have my own spread someday. I know my family has to go back. But I don't. Pa's been talking of selling our herd rather than trailing them all the way back to Beaver, and I'm gonna see if he'll sell them to me on credit and—"

Kumen held up his hand, smiling. "Slow down, son," he laughed.

Suddenly embarrassed by his excitement, Mitch shook his head. "I'll help them go back, of course. But hopefully I could make it back here before Escalante Mountain gets snowed in. But I'd need a place to stay. Just for a year. I could do whatever you need me to do. And I'll not be asking for any pay or anything like that."

Kumen's head cocked to one side slightly. "Do your parents know you're talking to me about this?"

Mitch's head dropped and he started kicking at the sand with the toe of his boot.

"I see. Well, then . . ." He rubbed at his chin, thinking hard. Finally, his head bobbed once. "Tell you what, Mitch. With your permission, I'll bring this up in our bishopric's meeting. See what Bishop Nielson thinks we should do. Would that be all right?"

"All right? That would be great!"

"Actually, we've already been talking about your family as a bishopric. Bishop Nielson's concerned about your mother. Making the trip back isn't going to be easy on her either. We're halfway through September, and if the snows come early on Escalante Mountain, they might have to hole up in Escalante or one of the other settlements, which means you'd be living out of your wagon through the winter."

"I know. I was thinking about that too." This was a slight exaggeration. Mitch's worries about Escalante Mountain getting snowed in had been regarding how it would affect him getting back to Bluff this year.

"You go on back to your cabin. Talk to your parents. Tell them what you're thinking. You'll have to have their permission or no one is going to take you in."

"Yeah," he said glumly. Talking to his folks was something he didn't even want to think about.

"I'll get back to you. We'll work something out, okay?"

"Thanks."

Kumen stuck out his hand. "Am I the first one you asked?"

"You were the first one I thought of," Mitch said as he gripped his hand and shook it.

"Then I'm honored." He started away. "I'll get back with you," he called again over his shoulder.

Mitch went back for the water buckets, but he didn't start back for the cabin right away. He went back and sat down in the swing again. His mind was firing off like a Gatling gun. Bam! Bam! Bam! Bam! Bam! The thoughts were coming that fast. The one thing he knew for sure was that it was going to be an uphill battle for him to convince his parents to let him stay in Bluff. So he had to line up some good answers to their objections before he went back.

It was nearly dark when he realized what time it was. He'd been gone longer than half an hour, of that he was sure. He jumped up, grabbed the buckets, and broke into a trot, sloshing water as he ran.

As he rounded the corner to their cabin, he stopped short. A lamp was still burning inside, casting a glow of soft gold outside by their wagon. Four or five figures were silhouetted in the light from the window. All were adults. Three were sitting on chairs. One was standing. One was seated on a log. The one standing turned at the sound of his footsteps.

"Mitch? Is that you?"

"Coming, Pa." Slowing to a walk to avoid spilling any more water, he quickly crossed the street and joined them. To his surprise, the entire bishopric was there with his parents. Kumen Jones nodded at Mitch but said nothing. Bishop Nielson and Lemuel Redd stepped forward and shook Mitch's hand as he set the buckets down.

His mind was reeling. They were supposed to be in a meeting. Then a thought struck him. Had Kumen already told his parents about Mitch's proposition? Had Kumen asked the bishopric to come and discuss it with his parents? His heart plummeted. He could imagine how his father must be reacting to that. And he hadn't talked to his parents, as he had promised Kumen he would.

He glanced quickly at Kumen, but his face was a mask, giving nothing away.

"Come," Bishop Nielson said. "Let us sit." As they all got settled, Bishop Nielson started right in.

"My dear Sister Vestland, vhen the meeting ended tonight, I vas vatching you. I vas thinking about you. And my heart vas very sad."

She was watching him intently. "I'm all right," she finally said.

He nodded. "I had an impression that perhaps you might like a blessing at the hands of the priesthood."

Her eyes flew open. Then she surprised them all. "Why?" she asked softly. "Why did you feel I needed a blessing? I'm not the only one struggling." She looked pointedly at Mitch.

Bishop Nielson smiled, and the kindness in his eyes was like a warm glow. "Dear Sister, I did not feel like you needed a blessing. Your Heafenly Father did. You vill haf to ask Him that qvestion."

Tears instantly filled her eyes, and after a moment her chin dropped. "Then yes," she whispered. "I would like a blessing."

The bishop got to his feet, took a small bottle of consecrated oil from his vest pocket, and then looked at Mitch's father. "Brodder Vestland, vould you like to do the anointing, please?" Then to his counselors, "Vill you join us as vell, brethren?"

As was customary, Mitch's father did the anointing by himself, using her full name, and then the others stepped up to join him. Each placed his hands lightly on her head. Mitch bowed his head and closed his eyes.

"Sister Gwendolyn Greene Vestland, in the name of our beloved Savior and by the power of the Holy Melchizedek Priesthood, I seal upon you this anointing and give you a blessing through the direction of the Holy Spirit."

Bishop Nielson continued with language commonly heard in blessings. He assured her that her Heavenly Father loved her and that He knew her heart. He assured her that her Father was pleased with her willingness to come with her family to Bluff in answer to a call from the prophet. He blessed her with improved physical health, and he blessed her family. When that was done, he was silent for several seconds. Then, in a softer voice, he went on. "Our dear Sister Vestland, the Lord knows how difficult it vas for you to come here, and He vants you to know that if He vere here vit us this night, He vould take you in His arms and tell you how much He loves you as His choice daughter."

A choked cry escaped from her lips. Mitch opened his eyes. In the lamplight he could see that her cheeks were wet.

Bishop Nielson was silent for several more seconds before he went on. "Dear Sister Vestland, you now haf a choice before you. It is a difficult choice, but the Lord vould haf you know this. Your sacrifice is acceptable to Him. He asks no more of you. The Spirit vhispers that you are free to return to your home with your family and vit His blessings."

Another sob. And now her shoulders began to shake.

Mitch felt his own eyes burning. But it wasn't for joy. In that moment, he knew he would be going back too. There was no way he could ask his mother to let him stay behind now. The sadness was like a knife, but with it came a peace as well.

"Go vit the Lord's blessings," Bishop Nielson continued, "if that is vhat your heart chooses to do. As President Smith promised this evening, you and your husband vill be blessed for coming and you can return vitout shame."

His voice suddenly dropped to a mere whisper, and Mitch had to lean in to hear it.

"But vee vould also say this unto you, our dear sister. The promise given by President Smith—that those who stay vill prosper and receive a double blessing—vas from the Lord too, and is also extended to you and your good husband should you choose not to return."

Mitch's eyes flew open and he stared at the bishop. *Was he encouraging her to stay?* But his hopes plummeted with his next words.

"But vhether you stay or go, I say unto you again, in the name of the Lord, either choice is acceptable to Him. You and your husband are free to choose vhat you feel is best for you and your family. And vee gif you this additional promise. Vhen you decide, if your choice is pleasing to the Lord, you vill be filled with peace in your heart and in your soul. You vill no longer be torn vit uncertainty. You vill know that the Lord accepts vhatever you decide." A brief pause. "And this blessing vee promise you in the name of Jesus Christ, our Savior and Redeemer, amen."

The bishopric shook hands with the Westlands and bade them good night. Mitch's father watched them walk away, one hand around his wife's shoulders. She had a handkerchief now and was wiping away the tears. Then Arthur Westland turned to his son. "Mitch, your mother and I would like some time alone to talk about this, if that's all right."

"Yes, Papa. I understand," he said softly. "I'm tired. I'll get my bedroll. Good night."

His mother's hand reached out and grabbed him by the

arm. "No. Stay, Mitch." She looked up at her husband. "I want him to stay. I've made my decision, if you agree, Arthur."

His father's head came up. He was staring at her. "Are you sure?"

"Yes."

Here it comes. Mitch couldn't bear to face her. They all sat back down again, his father and mother together in the chairs, holding hands. Gwen looked up at her husband. "This is your decision too, Arthur," she said, "not just mine."

"I have told you, my love, that whatever you decide is fine with me."

"Do you want to go back?"

Mitch held his breath. His father stared into her eyes for several seconds, and then his head bobbed firmly. "Yes."

"Not just for me? Be honest, Arthur. Is it just for me?"

This time there was no hesitation. "No, Gwen. I am ready. I believe that life here is not tenable any longer."

"No!" Mitch cried. Then he clamped his mouth shut. If the Lord gave her that choice, who was he to try to change her mind? "I'm sorry, Mama. I'll do whatever you and Papa think is right."

"Thank you," she murmured. "I know how much you want to stay." She hurried on before he could answer. "You'll be seventeen in January, Mitch. If you still want to come back next summer, then your father and I will give you our blessing, but we want you to come with us now."

He looked at the ground, the disappointment cutting through him. "So Kumen told you."

"Told us what?" his father asked.

"That I asked him if I could stay with him. I will go back with you, of course. But . . ." He stopped. His parents were exchanging shocked glances. He felt his heart sink. Kumen hadn't told them.

She nodded slowly, her eyes glistening in the lamplight. "I understand what is in your heart, son. And if you still feel that way next summer, then, though it will break my heart, I shall not stop you. But I can't bear to lose you now. I can't."

Knowing that he had lost, he numbly nodded. "Yes, Mama. I understand." He stood up, went over to her, and bent down and kissed her on the forehead. "Good night, Mama."

Mitch still shared the wagon next to the cabin with Johnny, but on this night he needed to be alone. He got his bedroll, careful not to wake his brother, and walked back down to the river. He found a stretch of soft sand not far from the Swing Tree and rolled it out. It was well after midnight before he finally accepted what had happened and went to sleep.

As he approached the cabin at about six the next morning, bedroll tucked under one arm, he was determined not to say another word that would make this harder for his mother. It would only be another year, and then he would come back. He was at peace with that.

As their cabin came into sight, the door opened and his mother stepped out. Mitch stopped short. He raised a hand to wave, but she turned away without seeing him and went to the wagon. For a moment he assumed she was checking on Johnny, but then he saw the large trunk in front of the wagon. This was the trunk they kept in the wagon because there wasn't room for it in the cabin. This was the large trunk she had gotten out when the Brethren had first come and started talking about closing the mission.

He sighed. Barely six o'clock in the morning and she had already started packing. That said a lot about her eagerness. He continued to watch her without her seeing him.

What he saw next puzzled him. As she bent over and opened the lid of the trunk, he realized that she had nothing with her. Then she reached down inside and came up with a folded quilt. He recognized it immediately. Just before they left Beaver to come here, the ward Relief Society sisters had made his mother a quilt as a farewell present. Was she looking for something, or just making room before she loaded the trunk up with other things?

What he heard next was like a stab to the heart. She was *humming!* Pain turned instantly to guilt. How could he resent a choice that brought her so much joy?

Determined to put on a brave face, he stepped out and started toward her. As he did so, the cabin door opened again and his father came out. He too turned toward the wagon without seeing Mitch. His parents spoke to each other, but he couldn't make out what they said. And then they did something very strange. Mitch's father held out his arms, palms up, and his mother laid the quilt over them. Then she bent down again and retrieved a blanket. That went on top of the quilt. Her lace tablecloth was next on the stack.

Loaded now, his father turned around and started back for the door. And that's when he saw Mitch. "Oh. Good morning."

His mother's head was almost inside the trunk as she rummaged for something near the bottom. She straightened quickly. "Mitch. There you are."

"Good morning, Mama," he said, starting toward them. "Mornin', Pa."

"Where were you last night?"

He shrugged. "I didn't want to wake Johnny, so I slept down by the river." He bent down and kissed her cheek, then peered into the trunk. Her Sunday dress and a petticoat were all that was left in it.

"What are you doing, Mama?"

"Unpacking."

"Can I help? Wait! Did you say *unpacking*?"

She seemed surprised by the question. "Yes, I think that's what I said."

"But—"

She tipped her head back and laughed at his perplexed expression. "Come sit down, son."

Her laugh was filled with merriment, as were her eyes. He realized that it had been a long time since he had heard her laugh like that.

"What's going on?" None of this was making any sense whatsoever.

She slipped an arm through his and pulled him over to the log. As they sat down together, his father reemerged from the cabin, his arms empty again. He sat down on a stool across from them.

"I tried to find you last night to tell you this, but . . ." She shrugged. "Before my head ever hit the pillow last night, I knew something was wrong."

'What?"

"Do you remember what Bishop Nielson said in his blessing? That when I made my decision, I would have peace?" He nodded as she continued. "Well, I realized what was wrong—I was not at peace in my heart."

"I'm sorry, Mama. I shouldn't have—"

One finger came up and pressed against his lips. "Hush."

Then came that smile again. "I thought to myself, 'What if we just stayed through the winter? Just one more season? Then what?'" Tears sprang to her eyes. "And just like that, I was at peace."

He was dazed. He didn't know what to say.

She poked him gently. "I don't like it. I wish I could blame you. But no, Mitch. This was the Lord's doing." She shrugged, "I went to sleep immediately after that and slept through the night. And when I woke up this morning, I was happier than I've been in a long time, so I decided I may as well get up and start unpacking."

To Mitch's astonishment, he found himself crying too. Tears filled his eyes, spilled over, and started trickling down his cheeks. He turned away, wiping quickly at them with the back of his hand, but not quickly enough to escape her attention.

She placed both hands on his shoulders and turned him back around. "Did it really mean that much to you to stay?" she asked.

He sniffed back the tears. "That's not why I'm crying, Mama."

"Then why? What is it, Mitch?"

He tried to say it but couldn't make it come out. He looked away, fighting for control.

"What's wrong, Mitch?"

"Nothing is wrong."

"Then what is it?"

He sniffed again and took a deep breath. Finally, he reached up and took her hands from his shoulders and clasped them tightly. "Oh, Mama," he exclaimed. "Don't you see? I'm crying because I don't know what I ever did to deserve you as my mother."

CHAPTER 9

October 13, 1884—Bluff City, Utah Territory

Gwendolyn watched from the doorway as her son folded his clothes and carefully put them in the bottom of the flour sack. "You do see the irony in all this, don't you?" she asked.

"Irony? How so?"

"I finally decide we will stay in Bluff, and three weeks later you decide to go to Colorado to see if you can get a job with the railroad."

Mitch stopped what he was doing. "If you don't want me to go, Mama, then I won't go."

"Of course I don't want you to go." She pursed her lips thoughtfully. "Are you really so determined to buy our herd from us?"

Arthur spoke up. "I am the only one offering him half price. Of course he is."

"How much are they going to pay you?" Martha wanted to know.

"Assuming they are still hiring, standard pay is two dollars a day."

Johnny's eyes got big and round. Martha was equally impressed. "That's a lot, right, Mitch?"

"Not for twelve hours of backbreaking work, it's not," he grumbled.

Johnny was still trying to work it out in his mind. Since he had never had a dollar of his own, he was struggling. "So how many nickels is that?"

Chuckling, Mitch paused long enough to ruffle his brother's hair. "That's forty nickels."

Johnny's eyes grew even larger and his mouth fell open. "Every day? Wow!"

Mitch laughed. To a boy who received maybe one nickel in a month, it was a pretty staggering fortune. "Would you like me to buy you something and bring it home?" he asked Johnny.

"Would you, Mitch? You're not just funnin' me, are you?"

"No, I'm not. What would you like?"

"A pop gun," he answered without a second's hesitation.

His mother looked surprised. "Why a pop gun?"

"Dan Perkins got one from his pa the last time they came back from Mancos. It's soooo neat. It sounds like a real gun."

Martha snorted. "Real guns don't go *pop*. They go *bang*!"

Arthur spoke up. "Martha, it's not necessary to correct your brother on everything he says."

"Yeah," Johnny said, sticking his tongue out at her.

"Nor is the tongue necessary," Gwen chided.

Putting the last of his woolen shirts in the sack, Mitch turned to his sister. "And what about you, Martha? What would you like me to bring back for you?"

"A new dress," she shot right back. "Pink with blue ribbons."

Mitch looked at his mother. "Do they make dresses like that?"

"Probably, but I'm not sure you'll find one where you're going." She looked at her daughter. "What if Mitch buys us a bolt of pink fabric and some blue ribbon and I make you a dress?"

"Oh, Mama. Would you?"

"Of course."

"And what would Martha's mama like?" Mitch asked.

"I think you've spent quite enough already," Gwen answered. "You'll be spending your whole salary if you're not careful. I'm willing to let you go for six months so you can get a start in life, but not if you're going to spend it all on us."

"Her color is lavender," their father spoke up, smiling at his wife. "If you can find a bolt of lavender cloth, I think she'd be right pleased."

Mitch looked at her, thinking she might protest. But after a moment, she smiled, almost shyly. "And some dark purple ribbon would be nice too."

"I'll do it."

"Never mind," she corrected herself. "What I really want is for you to come home for Christmas."

Mitch picked up the sack, pulled the drawstrings tight, and put it beside his boots. Then he went over and sat down beside her. "I'll try, Mama, but you saw the handbill. Twelve-hour days, six days a week, with Sundays off. It didn't say anything about holidays."

"Surely they'll give you the day off for Christmas."

Arthur shook his head. "Even if they did, it would be only one day. From here to Durango is a two- or three-day trip. There's no way he could get home and back in less than a week, let alone a day."

"How can they work in the winter? Maybe if the snow gets too deep, they'll have to quit for a time."

Mitch shrugged. "The handbill was dated in mid-September, so they must have some kind of plan for winter."

His mother nodded and looked down at her hands. "I'm going to miss you so much, Mitch," she whispered.

He had to look away. It was too painful to face the sorrow in her eyes. So he turned and stuck out his hand to his father instead. "Good-bye, Pa."

"Good-bye, son." Arthur pulled him in for an embrace. While they were close, he said, "It's not going to be a good environment, Mitch. You'll be working with some pretty rough men."

"Don't say that," Gwen cried.

"He will. I'm guessing they'll be hard-drinking and hard-living men. But just remember who you are and what you stand for."

"There won't be no partying for me, Pa. I'm bringing every dollar I make back to you and Mama, except for what I need to live." He hesitated. "I was just funning with you about half price, Pa. If you and Mama are going to farm, you'll need every dollar you can get. But I mean to get a herd, and then I'm going to look for a place to set up my own ranch."

"We'll see," his father said with a smile.

"Is this all my fault?" his mother asked. "You getting it into your head to have your own spread by the time you're twenty?"

Coming over to her, Mitch took both of his mother's hands. "You and Pa taught me to work hard, to be independent. Now that you've decided to stay here in Bluff—"

"Only until spring. That's all I committed to."

Mitch shook his head, laughing. "You ain't going back in the spring, Mama. You know that as well as I do. You ain't gonna leave here unless President Taylor says, 'Sister Westland, it's time for you to go back to Beaver.' Admit it. You are too stubborn and you've got too much faith to just up and quit."

"You say 'ain't' one more time and I'm going to pack up my belongings and leave this afternoon," she retorted.

"Sorry," he murmured.

"I'm not staying here just for you, you know," she said softly.

"I know that, Mama. You're doing it because it's the right thing to do. And it's the right thing for me to make my own way now, so you and Pa don't have to take care of me."

She put her arm around her son's shoulders. "You'd better write me, son, or you ain't never gonna hear the end of it. You understand me?"

His eyes were suddenly burning even as he laughed. "Yes, ma'am," he said meekly.

December 1, 1884—Bluff City

Martha came at a dead run, whooping and hollering. Gwen looked up from her needlework and gave Arthur a questioning glance. "What in the world?"

Then she shot out of her chair when she finally deciphered what her daughter was yelling about. "It's a letter from Mitch! It's a letter from Mitch!"

November 24th, 1884
C/O Mr. Pappy Carlson
D&RG Railway
Durango, Colorado

Dear Mother, Father, Martha, and Johnny,
I am so, so sorry that this is my first letter to you. Strange at it seems, this is the first chance I've had to write. I know that sounds like a lame excuse, but I'll explain.
It's nearly midnight now and everyone else in the bunk car is asleep. We have to be up at 5:00 a.m. and

ready to start work at 6:00, but I don't care. I'll write as
long as I can keep my eyes open.

Ben Perkins and I made good time to Durango. It is
about a hundred miles, but we made it in three days. Ben
got us a room in a rundown hotel here, and we got a bite
to eat. We were both exhausted, so I told Ben I was going
to wait until morning to see about a job. But then I had
this thought not to wait but to go straightaway.

I walked down to the train station and asked the sta-
tionmaster who to talk to about a job. He pointed to a
bunk car and told me the track foreman was in there.
When I found him and asked if he was still hiring, he
looked me up and down and then without a word found a
paper and had me sign it. "Good thing you came now," he
said as he showed me my bunk. "We're rolling out of here
in half an hour." I barely had time to run back to the hotel
to grab my things and tell Ben what was going on. So that
impression was a blessing from Heavenly Father. I started
to work only twelve hours after arriving.

The railroad is called the Denver and Rio Grande
Railway, but everyone just calls it the D&RG. With all the
mining going in this part of Colorado, they need railroads
bad, so they're pushing rail lines west as fast as they can.
I'm working on the line between Mancos and Durango.

I tell you all of this is so you know why I haven't written before. I left so quickly I didn't have time to get paper and pencil before we left Durango. When I asked the
guys if any of them could lend me some, they just laughed.
Most of them can't read or write, and the others hardly
ever write home. A couple of guys told me they've been
gone from home so long they don't even know if their parents are still alive.

We are back in Durango now for a couple of days
while we wait for more track to come. And that means we
got paid too. Twenty-four dollars! Yahoo! I'm rich!

My first purchase was writing stuff. Guess what my next purchases were? First was a hot bath for 35¢. I've been bathing in creeks, which right now are extremely cold. I paid an extra 10¢ to soak for an hour. Exquisite pleasure!

Then I spent $1 on a cheap hotel room. An extravagance, I know, but after two weeks of sleeping in a car full of men who snore, it was worth it. We call one guy Avalanche, because that's what it sounds like when he snores.

You were right, Pa. These men are so different from anything I've known. They are rough, many of them with little or no schooling and no sense of right or wrong. It has been a learning experience, and I'm so grateful to you and Mama. I never realized how important family is. I think about you all the time and miss you all so much.

But, here's some great news. Being a Mormon pays off. Now that winter is here, the work has really slowed down. So they announced yesterday that half of us were to be let go. Since I'm the newest guy here—and the youngest!—I thought for sure I'd be one of them. But the boss, who is this tough-as-nails old guy we all call Pappy, said he needed at least one guy who didn't come back every night so drunk he couldn't see straight. So I'm going to have work all winter. The bad part of that is that I definitely won't be coming home for Christmas.

Here's some more bad news, Mama. The foreman hinted that if I continue like I am, he may make me a track foreman in the spring. That's fifty cents more per day. But he'll only do that if I promise to stay on until we get the line laid all the way to Mancos, which would be sometime next September or early October. That means I wouldn't get home for almost a full year. But think about it: I'm saving about ten dollars a week now. If I do that for a year, I'll have over five hundred dollars. That would be enough for me to buy your cattle and perhaps a few more and start my own ranch. Please tell me that you think it's worth it, because even writing about it makes me want to cry.

Well, it's now past midnight, and I keep almost falling asleep over my pencil, so I'll quit for now. I hope I can write more regularly. Don't worry about me, Mama. Things are going well now. The first week or so was pretty bad. I had blisters on my hands so big that they had babies. But they're gone now, and I'm doing fine. I'm guessing I've also put on ten to fifteen pounds, and most of that is muscle from swinging a twelve-pound spike hammer twelve hours a day.

I love you all so much. I miss you every day. I'll write again soon.

All my love,
Mitch

January 31, 1885
C/O General Delivery
Mancos, Colorado

Hi to all.

Happy birthday to me! Now that I'm seventeen, I feel much older. (That's a joke.)

I celebrated my birthday by skipping the chow line at the camp and having breakfast at the little hotel in town. It cost me 50¢, but it was worth every penny. Yum! I had four eggs—cooked just like you cook them, Mama—a heaping plate of fried potatoes, six slices of bacon, and some toast. Very best of all, I had the lady bring me my own pitcher of fresh milk. It was as if I had died and gone to heaven. If I had had you all with me, it would have been the best birthday ever.

Pa, I'm glad to hear that the weather there has been relatively mild so that the stock is not having to forage in snow for their grass. My "cattle ranch fund" now has over a hundred dollars and keeps growing. I actually opened up a bank account here in Mancos a few weeks ago. On the weekends, my fellow workers often go through their week's wages in a single night at the saloons. I don't want them getting sticky fingers when they're looking for more funds.

That brings me to something for you, Mama. In one of your letters you reminded me of my promise to tell you everything so that you don't have to worry and wonder. So here goes.

This happened just before Christmas. Because I am a Mormon, all the guys think I'm very strange. Most of them drink and smoke or chew and other things I won't mention. I decided up front that I wasn't going to try to preach to them about right and wrong. I just say no thank you and walk away. Most of the guys have accepted that and don't bother me about it.

Anyway, it had snowed so much that we couldn't lay track for a few days. We were only six or seven miles from Mancos, so a bunch of us decided to walk into town. The others all went to the saloon, of course, but I went to the lobby of the hotel to read the newspapers. After a couple of hours, our foreman stuck his head in and asked me to round up the guys to head back.

So I went to the saloon and told the guys we had to go. We have two guys here who are cousins from Illinois. And they're two bad ones. Anyway, they claim to know all about Joseph Smith and the Mormons, so they have always taunted me. Well, when I started to leave the saloon, one of them grabbed me from behind and asked me to drink with them. I told them no, I didn't drink. They said it was time I started. One held me down while his buddy got a bottle of beer and tried to force it into my mouth. The other guys thought it was funny and started cheering them on.

Remember, Mama, I'm only telling you this because you made me promise I would.

I was fighting them like mad, but the one kneeled on my chest and jammed the bottle in my mouth, spilling beer all over me. He even chipped my tooth a little. I finally got an arm free and hit him in the nose with my fist. Blood spurted everywhere. Seeing that, the other guy whipped out his pistol, screaming at me.

Just then Pappy came running in with the pick handle he always carries with him. He yelled something and smacked the guy with the pistol across the back of the head, and he went down like a rock. Pappy kicked the pistol away and turned to the other guy, who was holding his nose and moaning. "You wanna fight the Mormon," he said, "that's fine. But there'll be no pistols. No knives. And you fight him one on one."

The guy straightened and his fists came up. But when he saw I was ready to fight, he changed his mind. He went over and helped his cousin up, and they left. Pappy went out after them. He must have fired them on the spot, because when the rest of us came out they were gone. We never saw them again.

Now, Mother. That only happened once. So don't worry about me. I think Pappy likes me. Last week, he made me foreman for one of the track gangs. He said he knew I was young, but since I didn't drink, he could trust me to not be drunk on the job. So, fifty cents more per day, starting as soon as the weather turns and we start laying track again. And yes, that does mean that I will be staying here until fall. That's the bad news.

The good news is we just learned that the load of track we were expecting around March 1st has been delayed for two weeks. So we have nothing to do until it comes. So the boss says I can take ten days off and come home. Mama, I expect to hear you squeal with joy at that news, even though you're a hundred miles away.

Well, I see I am up to three pages now. I guess that shows how glad I was to receive your letters. Please keep writing.

I love you all so much. I am so excited to get to see you again. Martha, Johnny, we're going back to Durango next week for some equipment, so I'll be sure to get you the things I promised.

I love you. See you soon.

Mitch

P.S. Oh, I almost forgot, Mama. I go to church whenever we are in Mancos on Sunday. It's a small branch, but they treat me like family. There are a few people here who once lived in Bluff, such as Stanford and Belle Smith. But I wanted you to know that every time I am in town on Sunday, I go to church and then get supper and good company for the rest of the day. It has been wonderful.

Notes

Because the San Juan pioneers lived largely in a barter economy, cash was hard to come by. To get them through the winter when they couldn't farm, the men from Bluff often freighted supplies or went to Colorado to work in the mines or for the railroad.

The railway lines described here are actual lines that were constructed within a few years of the time of this chapter.

CHAPTER 10

October 8, 1885—Mancos, Colorado

Mitch was striding along, trying to remember all that he needed to buy at the trading post and wishing that he'd written it down. He was thinking mostly about Christmas. He could purchase much more here in Colorado than in Bluff. He had agreed with Pappy to stay on until December 1st for a bonus of twenty-five dollars. That meant he was done with railroading in about six more weeks. And he would be home for Christmas.

"Hey, Westland."

He turned around and saw Pappy coming toward him. His head was down, but there was no mistaking who it was. The lean hips, long legs, and broad shoulders would have been enough, but the corncob pipe he forever clenched in his teeth was the dead giveaway. He lifted a hand. "Hi, Pappy."

"Where you going in such a hurry?"

"Wanna get to the trading post before it closes."

"I'd suggest you go the other direction and stop by the post office."

"The post office? Why? I was there yesterday afternoon and picked up my mail."

Pappy's leathered face was a study in not caring. "Suit yourself, but the postmaster told me there's a letter."

"For me?"

"No, for the Easter Bunny." He shook his head in disgust before taking out a match and striking it on his Levi's jeans. When it flared into life, he touched it to the end of his pipe and sucked furiously until it glowed red. Flipping the match away, he drew in deeply and then exhaled two streams of smoke from his nostrils.

There was something in the way he did the whole ritual that had always fascinated Mitch. And while he hated the smell of cigarettes and cigars, he didn't mind the smell of pipe tobacco.

"Well, ya gonna stand there and gawk at me or go get your letter?"

Chuckling, Mitch raised a hand, turned around, and pushed past him. "Thanks, Pappy."

"Hope it's bad news," he grumbled as Mitch started away.

"Hope so too," he called back cheerfully. "Anything to break the monotony."

Pappy was right. The postmaster had a letter for him. To Mitch's surprise, it was from his father. That was strange. His father hardly ever wrote to him. He'd sometimes add a paragraph or two to Gwendolyn's letters, but that was all.

Finding a place where he was alone, Mitch slit the letter open with his knife and began to read.

October 4th

Dear Mitch—

I am sending this letter with a freighter from Durango rather than waiting for it to go out with the regular mail. I believe we have a situation that requires some immediate action on your part.

The new stake president, Francis A. Hammond, arrived here three days ago with his family and a few other families. He plans to stay here in Bluff for a week or two while he gets to know the people. Then he plans to visit the Saints in Colorado and New Mexico. In fact, someone has told him about Mancos and he's interested in seeing if that area might be a good place for him to settle. When I heard that, I told him that you were working for the railroad in the Mancos area, and he promised to look you up.

But listen to this. The next night, we had a potluck supper and dance at the new co-op store and dance hall to welcome him and the others to San Juan County. Before the dancing started, Bishop Nielson invited him to speak to us for a few minutes. President Hammond has a very warm personality, and both your mother and I were favorably impressed with him. If he chooses to settle in Bluff, we will be most pleased.

But he said something I think you need to hear. He commented on how desolate and dry the land up between Thompson Springs and Moab was. But then he said that they had found a place that might have promise for some settlement. Now listen to this: he said it was the area around the north and south branches of Montezuma Creek, the area that we call the Blue Mountain country.

Yes—the very place that we have talked about. The very place that you said you are interested in because of the rich rangeland up there.

Now, are you ready for this? He said it is his opinion, and Salt Lake City agrees, that it is time for our little colony to be divided and new settlements started, as President Smith and Elder Snow described when they were here a year ago.

Mitch gave a low cry and read that sentence again. "Oh, my," he breathed.

This is no surprise to us, of course. We have been going to the Blue Mountains for timber for about three years
now, and several families have expressed an interest in
settling there. Well, that time has now come.

This morning I was down helping Lemuel Redd and
Kumen Jones get their corn in, and they told me that the
bishopric met with President Hammond last night. He
said that it was too late to do it this season, but as soon as
the snow starts melting in the spring, he wants to send a
party of interested men north to explore the whole region
and identify possible sites for two or more settlements.

Mitch half closed his eyes and looked up at the sky. "Oh,
Pa, tell me you told them that I'm interested. Please. Please."

I, of course, mentioned to them that you are very interested in finding a place to start your own ranch next
spring.

"Yes!" Mitch punched the air with his fist.

But before I could ask them to put your name up for
consideration, Lem said to me, "I already have Mitch on
my short list." Kumen smiled and said, "So do I."

Now, here is the thing of urgency. If you are interested,
you will have to leave immediately after you get this letter
to be back in time for the negotiations and decisions. Your
mother, who is standing behind me as I write, is saying
very loudly so you can hear: "This is what you've been
waiting for, Mitch. So come home. Come home now."

I know you promised your foreman that you would
stay until the end of November, but you have already
given him a full year. So you have a decision to make. But
you have to make it quickly.

Pray about it. We trust that you will do the right thing.

Love, Pa.

P.S. In case you don't know your mother's feelings on this question, she paid the teamster one dollar to wait until I could write this letter so we could get it to you immediately.

October 12, 1885—Bluff City

"Mama! Mama! Mama!"

Gwen looked up with a start. It was Martha's voice. She quickly walked to the window and picked up a cloth to wipe the condensation off so she could see. There was a pot of stew on the stove and all of the windows had steamed up.

They were still a block away, but she instantly saw who it was.

"Oh, my goodness!" She dropped the cloth, yanked on the strings of her apron, pulled it off, and threw it at a chair. "Johnny!" she cried. Her son was lying on the bed reading a book. "Mitch's home, Johnny. Mitch's home! Go get your father."

Brushing her hair out of her eyes, she plunged out the door.

"All right, children," she chided. "Let Mitch come inside. Let him put his things down. Then you can give him all the hugs you want."

They stepped back and she watched her son come in, this stranger that she still knew so well and had missed so fiercely. He dropped his bedroll and pack behind the door and then took off his hat and coat. Holding out his arms, he grinned. "Okay. I'm ready."

Johnny and Martha rushed in and threw their arms around

him. Gwen was only a split second behind them. Arthur stood back, letting them have their time, smiling proudly.

Finally, Mitch was able to move over to the table and sit down, Martha on one side of him, Johnny on the other. "Did you bring us anything?" Johnny blurted.

His mother sighed. "Be polite, son."

Mitch pulled a face. "Sorry, buddy. Not this time. I didn't have time. I got Pa's letter, went straight to the foreman to tell him I was quitting, gathered my things, and took off."

Johnny's shoulders slumped. "That's all right."

"How's the pop gun? Is it still working?"

"Oh, yeah. It's great! The string broke once, but Pa fixed it for me."

"And I love my pink dress," Martha said.

Reaching out, Gwen laid a hand on her youngest's shoulder. "All right, son. Now it's our turn." She looked at Mitch. "So how did you get here?"

"I walked most of the way. Couldn't find any wagons headed this way. And besides, they're too slow if they're loaded." He glanced at his father. "Once I got your letter, there was no holding back. I was on my way."

"How long did it take you?" Martha wondered.

"This is my fourth day. I figure I made about twenty-five miles a day."

Reaching across the table, Gwen took both of his hands and held them tightly. "It is so good to see you, son." The tears started immediately, and she choked back a soft sob. "So good."

The silence was awkward for a moment, but then Arthur spoke. "So, how did your boss take the news that you were quitting?"

"Oh, he was mad. Furious. Swore a blue streak. Said I

couldn't just up and walk away. So I told him I had no choice."
He was suddenly studying his hands. After a moment, he
looked up at his mother. "But I'm going back."

She gasped. "No, Mitch!"

"Yes, Mama." He went on in a rush, before she could protest further. "He said I could take off the time I needed now.
And he promised that I can come home again for Christmas.
But the railroad's starting a new spur line up to the mining
country around Telluride. They've already surveyed a route,
and we've started grading the right-of-way between Mancos
and Dolores. We can do a lot of that during the winter."

His mother said nothing. Nor did she look up. He reached
across and laid a hand on hers. "That wasn't my plan, Mama.
But he's offered me a hundred-dollar bonus if I'll stay."

"You said it was my fault that you went to Colorado. But if
I had known it was going to be for over a year . . ." she shook
her head. "There are more important things than buying more
cows."

"If you do get included in that exploring party," his father
said, "they plan to leave in March, as soon as the snow's out of
the high country. President Hammond wants the first families
moving up there by June."

"I know that, Pa. And I'm going to be with them. But if I
can work until then, that's another hundred and fifty dollars I
can earn. I'm going to need it, Pa, what with buying cattle and
lumber and whatever else I'm going to need." He glanced at his
mother. "Then I'm not ever going back, Mama. I promise."

Abruptly his mother stood. "No more talk about leaving.
Not now. Right now we're going to have supper, and then we're
going to let Mitch sleep for as long as he wants."

"Yes," his father agreed. "While you're getting that ready,

I'd like to take Mitch over to meet President Hammond. And we'll stop in and say hello to Bishop Nielson."

She nodded. "All right. But the stew will be ready in an hour. Don't you be late."

"We won't, Mama," Mitch said, flashing her a big grin. "We wouldn't dare."

October 15, 1885

Francis A. Hammond was an impressive man. In his early sixties, he was slightly taller than Mitch and solidly built, with broad shoulders and a trim waistline. His face was somewhat long and narrow but pleasant looking. He had a receding hairline, though his dark hair was thick and plentiful with some natural wave to it. His full beard was mostly grey.

Over the next two days, as the men of Bluff got together to discuss this exciting new development, Mitch learned more about their new stake president, and everything he learned was impressive. He was a native of New York state. Like so many of that time, he had little formal schooling. His father was a shoemaker who tanned his own leather and also made saddles and harnessing. Francis learned each of those trades from him.

But at fourteen, Francis decided to go to sea. As a deckhand on a whaling ship, he traveled from the Arctic Ocean to South America and from Cape Horn to Hawaii. After an accident at sea nearly broke his back and cost him his life, he set up a shoemaking business in San Francisco. There he met the Mormons who had just arrived from New York on the ship *Brooklyn*. Liking what he saw, he joined them and eventually moved to Utah.

After three days of discussion and debate, the plans were laid and the members of the exploring party selected. They would leave in early March, or as soon as the weather permitted. They planned to take a week to ten days. Twelve names were selected. Squarely in the middle of the list was the name of Mitchell Arthur Westland, future rancher.

October 17, 1885

"Must you go back, Mitch?" Martha's cheeks were wet with tears. "You just got here."

"I know, I know," he said, sweeping her up and sitting her on his lap. "I've only been here for five days, but remember, it took me four days to get here and it will take four more to get back. But I'll be home for Christmas."

"That's what you said last year," she pouted.

"No, last year I said I would *try* to be home for Christmas. I didn't even have a job at that point, Martha." He stroked her cheeks, wiping away the tears. "But this time, I promise that I *will* be home."

"And we're holding him to that promise," Gwen said fiercely. Her eyes bored into his. "Right?"

"That's what the boss said. If he tries to back out on his word, I'll just quit."

Setting Martha down, he got to his feet. Johnny leaped up and grabbed his pack for him. He looked at his mother. "Can we walk with Mitch to the edge of town?" he asked, eyes pleading.

"Yes, but no farther."

"I've got to get some jerky and a couple of other things at the co-op trading post. You can go that far with me."

That brought his mother's head up. "You're going to the co-op?"

"Yes. Can I get you something?"

She hesitated and then shook her head. "Never mind. It can wait."

He came over and shook hands with his father and then kissed his mother on the cheek. "I *will* be home by Christmas. You have my word."

As he and the children left, Arthur turned to his wife. "If you were thinking of the Zimmer girl, she's not at the co-op today. I saw her hanging laundry with her mother."

"I know. I saw her too. I just forgot." Then she smiled at him. "It's all right. There's plenty of time."

Arthur gave her a chiding look. "How old is she now?"

"Fifteen. She'll be sixteen in May."

"Isn't that a little young?"

"Of course it is. I wasn't going to ask him to introduce himself. But her family is new enough in town that I don't know if he's even seen her yet."

"Hmm." Losing interest, Arthur started to turn away.

But Gwendolyn continued, "I was only fourteen when you and I first met."

"Ha!" he cried. "You were fourteen when we were assigned to the same handcart company. I was eighteen. You were just a scrawny little kid in the company. I didn't even notice you back then."

"Of course you didn't," she cooed. "You're a man. That's why your mother and my mother had to make sure it all worked out. It took them four years to get your attention. You didn't know it, but you never stood a chance."

He laughed and came back over to her. Taking her in his arms, he said, "That's right. Once you grew up, I never stood a chance."

She kissed him, still smiling. "I'm just looking out for our boy, the same way your mama and my mama did for us."

————————————

Notes

For readers who may wonder if people at this time really wore Levi's jeans, the answer is yes.

In 1870, a tailor named Jacob Davis was looking for a way to strengthen trousers for hard-working men. He used a heavy-duty, dark blue denim cloth but found that miners, teamsters, lumberjacks, and cowboys gave their pants such a hard workout that they kept tearing in critical places. He came up with the idea of hammering copper rivets into the corners of the pockets to strengthen them and triple stitching the places that took the most stress.

Davis went into partnership with a successful merchant in San Francisco named Levi Strauss, and they got a patent in 1873. The pants were an instant hit. Within eighteen months, thousands of people in San Francisco were wearing "Levi's waist-high coveralls," as they were first called. People quickly shortened that to Levi's jeans or simply Levi's. Though the brand name is often written without the apostrophe, which shows possession, the official brand logo still includes it.

President Francis Asbury Hammond was probably called by Church leaders in Salt Lake City in the fall of 1884, shortly after Platte D. Lyman was released as stake president. The details of his early life come from his biography (see *LDS Biographical Encyclopedia*, 351–53). He lived in Bluff for a number of years and then in Mancos, Colorado, before eventually moving to Moab. While in Bloomfield, New Mexico, in November 1900, probably on stake business, he suffered an accident that took his life.

CHAPTER 11

March 24, 1886—North Montezuma Creek,
near the Blue Mountains

The surveyors of the U.S. Geographical Survey who came through the area during the 1870s called them the Sierra Abajo, a Spanish phrase meaning "lower mountains." This title seems to have been given because the highest peak in this range was only a little over 11,000 feet. But in the La Sal Mountains, just forty-five miles to the north, there were five peaks over 12,000 feet.

But the residents of San Juan County had always called them the Blue Mountains, or just the Blues, because the pine-covered slopes took on a bluish tinge when the light was right.

Compared to Bluff and the desert country along the San Juan River, the eastern slopes of the Blue Mountains were an incredible paradise. The spring grass was just coming up, but judging by its abundance, Mitch guessed that by summer it might reach the horses' bellies. Several streams came down from the heights, their crystal-clear, ice-cold waters teeming with trout. The ravines through which those creeks ran were lined by groves of willows, maples, cottonwood, and quaking aspen. The sloping mountainsides were covered with oak and stately pines that came down almost to where the ground began to level out. That meant they had "sawable" lumber within a few miles of where the settlements would be. As the explorers rode along, they were constantly spooking mule deer out of the brush and trees. Sage grouse would explode from their cover with a whir of sound that startled the horses.

Perfect cattle country, Mitch thought. Plenty of water, plenty of feed, and summer range within half a day's ride. And now, with a year and a half's worth of railroad wages in the bank and his father still willing to sell his cattle for fifty cents on the dollar, Mitch was ready to make his move. He had turned eighteen in January. That was young for starting your own ranch, but he knew he was ready.

Then he frowned. Winter would be more of a problem. The elevation at the base of the mountains was just a little over 7,000 feet, about 3,000 higher than Bluff. It would definitely be cooler in the summer, but he guessed the winters might turn brutal. Right now, with the sun just going down behind the highest ridgelines and a stiff breeze coming out of the northwest, it was cold enough to see his breath and to make him grateful he had on his woolen long johns and leather gloves.

When they left Bluff three days before, the early morning temperature had been near fifty degrees. By morning here there would be frost on the ground, maybe even ice on standing water. But that was all right, Mitch decided. Build some lean-to sheds that blocked the north winds, put up plenty of hay before winter set in, and they could ride out even a tough winter.

At the sound of horses, he turned in his saddle and looked to the south. William Adams and his two sons, George and Fred, were coming at a steady walk toward him.

"What do you think?" George asked Mitch.

Grinning, Mitch responded, "Thinking as a man who wants to spend his life running cows, I think it's fantastic. As a man who wants to spend his life as a farmer, what do *you* think?"

William Adams turned in his saddle and looked to the east. From where they were, the ground gently sloped away for miles into a broad plain whose smooth surface was broken only by the few ravines that marked the creek beds. "I never expected this," he said, half in awe. "I think we might even have some success dry farming up here."

Cocking his head to one side, Mitch gave him a quizzical look. "I thought we had dry farming down in Bluff. Isn't that the problem? It's a little too dry for farming?"

William laughed, as did his two boys. "That's irrigated farming, Mitch. That's why we've struggled so much. With the Big Ditch being wiped out by the river, it's hard to grow anything down there. But up here—" he turned completely around to gaze up at the mountains. "You've got a thousand acres or more that are flat enough to not need a lot of grading. And this close to the mountains, it'll get enough rain to keep crops growing without having to dig ditches and turn water on it. Put in wheat or oats first thing in the spring and I'll wager by fall we're getting fifteen, maybe twenty bushels per acre."

George was nodding vigorously. "Not only that, but remember that little valley we came across about six miles south, where South Montezuma Creek runs?"

"Yes." Mitch remembered it well, because he had thought of it as a possible settlement site.

"Did you notice how green and verdant it is? That's going to be a great place to farm. Maybe run some milk cows, start a dairy."

"Ugh," Mitch groaned. "The problem with milk cows is you have to milk 'em twice a day. Give me beef cattle any day."

"Actually," William went on, "I think we go back and

recommend both sites as settlements. One here on the North Fork, one down there on the South Fork."

"You've got my vote on that," Mitch said. His exultation was soaring.

Standing in the stirrups, William surveyed the land around them. "Have you picked out a spot for yourself?"

"I have." Mitch pointed to the north. "Starting right about where that line of cedar trees begins. I'd like to build a ranch house right there. There's a spring just a hundred yards from there. That's assuming everyone agrees."

All nodded in agreement with that. William Adams wheeled his horse around. "Well, we promised to meet the others about now down on the South Montezuma, so we'd better get moving. Our brethren back in Bluff are anxious for our report."

April 7, 1886—Bluff City

There weren't a lot of people out and about yet on this chilly morning—chilly for Bluff, not for North Montezuma Creek. But every cabin and house had smoke rising from the chimney, and Mitch could smell bacon and eggs and oatmeal in the air. He drew the smell in deeply.

As he came around the corner and started up the street for the trading post, he saw Kumen Jones out behind his house saddling his horse. Mitch changed directions and headed that way. Kumen looked up and waved when he saw him. "I heard you brethren got back last night. Welcome home."

Mitch got down from his horse and they shook hands. "Thanks."

"Can't wait to hear your report tonight."

"We're anxious to give it. It's incredible country."

"I know," Kumen agreed. "I've ridden up that way several times."

"So you think the place has promise?"

"Absolutely."

"Good. How have things been here?"

"Good."

Mitch smiled to himself. That was Kumen. Not much for wasting words. He raised his hand. "See you tonight."

"Right. Oh, Bishop Nielson and President Hammond might look you brethren up today to get a preliminary report."

"I'll be home."

"I'll tell them."

Mitch stopped at the store that Ben Perkins and his wife had attached to their house and chatted with Mary Ann for a few minutes. Ben was on his way back from Colorado with another load of freight. Farther on, he waved to Lem Redd, who was up on his roof patching a spot that looked ready to collapse.

It was good to be back, he thought. His family had only been here a year—well, actually two, but one of those he had spent in Colorado—but this felt more like home to him than Beaver ever had. These were good people, people you liked to sit across a campfire with, people you wanted at your back if you were going after horse thieves or facing down Moenkopi Mike.

As he approached the co-op store and dance hall, Mitch noted his amazement at this new structure. It was by far the largest building in Bluff. The San Juan Co-op Association had worked with the town to build a spacious store on the ground floor and a large meeting hall on the upper floor. Though their town meetings were often held up there, everyone called it the dance hall, for that was its primary use. He was impressed. Just as President Smith had promised, Bluff was beginning to prosper.

Mitch was glad to see that there were no other horses tied up outside the co-op. If you happened to arrive after a new load of freight had come in, you could end up waiting as much as half an hour to pay for your purchases. He swung down, tied his horse, and went in.

Removing his hat as he entered, he stopped for a moment to let his eyes adjust to the dimmer light. He saw a woman at the counter waiting to make a purchase, but no one was help-ing her at the moment. With the light coming in from the win-dows behind her, he didn't recognize who it was. Not in a hurry, he moved toward the small counter in the back that held the guns and ammunition.

"Be right with you," a pleasant voice above him sang out.

He turned and looked up. Along the narrow catwalk that served as a makeshift loft, a woman came into view. She was carrying a small barrel of what looked like pickled cod. Mitch raised a hand to signal he had heard her, but she didn't see him.

When she came down the stairs, she was only ten feet or so away from him. "Oh," she said, momentarily startled. "Hello." Her smile was warm and welcoming. A dimple on her left cheek flashed briefly. She was not a woman, as he had thought. She was a girl about his age—one that he wasn't sure he had ever seen before. "I'll be right with you, Brother Westland."

As she turned and moved toward the front counter, he stared after her. *She knows me?* And then came another thought. *Am I supposed to know her?*

Puzzled, he moved on to the gun counter and checked to see if they had what he was looking for. A few moments later, he heard the woman at the counter say something. The girl responded with, "It's pretty heavy, Sister Wahlquist. I can have Alma deliver it to your cabin."

"That would be nice. Thank you."

"You're welcome. He should be back in about half an hour and I'll send him right over." She followed the woman out, saying something about the weather. A moment later, she appeared again, coming toward Mitch.

"All right, how may I help you?"

"Um . . . I need a box of thirty-thirty shells and—no, make that two boxes."

She slid open the glass door and pulled out two boxes of Remington 30.30 center-fire shells and set them before him.

"Good. And a box of .45 caliber for my pistol."

She retrieved another box.

"Good. And do you have a gun-cleaning kit?"

"We do. For your rifle or your pistol?"

"Pistol." He smiled sheepishly. "I lost mine while we were crossing a creek."

She set the ammo for his Colt .45 beside the other shells and then rummaged for a minute. "Ah." She held up a small tin box. "How about this?"

"That'll do," he said, impressed with how well she knew what she was doing. "Thank you. How much do I owe you?"

Her lips pursed as she concentrated, touching his purchases one by one. That gave him a moment to study her, and he liked what he saw. She was shorter than him by quite a bit, about the size of his mother, he guessed. Five foot three, or maybe four. She was slender but shapely. But it was her face that arrested his gaze. Her nose was petite with a slight inward curve to it. Her lips were soft and full. The lines of her face were also soft, with skin that was browner than he would expect this early in the year. She evidently spent some time outdoors. But it was her eyes that held him. They were large, slightly almond shaped, and a lustrous deep brown that drew you in and made you like her immediately. Very nice indeed. She looked vaguely familiar, but he couldn't place her. But then, several new families had come to Bluff while he'd been in Colorado.

He realized she was giving him a curious look. "Is there something else?"

"Uh . . . No. That's it."

"That'll be one dollar and eighty-five cents. Let's go up front and I'll ring it up on the cash register." She gathered up his things and moved past him. He fell in behind her.

He handed her two dollar bills, and then as she was about to make change, he had a thought. "Can you give me fifteen cents' worth of candy instead?"

"Sure. What would you like?"

He shrugged. "I don't know. Just pick what you think they'd like. My sister is twelve. My little brother is nine."

"Ah, yes. Well, Martha loves lemon drops, and Johnny is definitely a licorice man. Is that okay?"

He was staring at her again. "Yeah. Sure."

She laughed at his expression and then got the candy and put it into two separate small paper sacks. When she handed them to him along with his other purchases, she smiled up at him again, and the dimple reappeared. "Welcome home."

"Uh . . . thanks."

"The whole town's anxious to hear about what you brethren found up there."

He nodded, getting more bewildered with every sentence. He waved, gave her a smile that he suspected showed just how stupid he was feeling, and then walked out swiftly.

"No, Johnny," Gwendolyn said, shaking a finger at her son. "No candy until after breakfast." She took the licorice from him, put it back in the sack, and put it in the cupboard. Without waiting to be told, Martha relinquished hers as well. Satisfied, their mother went back to the stove and began stirring the pan of cracked wheat that was just starting to boil.

"Uh . . . Mother?"

She turned her head. "Yes?"

Mitch hesitated, knowing that what he was about to do would trigger her motherly instincts in a way he wasn't sure he wanted, but he decided it was worth it. "There was . . . uh . . . this girl working at the co-op store. I didn't recognize her, but she . . . uh . . . called me by name. Like she knew me. And she knows who Martha and Johnny are."

His mother put the stirring spoon in the porridge and turned around slowly. A smile stole across her face. "Yes. And what about her?"

"Well . . . uh . . . she acted like I should know her."

"You do know her, silly," Martha squealed. "That's Edie Zimmer."

"E-who?"

His mother came over to him, trying hard not to show her delight. She cocked her head to one side. "You don't remember, do you?"

"Remember what?"

"It was about a year ago, that first time you came home from Colorado. You and I went to the co-op store. She was there putting out stock. I wanted to introduce you, but you wrinkled up your nose and said, 'That skinny little thing? How old is she? Twelve?' And you wouldn't let me introduce you."

He reared back, his jaw going slack. "She's *that* girl?"

"The very one," she confirmed, her eyes dancing with amusement. "Her name is Edna Rae Zimmer and—"

"But everyone calls her Edie," Martha said, "and she's one of my best friends."

"Her family came here just a few weeks after you left for Colorado. They're from Richfield."

"But . . ." He still wasn't sure this could be the same girl. "I don't remember seeing her since I came home."

"Of course you don't. I don't think you went to the store while you were here at Christmas, and then you were off to Colorado again." She gave him a chiding look. "Then you were here, what? Four days before you headed north? In fact, you haven't been here much at all during this last year and a half, mister. No wonder you feel like a stranger in town."

He sat down, feeling pretty foolish. "And that's really her?"

She clapped her hands in delight. "It is, Mitch. But she has changed a little."

"How old is she?"

"She's fifteen. But her birthday is next month. That's only two years younger than you, my boy."

———————————

Note

A party of ten to twelve men left Bluff in early March of 1886 and rode north to explore the area that President Francis Hammond had earlier recommended as possible sites for two new settlements. They explored routes and potential sites along the way but focused primarily on the area just east of the Blue Mountains (most modern maps call them the Abajo Mountains). They were very impressed with what they found there, including the possibility of dry farming. They returned via a more westerly route, following Elk Mountain down to Butler Wash, which is a few miles west of Bluff (see *Lariats*, 82–83; *Saga*, 91–92).

CHAPTER 12

April 23, 1886—Bluff City, Utah Territory

No, Mama. Absolutely not."

Gwen just smiled.

"I mean it, Mama. I am not going to the dance. I am not going to go to the co-op and ask her to let me sign her dance card. What if she finds out what I said about her?"

Martha, who was just outside the door with Johnny, enjoying the spring sunshine, stuck her head in. "She knows. I already told her."

Mitch groaned. "No! When?"

"Right after you came back from up north. She thought it was really funny."

"Martha," Gwen said, trying to hold a straight face. "It isn't your place to say things about Mitch to Edie."

"That's right," Mitch snapped. "And if you're going to be telling her everything you hear, then that settles it. I'm not doing anything with her. Not ever."

"Martha," Gwen said, "no more. This is between Mitch and Edie. Do you understand?"

Martha put her hands on her hips and glared at her brother. "Yes. But I hope she won't dance with you. You are so grumpy these days."

"All right," their mother said. "That's enough. Shut the door behind you."

When she did, Gwendolyn came over and sat down beside Mitch. "Okay. Now you listen to your mother."

He rolled his eyes but finally nodded.

"You aren't the only boy in Bluff who thinks she's a lovely young woman. She even has some of the cowboys ride in and ask her if they can sign her card. So if you don't get over there today—right now would be best—her dance card will be full. You're leaving Monday with the cattle for Butler Wash, right?"

"Yes."

"And you'll be gone for how long?"

"A couple of weeks."

"And then what?"

"Well, I'm hoping and praying I'll be one of those who Bishop Nielson and President Hammond choose to call to the Blue Mountain Mission."

"And if you are, you'll be back in Bluff when?" She was giving him a look that said, *Why am I the one doing all the thinking for you?*

He looked away. "No telling. The men talked like we'd go up this summer and start some cabins and stuff before winter but not take the families up until next spring. But since I don't have a family—" At her look, he quickly corrected himself. "I mean since I'm not married and don't have a family of my own, I might just stay on through the winter."

"That's what I thought." Up came her finger, and she pointed it right at his nose. "So you get out of that chair right now and get down to the store and talk to her."

The door popped open. "She's not at the store," Martha said. "She's at the schoolhouse helping our teacher."

"Stop eavesdropping!" Mitch yelled. Then to his mother, "I'm not even sure I'm going to the dance."

There was a soft explosion of exasperation, and Gwen turned toward the door. "Martha?"

Mitch jumped. "What are you doing?"

"Martha! Come in here."

A second later the door opened again and his sister stuck her head in. "Yes, Mama?"

"I want you to go over to the school. Find Edie and—"

"Mother," Mitch warned.

She didn't even glance at him.

"Tell her that Mitch wants to sign her card for some dances but he's too scared to come and do it himself."

He jumped up. "*Mother!*"

With a squeal of joy, Martha slammed the door and took off like a shot, whooping and hollering.

"All right!" Mitch yelled. "I'll do it."

Gwen walked to the door, stepped outside, and shouted at Martha. "Never mind. Mitch's found his courage."

"You are a tyrant, you know," he said.

"I know. And someday you'll thank me for it."

He chose a position where he could watch the schoolhouse from the shade of a cottonwood tree. His hope was that anyone coming out from the dimmer light inside the school into the bright sunlight wouldn't immediately see him in the shadows. From time to time he saw movement through the windows, but he couldn't tell if it was Edna Zimmer or Ida Nielson, Bluff's schoolteacher. Several times he almost gave up, but knowing what he would face if he came home empty-handed kept him in place.

In reality, fear of his mother was secondary. For all of his embarrassment and feeling like the fool, he really wanted to ask Edie for a dance and was glad his mother had taken charge. In the two weeks since returning, he'd been in the store four times, but he had only seen her twice. Both times he had only been able to talk to her for a minute or two before other customers came in. But he thought about her all the time. He could picture every detail of her face and how her eyes came alive when she smiled. So he told himself he'd wait fifteen more minutes. When those fifteen minutes were up, he told himself to go another ten, promising that this time would be the last.

Finally, after almost an hour, the north door opened. He stepped back quickly behind the tree trunk, fingers crossed that she would be alone. Martha, who was a fountain of information, said that Edie came to the school as it got out each day to help Ida clean up and correct papers. But she usually left before Ida because she worked at the co-op each afternoon.

Martha was right. Mitch was relieved to see that it was Edie who came out the door and shut it behind her. But that elation turned to panic when she turned and looked directly at him and then waved and came straight over to him.

"Why didn't you come in?" she asked, somewhat shyly.

"You saw me?"

"Yeah, about an hour ago."

"Uh . . . Martha told me that you help Sister Nielson after school. I didn't want to interrupt."

"Are you waiting to see Ida?"

"Uh . . . No. Not really."

She gave a satisfied nod. "Good. How can I help you?"

All Mitch could think of at that moment was how much he wished to be back up at the Blue Mountains, or laying track near Mancos, or anywhere but right there at that moment.

"Well?" She cocked her head and smiled at him.

That didn't help him at all. "Um . . . well, I . . . Look, I know you don't know me very well, but I was wondering—"

The smile broadened. "Actually, I feel like I know you quite well. Martha's told me all about you."

He exhaled in exasperation. "Yeah, that's what I hear. Little sisters. What a pain. Do you have one?"

"No. I'm an only child." Then she brightened. "Don't be too hard on her. She worships you, you know. Every time you sent a letter, she'd tell me all about it." She paused for a moment. "So here we are. Just you and that skinny little freckle-faced kid."

He groaned aloud. "Sorry. That was over a year ago, and I . . ." He didn't know how to finish that, so he just let it trail off.

Again came that quiet laugh that was like the murmur of a rippling stream. "Don't be embarrassed. To be honest, I take it as quite a compliment that you didn't recognize me."

"I didn't. I mean, you didn't look at all familiar to me."

They both fell quiet for a moment. He wanted to look at her but kept his eyes on the ground, the only neutral place he could think of. Finally, she bent down a little and looked up into his face. "So . . . ?" she asked slowly.

Straightening, he knew it was time to do it. "Look, I was . . . uh . . . I was wondering if I could sign your dance card for Saturday night."

His hopes shot up as he saw the look of surprise instantly followed by pleasure. "Yes. I would like that very much."

"Uh . . . So would I."

She half turned, looking down the street. "Unfortunately, I left my dance card at the store."

"Oh."

She waited, and when he started looking at the ground again, she nudged him gently with her elbow. "You could walk with me to the store and I could get it." His head came up and she smiled again. "And then you could sign it."

Face flushing, he realized he was acting like an idiot. "Yeah. I can do that. I mean, I would like to do that."

"Good."

She started away and he quickly fell in beside her. "Sorry, I'm not very good at talking with girls."

"And why would that make you sorry?"

Again panic flashed in his eyes. *Why does she keep asking me these questions that I don't know how to answer?*

She touched his arm briefly. "Sorry, that was a dumb question." Then she laughed. "Let's see, how many times have we said we're sorry in the last minute?"

He managed a crooked grin. "I'm not sure. But I'd like to stop if you would."

She stuck out her hand in front of him. "Deal."

Taken aback, he stared at it for a second and then gripped it. "Deal."

They fell silent, content to walk slowly along side by side. As they approached the store, she suddenly looked up at him. "Do you prefer to be called Mitch, Mitchell, or Brother Westland?"

"Mitch," he said right back. "My family calls me Mitchell sometimes, and that's okay, but everyone else calls me Mitch."

He wrinkled his nose, remembering what she'd called him in the store. "Definitely not Brother Westland."

"Okay, Mitch."

"And what about you? Martha tells me that you—"

"I like Edie. Or Edna Rae. But not just Edna."

"Okay, Edie." He glanced quickly at her and away. "I like it."

They were approaching the store. "My dance card's behind the counter. Do you want to come in, or should I bring it out?"

"Uh . . ."

"Maybe it's better out here. Or maybe in the back." The dimple had appeared, and he could see she was teasing him. "We wouldn't want people talking."

To his surprise, he chose boldness. "Or, how about this? What time do you finish work?"

Her eyebrows lifted. "At six."

"What if I came and walked you home? I could sign your card then."

A tiny smile stole across her face. "It's only three blocks," she teased.

His face went serious. "But I hear it's a dangerous neighborhood."

Now the laughter burst from her like a song. "Yes, I've heard that too."

"Good. I'll be right here at six o'clock."

"Can you make it 6:10? It takes us a few minutes to close up."

"I'll be here at 6:09 . . . Edie."

She touched his arm for just a moment. "Good. So will I . . . Mitch."

Mitch suggested they walk for a while. Edie agreed but said she had to stop off and tell her parents why she wouldn't be home. Mitch waited outside, curious about exactly what was being said inside, but not curious enough to go in. When she came back out she wore a light sweater. It was dark now, and the warmth of the day was dissipating rapidly.

"Where would you like to go?" he asked as they started away.

"Somewhere quiet."

He nodded and took the next turn and headed for the river. They walked slowly, their shoulders close but not quite touching, not saying much yet. He was glad, because that gave him time to collect his thoughts. Her mental quickness kept him off balance about half the time.

A half-moon was just rising. A light rain from the previous night had left the air clear, so they had no trouble seeing in the moonlight as they reached the river and turned west.

"Want to go to the Swing Tree?" she asked.

"That would be great." Then after a moment, Mitch spoke again. "Zimmer? Is that German?"

She nodded. "Actually, Swiss-German. My grandparents on my father's side were from Bern, Switzerland, but they moved to a little village called Sulz, just outside of Mannheim, Germany, to work in a factory that made steam engines."

"And are they still living?"

"Opa died last year. Oma lives with my aunt and uncle in Richfield."

"Are those their names?"

She smiled. "No. Sorry. That's what I always call them. It means *grandpa* and *grandma* in German."

"And that's where you're from too, right? Richfield?"

"Yes."

"That must have been hard on your father to come here and have to leave his mother behind."

"Very. And Mama too. She's also close to my grandmother. But I miss her the most. She and I are very close. Papa calls us kindred spirits." Her brows had furrowed as she spoke, but then she brightened. "I miss her very much, but Oma has agreed to move out here next year. She has bad arthritis, and the doctor says this dry climate would be good for her."

"Yes," Mitch said with a droll smile. "We do have an abundance of dry climate in Bluff." Then he had another thought. "Were your grandparents members of the Church?"

"Yes, they were baptized in Germany." They had reached the great old cottonwood tree with the long rope swing on it. The river, not yet fully into its spring flood stages, filled the air with a soft murmur. Mitch was happy to see that no one else was there. Edie increased her pace, smiling back at him over her shoulder. "Can I swing first?"

"Of course. Want me to push you?"

"Of course."

As she reached the swing, Edie turned around and backed up to it, grasping the ropes with both hands. The swing's seat was quite high off the ground. For Edie it came to her waist, so when she tried to pull herself up, she didn't quite make it. Mitch stepped in behind her, took her by the waist, and lifted her up.

"Thank you," she said, tipping her head way back and looking at him.

The swing seat was wide enough for two adults, and for a

split second Mitch considered asking if she wanted him to sit beside her. But he shook it off. It was one thing to be bold, but quite another to be insanely bold. He stepped around behind her, grabbed the ropes, and began to pull her back.

"Higher," she said.

He backed up another three feet.

"Higher!"

Arching his back, he pulled her up until her feet were nearly level with his eyes and then gave her a mighty shove. She squealed in delight as she shot away from him. Laughing merrily, she stuck her feet straight out, tipped her head back until she was almost laid out flat and her hair was flying out behind her, and began to pump.

He moved away and sat down where he could watch her face, now pale and ghostly in the moonlight. And, to his surprise, he found himself totally content.

She swung back and forth, her eyes closed, for six or seven minutes. At about five minutes she asked if he wanted to trade places, but he said no. He was enjoying just watching her too much, though of course he didn't tell her that.

Finally she stopped pumping and let the swing begin to slow, the arcs growing shorter and shorter until she was nearly stopped. Then she hopped down and came over and dropped down beside him on the sand.

"It is a perfect night. This is so beautiful."

"Yes."

"I love it." She lay back on the sand, cupping her hands beneath her head.

He turned to face her. "So," he said, "your grandparents were converted in Germany?"

"Yes. Missionaries came to Mannheim about the time my

father was ten years old. His family was pretty disillusioned with the Lutheran Church, and when they heard that some missionaries from America were going to preach one night, they decided to go. Grandpa connected immediately. Grandma was a little more stubborn." A dimple showed in her left cheek as she smiled. "But Opa convinced her to pray with him, and that was it."

"So then they came to America?"

"Not at first. They didn't have the money. But Grandpa and some others got sick somehow at the factory where he worked. I'm not sure what happened, but I guess it was pretty bad. The factory refused to do anything to make it safer or to pay for their doctor bills, so Grandpa and three or four other workers got a lawyer and sued the factory. And they won. Each of them got a pretty decent settlement. And with that, Grandma and Grandpa had enough to come to Zion, and so they did."

"And ended up in Richfield. Did they learn English then?"

"No. Well, just a few words. But they spoke German in the home."

"What about your father? You say he was ten when they came here."

"Yes, but he was the opposite. The kids in school made fun of him. Called him the 'dumb German.' So he learned to speak English without an accent and still refuses to speak German, except with his mother, which irritates Oma greatly. She received her patriarchal blessing a few years after they arrived in America, and it says that through her posterity, her family lines and Grandpa's family lines will receive the gospel. So she's determined that her children and grandchildren will speak at least some German so they'll be ready for their mission calls when they come."

Again that bewitching smile flashed at him. "Papa says that's why he tried to forget German. He doesn't want to go to Germany on a mission."

Mitch leaned in, surprised at all she was sharing. "So do you speak German?"

"Quite a bit, actually."

Mitch sat back, marveling. "Wow."

Edie sat up, brushing the sand off as best she could. "Wow what?"

"Just, wow. I'm impressed."

"I'm afraid I have been thoroughly indoctrinated by Grandma. I plan to teach German to all of my children."

"Your grandmother must be quite the woman. I hope I can meet her someday."

"You will, next spring, I hope. If not next year, Papa says we'll bring her out the next. I wrote her and told her she has to come because I am barely using my German at all."

"Wow," he said again. "I've never had a girlfriend who spoke German before."

She hooted and then slapped him playfully. "You've never had a girlfriend, period. Remember, I have my sources on that." Then suddenly she sobered and looked away.

"What?"

"Are you saying I'm your girlfriend?"

In one instant he went about four shades of purple. In the moonlight, his face almost looked black. "No! I didn't mean that." He was stammering and shaking his head. "I'm sorry, Edie. I didn't mean it that way."

He looked away and just shook his head. "You are so stupid, Westland," he muttered to himself.

She leaned in and smiled sweetly. "The German word is *dummkopf,* if that helps."

He lumbered to his feet. "It's getting late. I'd better get you home before your father comes looking for you."

She got to her feet now too, sorry she had teased him. Then she jerked her head up. "Wait a minute," she said, giving him a sharp look.

"What?"

"Is this your way of trying to get out of signing my dance card?"

Instantly he was red all over again and stammering pro-testations. She reached out and took his hand. "Mitch, it's all right. I'm only teasing you."

"I didn't forget. I just . . ."

She reached in the pocket of her sweater and drew out the card and a short pencil. "Mr. Westland," she said solemnly. "Would you like to sign up for a dance with me on Saturday?"

He smiled faintly. "I would."

Handing him the card and the pencil, she went on. "Very good. I would like that too." She stepped closer and pointed to the card. "You'll notice that I still have four places that are not yet signed. You can choose any one you like."

"Four out of fifteen?" he drawled, "and the dance is still three days away. Whatever shall you do?"

She poked him hard. "Don't be sassy. Do you want to sign it or not?"

He nodded and turned the card a little so it caught the moonlight fully. "I see dance number three is open, so I'll take that one." He laid it on the back of his hand and signed it and then held it out for her. She folded her arms without taking it and moved back a step.

Taken aback, he stared at her for a moment. Her face was unreadable. "What's wrong?"

That impish, teasing smile appeared again. "I said you could sign *any* dance you like."

Now he got it. "Hmm." He looked at the card again. "Then I think I will also take number seven." He signed it with a flourish and again held out the card. She stepped back another step, still smiling.

"And perhaps, numbers thirteen and fourteen as well."

Laughing merrily, she came forward. "I think you'd better leave fourteen for someone else or my father will wonder just who you are."

"Done," he said, feeling a little lightheaded at what had just happened. He signed number thirteen and handed her the card.

As she slipped it back into her pocket, she smiled demurely at him. "Thank you, Mr. Westland. I look forward to Saturday evening."

"Not nearly as much I do," he said gallantly. "And now, I think I'd better take you home."

When he entered the cabin, the first thing Mitch looked at was the clock. It was twenty past eight. Then he looked at his mother and father, who were seated together reading a book. Martha and Johnny were already asleep in the corner bed. His mother didn't even glance at him. Instead she turned to his father and said, "Well, I certainly didn't think it would take two hours to apologize for calling her a skinny little freckle-faced kid."

His father grunted. "You know Mitch. He probably gummed it up and will have to do it again tomorrow night."

Mitch fought the urge to laugh. "It's warmer tonight. I think I'll sleep in the wagon."

"Good night, dear," she said, waving him away.

Chuckling, he grabbed his bedroll from beneath the bed and went to the door. "Good night, Mama. Good night, Papa."

His mother looked up and smiled at him. "Sweet dreams, dear."

Notes

Ida Evelyn Lyman Nielson, Bluff's first schoolteacher, came across the Hole-in-the-Rock Trail with the original company of San Juan pioneers. She was a sister of Platte D. Lyman, who led the company. She took great pride in telling people that she drove a span of mules down the Hole in the Rock when she was only twenty-one. It was on that trip that she met Hans Joseph Nielson, commonly called Joe, who was the son of Bishop Jens Nielson. Eighteen months after their arrival, Joe and Ida took a wagon back to St. George, where they were married in the temple in November 1881. Her first payment for teaching was an old cow named Blue (*Saga*, 321).

The Old Swing Tree is mentioned in most of the histories of San Juan County. Situated right on the banks of the San Juan River, it quickly became a favorite gathering spot for individuals and groups. Sometime in the 1890s a flood tore out the tree, taking the swing with it (see the Hole-in-the-Rock Foundation's brief article on the swing and their efforts to pinpoint its exact location at http://www.hirf.org/Newsletters/News_12.pdf).

Regarding nicknames, it is clear women and girls as well as men and boys commonly took on nicknames in those days, just as they do today. Some of these are what you would expect—"Becca" for Rebecca, "Liz" or "Lizzy" for Elizabeth, "Lem" for Lemuel, and so on. Some readers might think that Edie would not be a natural nickname for Edna because there is no long *ee* sound in Edna. But back then, several women had nicknames that were obviously derived from their formal name but altered the sounds a little. Some examples are "Sally" for Sarah, "Feenie" for Parthenia, and "Nean" for Cornelia.

CHAPTER 13

May 13, 1886—Bluff City, Utah Territory

Mitch reached out and took Edie's hand. She squeezed it but didn't look up. "Is this going to make your father mad at me?"

Her head lifted in surprise. "What?"

"Me holding your hand when they're right in the next room and can see us."

That won him a fleeting smile. "No. I've told you. Mama and Papa really like you. They really like your family."

"How is he able to hide it so well?" he whispered.

She poked him, but this time there wasn't even a hint of a smile.

He pulled her so she was half facing him. "What's wrong, Edie? Why so down tonight?"

She looked at him in dismay. "You have to ask?"

Mitch let out a long sigh and then another. "I'm sorry. I don't want to go."

"I know. I know you have to, but . . ."

He put his arm around her, stealing a quick glance to see if her father was watching. He wasn't, so he pulled her closer. "Now that I've got my own herd, it's different. If I don't get them plenty of grass, I could lose everything I've worked for."

"I know that, Mitch," she said with some exasperation, "but that doesn't make it easier."

"I'll only be out in Butler Wash for the first ten days. I'll come back here before I take them up to Elk Mountain."

"And then you'll be gone all summer."

He nodded, not happy with that thought either. "Unless President Hammond decides to send us up to the Blue Mountains this summer. Then I'll take the herd north and meet them there."

She nodded, but said nothing.

"But I'll come back and see you before we take them to the high country."

"You'd better."

He grinned. "You think I'd risk the wrath of you *and* my mother? I'm not that much of a *dummkopf*."

And that finally won him an actual laugh. She laid her head on his shoulder and snuggled in against him. "I'm sorry to be so sour on our last night together. It's bad enough that you're leaving tomorrow, but . . ."

"But what?"

"Nothing."

He turned to face her, taking both of her hands in his. "No, tell me, Edie. What?"

Suddenly her eyes were glistening. "You just picked a really bad day to leave."

"What do you mean? Why is this a particularly bad day?"

She wiped angrily at her eyes. "Sorry. I hate it when I cry."

He leaned closer. "Why is this a particularly bad day?"

"Because it's my birthday," she murmured.

For several seconds he just stared at her in horror, and then he slowly shook his head. "Oh, Edie, I'm so sorry. Why didn't you tell me?"

She sniffed back the tears. "Because I'm not supposed to have to tell you. You're supposed to just know."

"That's not fair," he said in dismay.

"I know. But a girl can hope, can't she?"

"Aw, Edie. What can I do to make it up to you?"

"Stay home."

He got to his feet. "I wish I could." He sighed. "I'd better go."

She started to cry. "Now I've hurt you, haven't I?"

"No." Then he touched her arm. "Look, there's something I have to tell your mother."

Her eyes widened. "My mother? Right now?"

"Yes." He touched her cheek. He turned and looked across the hall into the kitchen. Her mother was already getting to her feet. "Now?" Edie heard her ask.

Mitch nodded.

Her mother turned and left the room, going into their bedroom. Mitch came back in and rejoined Edie. She was staring at him, completely mystified. "What are you doing?"

He held up a finger. "Just a minute."

A moment later, her mother reappeared, holding one hand behind her back. But instead of sitting down, she kept coming toward them. To Edie's further surprise, her father stood up and fell in behind her mother.

"Mitch," she hissed. "What's going on?"

Up came the finger again, this time accompanied by a sly grin. "Patience, Edie."

Caroline Zimmer crossed the hall, entered the small sitting room, came up to her daughter, and kissed her on the cheek.

"Happy birthday, honey." Out came the hand from behind her back, and Edie saw that she was holding a small box wrapped in brown paper and tied with a string.

"But, Mama." She was staring at the package. "You and Papa already gave me my dress." But even as she said it, she reached for the box.

Her mother jerked her hand away and then, smiling, turned and handed the box to Mitch. "But, my dear," she said to her daughter, "this isn't from us."

Mitch, grinning like a six-year-old on Christmas morning, stepped forward. He too bent in and kissed Edie on the cheek. Then he handed her the box. "Happy birthday, Edie."

Dumbfounded, for a moment she didn't know what to say. Finally, she blurted, "This is from you?"

"Yup," he drawled.

"You remembered?"

"Yup." He was having a hard time not laughing at her expression.

With a squeal of joy, she threw her arms around him. "What is it?"

She didn't wait for his answer. She tugged at the string and then ripped the paper off and let it fall to the floor. What was left was a plain white box about twice the size of her hand. She looked at him again, her face radiant with joy. "What have you done?"

"My goodness, Edna," her father said. "Just open it and see for yourself."

She did. Inside was a small wooden box made of polished wood. Gingerly she took it out and examined it. It had a hinged lid, which she opened. A soft "Oh" followed as a tiny figure of a ballet dancer with her hands over her head started twirling around in graceful pirouettes. At the same moment, a soft sound, like a dozen tiny bells, began to play. It took her only three or four seconds to recognize the melody. She had played it as a young girl when they were back in Richfield and had a piano. It was one of Stephen Foster's most popular pieces, "Beautiful Dreamer."

When she finally looked up, tears were streaking her face. "Where did you ever find it?" she whispered.

"When Ben Perkins made that run to Durango last month, I asked him to see if he could find a music box for me. I was hoping he could find one with a German song," he said with a lopsided grin, "but he only had two choices. It was either 'Beautiful Dreamer' or 'Old MacDonald Had a Farm.'"

"It's beautiful, Mitch. Perfect in every way."

"Happy birthday, Edie."

Once again, she threw her arms around him. Mitch quickly glanced over at her father. He was not smiling. But as he looked closer, Mitch could see that he didn't really look angry, either. So he hugged her back.

June 6, 1886—Butler Wash

Mitch was staring into the campfire, thinking of Edie, when he heard a voice call out. "Halloo the camp."

The men around the fire stood up. A few moments later, Joe Nielson came riding in, leading two pack mules. He swung down and came over to the fire. It had been a warm day, but night came on quickly in the desert, and with it, the temperature dropped surprisingly fast. Mitch guessed that it would be in the forties by morning, and most of the men had put on light jackets.

"Evening, boys," Joe said. "I got a load of grub for you. Beef and venison jerky, some canned peaches and apples, molasses, cracked wheat, sugar, and some freshly baked loaves of bread, courtesy of your sisters in the gospel."

There were murmurs of appreciation all around.

"When are you headed for Elk Mountain?"

Lem Redd spoke up. "First thing in the morning."

"That's what I heard, so I thought I'd better get out here today."

He reached in the pocket of his shirt and looked at Mitch. "And, I also have a letter here for Mitch Westland. Anyone know if he's in camp?"

The men whistled and clapped as a red-faced Mitch stood up and walked over to Joe, who handed it to him. "There's no return address," Joe said sardonically, "but I'm guessing you've got a pretty good idea who it's from, right?"

Mitch took it without answering, turned and bowed deeply to his fellow cowboys, and then said, "My apologies, brethren, but I have a matter of some importance to attend to." He waved again as the heckling came back at him in a wave.

When he was far enough away that their voices were only a murmur, he eagerly ripped the envelope open, removed the letter, and held it up to his nose. He smelled it immediately—just the faintest touch of lavender. Then, turning so that the last light from the evening sky illuminated the page, he began to read.

Dear Mitch,

Sorry for the shortness of this letter. I've been working on a longer one that I will send the first time someone takes more supplies up to you. But I heard that Brother

Nielson was coming out to Butler Wash this evening, so I dashed this off and asked if he would take it with him.

We heard some disappointing news today that I think you should know about. President Hammond received word that there is a committee in the House of Representatives in Washington who are considering turning all of San Juan County into a Ute Indian Reservation.

Mitch stiffened. "What? They can't do that."

Pres. Hammond thinks it is all just talk and nothing will come of it. But he is also wondering if it is wiser not to send families up to the Blue Mountain Mission until this is resolved.

"No!" He stomped his boot on the ground and then gave a stone a savage kick. "No! No! No!"

That is not for certain yet, but I thought you ought to know.

Sorry, I can hear Joe's horse outside. Got to run.

I listen to "Beautiful Dreamer" every night before I go to bed. I love it. I miss you so much.
                                    —Edie

*June 6, 1886—Barton Trading Post—The Rincon,
San Juan County, Utah Territory*

They were headed slowly up Butler Wash at a leisurely pace, the cattle out front stirring up clouds of dust, the four men hanging back with bandannas over their noses and mouths.

"Hey!" Mitch Westland exclaimed as he felt a sudden lightness around his waist. He glanced down in time to see his six-shooter, holster, and belt slither down his leg. They hit the ground with a soft thud. "Great!" he muttered, pulling up his horse. He swung down, not sure what had just happened.

About twenty yards away, Lemuel Redd pulled up. "Problems?" he called.

Picking up his belt, Mitch dusted off the pistol and then examined the belt. "Darn!" Then he held it up. "My buckle just tore free from the leather."

Lem rode over to look. Mitch was fiddling with the buckle, muttering to himself. "It's clean busted off," he said, holding it up for Lem to see.

"Do you have an extra one?"

Mitch shook his head. "Never carry one. Do any of you?"

Hyrum Perkins and George Decker had come over to see as well. All three shook their heads. "Just use a piece of rope," George suggested, trying not to snigger.

"That might hold up my pants, but not my gun, too." Disgusted with himself for not noticing it sooner, he looked up. "I'm going to have to go back to Bluff. I can't be worrying about my pants falling off all summer."

"I think that might be a problem for all of us," Lem drawled, straight-faced. But then he shook his head. "Bluff is eight, maybe ten miles back. The Barton place is just couple of miles straight south of us."

"Oh, yeah," Mitch said, surprised that he hadn't thought of that. "I wasn't thinking about the trading post. Good idea." Putting the belt and pistol in his saddlebag, he mounted up again.

Lem removed his hat and wiped at his forehead with his sleeve. "We'll be following Butler Wash all the way up to where it narrows. But you should catch up with us long before that."

"Right." He wheeled his horse around. "See you in a while."

Mitch didn't really know Amasa Barton or his wife, Feenie. When he had returned from Colorado, the Bartons were gone from Bluff. Mitch learned that Amasa and his wife had started a small trading post down on the Rincon, about eight miles downriver from Bluff. Rincon, Spanish for "corner" or "nook," took its name from a wide, lazy, U-shaped bend in the river that enclosed a substantial area of mostly flat sand and red rock.

When Mitch approached the trading post, he saw that a wooden boat was beached not far from it. Several Navajo women and children were standing outside, seeming perfectly impervious to the heat. Mitch tied his horse to the hitching post and raised a hand in greeting. "*Yah-ah-tay.*"

The women looked up in surprise and then quickly away, but the children, especially the younger ones, waved shyly and answered back with the same greeting. Mitch smiled at them. There were five of them. With their chubby, round faces, jet-black hair, olive skin, and large, dark eyes, they were beautiful. But in the midst of them was a little white boy, younger than the rest, a towheaded blond with brown eyes.

Removing his hat, Mitch pushed open the wooden door and stepped inside. The rush of cooler air felt wonderful on his face as he looked around. Amasa Barton was behind the counter, serving two Navajo men, one young, one older. He waved a hand. "Be right with you, Brother Westland."

Mitch waved back and started moving around the store, looking for belts. A movement caught his eye. He turned to see Sister Barton haul herself up out of a chair of rough-hewn lumber. Beside her was a handmade bassinet with a baby in it. "Good morning, Brother Westland. Mitch, if I remember right."

"Yes, Mitch. Good morning." He had wondered as he rode

down if she might have had her baby yet. Now he had his answer. "How are you, Sister Barton?"

"Feenie, please," she said with a pleasant smile. "My name is actually Harriet Parthenia Barton, but I prefer just Feenie. How can I help you?"

Mitch held up the belt and explained what had happened. Her smile broadened. "A cowboy emergency, eh?"

Laughing, he nodded. "For sure. We're taking the herd up to Elk Mountain, so I won't be down all summer."

"Then that's more than an emergency; that's a crisis." Her laughter was soft and pleasant. She walked slowly and with some care over to a rack in the corner and motioned for him to follow. "Do you want a new buckle as well or just the belt?"

He shrugged. "The buckle is fine, but if I have to take both, I can do that too."

"Oh, no. Amasa can fit your buckle on whatever you like. And he can shorten it if you need it." Before Mitch could respond, Feenie moved over to her husband and whispered something in his ear. He turned to look and then said something to the two Indians. They nodded, and Feenie stepped in to take his place. Amasa came over to join Mitch. Extending his hand, he gripped Mitch's in a powerful handshake. "Understand you have a problem."

As Mitch moved steadily up Butler Wash, liking the feel of his pistol on his side again, his thoughts kept coming back to Sister Barton, or Feenie. He couldn't quite get her out of his head. What a remarkable woman. Two children under the age of two. Out here, more than an hour's ride from Bluff, standing by her husband in his new endeavor, obviously taking a role in running the store, being a mother, wife, and cook, dealing with Indians and cowboys day in and day out. And yet she was happy, pleasant, and seemed to be contented with her lot.

And that, of course, turned his thoughts to Edie. She was just sixteen—still a girl in some ways, yet fast becoming a woman. He thought he sensed in her that same kind of strength and faith, but it was still too early to tell. It would take some watching. But then, he wasn't ready for marriage yet. He was only eighteen—just barely a man. And he had things he needed to do first—get his own spread, build a house on it, increase the size of his herd, maybe start adding some horses as well. Give him three years and then he'd be ready. And in three years, Edie would be nineteen. Then he would know for sure if she was a woman like Feenie Barton.

But as he thought about her laugh, her enchanting eyes, that dimple that appeared and disappeared like magic, he realized that he was hoping more and more that she might be the one.

Notes

"Beautiful Dreamer" was written around 1862 and was one of Stephen Foster's last songs.

One source says that in early 1885, Amasa Barton discussed his plans to move out to the Rincon with Bishop Nielson and that the bishop discouraged him from doing so, citing the counsel they had received from Church leaders to stay close together (*Saga*, 68). That may be the case, but we should remember that when President Joseph F. Smith and Elder Erastus Snow came to Bluff in the fall of 1884 and asked the members to stay on, they also gave permission for the pioneers to move out of the fort and start establishing homes farther out from the town. Other families had done the same. One had even started a dairy near Elk Mountain, which was right in Indian country.

CHAPTER 14

June 9, 1886—Barton Trading Post—The Rincon,
San Juan County, Utah Territory

Three days after Mitchell Westland left the Barton Trading Post, while Feenie's mother was still preparing breakfast, Amasa Barton glanced out the window and made a soft exclamation of surprise. Down at the river a boat was approaching the beaching area. In it were two Navajo men. This was a surprise only because normally the Indians didn't start coming until 8:30 or 9:00 in the morning. He shrugged it off.

"Grandma Hyde, I've got some customers. I'll be back in a few minutes." He retrieved the keys to the store and went out.

Farther on by the milk house he saw a small group of Utes who had come in and camped the evening before. They were watching him with stone faces. Their leader was an older man named Cheepoots, but everyone called him Old Chee. His two teenage sons, Posey and Scotty, stood beside him. There were also three women and some children, but they were staying back for the moment. Amasa raised a hand and called a greeting, but knowing that the Utes and the Navajo were longtime enemies, he didn't worry about them. They would stay out back until the two Navajo left.

By then the boat was landing. Amasa recognized one of the men in it. It was an older Navajo whom Barton knew well. He had worked for the Bartons off and on for several years. In fact, he had lost an eye one day helping in the blacksmith shop when a piece of metal broke off from something Amasa was hammering on and hit the Indian in the eye. Now everyone called him Old Eye. He was mostly gentle and amiable, and he still came over from time to time to help in the trading post.

Barton didn't recognize the other man at first. But as they started up the bank toward him, he realized he looked familiar. He was much younger than Old Eye, probably in his mid-twenties. His countenance was dark and ugly, and he was powerfully built. He walked with the natural swagger of a bully. He also had a pistol stuck in his waistband and carried a short piece of lariat curled up in his hand. And then it came to Barton. This was Atsidi, "The Hammer." Barton had not dealt with him before, but he knew his reputation. His name said it all. He was a bully, mean and vicious and hot-tempered.

Wishing he had brought his pistol out with him, Barton considered going back for it but then changed his mind. They would see him, and that would not be good. Besides, he had dealt with angry young natives before. So he turned and unlocked the door to the store and went inside.

Old Eye led the way inside and immediately stated his purpose. Atsidi stepped back, watching with a sullen expression. Through Old Eye's limited English, Amasa's limited Navajo, and a lot of sign language, Old Eye reminded Barton that a few days before he had traded some of his wife's jewelry for some goods in the store. Now he wanted the jewelry back. He withdrew an old broken pistol and offered that in trade.

Barton shook his head. "Now, Old Eye, you know that pistol is not worth anything. You've got to offer me something better than that."

The young man stepped forward. "You trade," he said angrily. "The Man with One Eye want jewelry back."

"I'll give him the jewelry back, but not for that old pistol."

Atsidi raised a fist and started yelling. "You cheat old man. You bad man. You no cheat my friend."

Stunned by this sudden hostility, Barton looked at Old Eye. His head was down, and he was staring at the worthless pistol. Barton had a sudden intuition that this young buck had set this up and that Old Eye was a reluctant partner. He turned calmly to the younger man. "This trade is between me and Old Eye."

Atsidi would have none of that. "You give Old Eye jewels. You take gun." He let his hand rest on the butt of the pistol stuck in his belt. "You do it now."

Feeling a little chill and not liking what was happening here at all, Barton had an idea. "You hungry, Old Eye? We're just having breakfast. Would you sit at our table with us?"

The two men exchanged glances. Atsidi finally gave a curt nod. Only then did Old Eye nod. Not a good sign. The old man was clearly afraid of his companion. Barton walked to the door and pushed it open. "Feenie! We have company for breakfast."

He knew this would not be a surprise to his wife. They often fed the Indians who came to trade with them. It was a way to make friends.

The three men ate quickly while the two women sat in the corner. Feenie tried to talk to Atsidi, but she might as well have been talking to a rock. He refused to even look at her. Old Eye kept his head down, barely speaking. Barton's feeling that Atsidi was coercing Old Eye into something grew stronger, as did his uneasiness. Feenie and her mother sensed something too, and Feenie kept warning her husband with her eyes. So

Amasa stood up as soon as they were done. "Let's go see what we can work out for you, Old Eye."

Back in the store, Barton tried again. "I'll be happy to give the jewelry back, Old Eye, but I have to have something more than that old pistol. Do you have any money?"

Old Eye shook his head. The younger Navajo, who had moved off to one side, was growing increasingly angry. He still carried the piece of rope in one hand and kept slapping it against his leg. He hissed something at the old man.

Barton decided this had gone far enough. His warning senses were tingling, but he knew he could show no fear. "If you won't trade," he said to Old Eye sternly, "then you go now."

He started around the counter to usher them out. As he did so, Atsidi quickly moved around behind Barton. Barton started to jerk around to see what he was doing, but it was too late. The rope was in both of Atsidi's hands now, and Barton saw that it had a noose on one end. With a practiced flick of his wrist the Indian threw the rope over Barton's head. Instantly, the young buck jerked back hard, screaming at Old Eye to do something.

Clawing frantically at the rope around his throat, Barton kicked back at Atsidi, but he jumped clear. Quick as a cat, Old Eye darted around and grabbed the rope too. Both men yanked hard, pulling Barton backward up onto the counter. A box of trinkets crashed to the floor. "Outside!" Atsidi screamed. "Get him outside."

Amasa Barton was a big man, and years of blacksmithing had left him strong as an ox. But with two men pulling on the rope, he was fighting frantically for breath. Somewhere he heard Feenie screaming. Through the window, he saw her come out of the house carrying his pistol. That sight filled him with terror. He dug at the rope, pulling it loose enough to shout at her. "No, Feenie. Hide the gun! Go back!"

That momentary distraction was just enough for the Indians to pull Barton over the counter. He crashed to the ground. He was stunned for a moment, disoriented and confused. Then he realized they were dragging him outside. His head cracked on the counter, further dazing him.

Digging at the rope and fighting desperately for breath, Amasa struggled to get free. He clutched at anything to stop them from taking him outside. The Indians got him halfway out the door and had to stop. Both bent over, gasping for breath. Barton turned his head toward the house in time to see Feenie dart inside. He felt a rush of relief.

Raging now, Atsidi yanked out his pistol and fired a shot at her. "No!" Barton screamed. He turned his head and felt a thrill of joy. Feenie was gone and the door was shut behind her. Then, just as he started to lose consciousness, Barton saw something else—something he didn't understand. Old Eye had let go of the rope and backed off a few steps. He was clutching at his chest, where a blossom of red had appeared on his shirt. Blood was oozing out from between his fingers. Staring at his companion in utter shock, Old Eye staggered backward and then broke into a stumbling run. Then Barton lost consciousness.

Things were happening very fast now. Grandma Hyde, who was watching from the window, saw her son-in-law go down and heard a shot. Thinking the Indians had killed him, she burst out the door, sobbing and screaming at Atsidi to leave him alone. Atsidi's reaction was swift and unhesitating. He stepped forward to stand over the unconscious man lying facedown at his feet. He aimed his pistol and fired a shot into the back of Amasa Barton's neck.

At a full run now, Grandma Hyde, nearly hysterical, threw her shoulder into the Navajo and knocked him away. She instantly dropped down beside her son-in-law and started loosening the rope. Dazed at the speed with which things were happening, Atsidi jumped back. For a moment it looked as if he would shoot the old woman, but then he turned away and ran stumbling around the store to find his wounded companion.

Old Eye was behind the store, sprawled on the ground, dead from a gunshot wound to the heart. Hoisting the body of his fallen partner onto his shoulder, Atsidi came back around to the front of the store. Yelling at the old woman to get back, he walked up to Barton a second time, still carrying his dead companion. Cursing and shouting, he fired another shot into the back of Amasa Barton's neck. Then, in a lumbering run, he headed for the boat, carrying Old Eye with him.

For several seconds it was as if time had been frozen in place. Grandma Hyde was bent over Barton's body, examining his wounds, which were just inches apart. Feenie came at a dead run out of the house and fell down beside her husband. "Amasa! Amasa! Amasa!"

Through all of this, the little band of Utes had sat back in silence, watching events unfold. Now, Old Chee and his two sons came forward and asked if they could help. Though numb with shock, Feenie nodded. "Help me get Mr. Barton into the house," she said.

She glanced toward the river and saw a solitary figure frantically rowing the boat back across to the south bank. Knowing this might not be over, she stood up. Chee and his son Posey knelt down and lifted Amasa.

"Careful! Be gentle," Feenie cried. Her mother came up behind her and slipped an arm around her as she nearly collapsed.

"Where you want him?" Old Chee asked.

"In the house." She pointed. Then she instantly changed
her mind. "No. That's the first place they'll look. Take him
around back. By the shed." She led the way now, finding a
place in the shade where they could lay him out.

To the Utes' surprise, as soon as Amasa was down, the
white woman leaped up and ran into the house. All was silent
for two or three minutes, and then she came running back with
a fistful of money in one hand and a folded paper in the other.
She was waving it at the father and his two sons. "We are in
grave danger," she cried. "I need you to ride like the wind to
Bluff and bring help. Here is fifteen dollars. Take it. But please,
please, bring help."

Posey, the older of the two boys, stepped forward, turning to
his father. After a moment, Old Chee nodded. Posey snatched
the note and the money from her hand and sprinted for his
horse. Moments later, the clatter of hooves on stone sounded
loudly and then slowly faded away.

Feenie Barton watched him go before turning to her mother.
They fell into each other's arms and sobbed and sobbed. Then
Feenie got to her feet. "We need bandages, Mama. And hot
water."

June 12, 1886—Elk Mountain

Lemuel H. Redd Jr. was half asleep in his saddle. Mitch
Westland was rapidly sinking into the same torpor. Knowing
that if he gave in he'd be awake half the night, he straightened,

looking out west. "Looks like there are some thunderheads building up out over the Henry Mountains."

Lem's head came up. He tipped his hat back and looked in the direction that Mitch was pointing. Way off to the northwest, thirty or forty miles away, a large slice of the sky was dark gray. He stood up in the saddle, shaking off the weariness. "Lots of moisture in the air right now," he allowed. "That and the afternoon heat make a bad combination."

"Wind's out of the northwest," Mitch observed. "Think it could come our way?"

"Not sure. Probably not much rain in them. But we may see some dry lightning."

"Cows hate dry lightning as much as they do wet lightning," Mitch observed.

George Decker, who was about thirty yards away, nudged his horse into a walk and came over to join them. "Wanna start pushing them together, just in case?"

Lem studied the sky for another moment and then grunted. "Not like we're busy doing something else right now. Yeah, let's do it. Better safe than sorry."

George wheeled his horse around. "I'll tell the others."

They took their time. Mitch let his horse pick his way along until they spotted more cows. As he was headed back to the open meadowland, pushing along six head, he pulled up. In the distance he could hear the soft drumbeat of a horse's hooves. And they were coming fast. He stood up in the stirrups and looked to the east. But with the trees, he couldn't see much more than fifty yards. He sat down again, pulled his rifle out of its scabbard, and kicked his horse into a trot in that direction.

Lem, George, and the others joined him. They pulled up, peering ahead where the wagon track came into the meadow.

All had their rifles out now. As Mitch rode up, Clint Gurr, who was about fifteen, turned. "You think it's Indians?" he asked, clearly nervous.

"It's only one horse," Lem replied. "And it sounds like it's shod."

The Gurr boy gave him a strange look but said nothing. Less than a minute later, a single rider shot out from the pine trees, bent low over a heavily lathered horse. Mitch shook his head as he lowered his rifle. One rider. A shod horse. Lem was astonishing.

It was Henry Johnson, who farmed the little plot next to Ben Perkins's place. He took off his hat and waved and then spurred his horse all the harder. They all swung out of their saddles as he pulled up and leaped off his horse.

"Got big trouble in Bluff," he exclaimed breathlessly, without preamble. "Bishop Nielson wants one man to stay here with the cattle and the others to come down as fast as you can."

"What is it, Hank?" Lem asked in alarm.

"Amasa Barton's been shot. He's dying. May even be dead by now."

There was a collective gasp. "What happened?" Mitch asked.

"Three days ago, two Navajo came to the Barton Trading Post out on the Rincon." As their horror grew with every word, he quickly sketched out what had transpired. Mitch went white. Amasa dead? Or nearly so? And what of Feenie? And the grandmother?

"But Amasa was still alive when you left?" Clint asked.

"Yes, but there's big trouble brewing. When Posey arrived with Feenie's note, everyone sprang into action. Kumen Jones and Platte Lyman made it back there in an hour and a half. Jo

Barton arrived an hour after that. But before that, the Navajo they call Atsidi had come back with six or seven other young bucks. Knowing they were coming to make sure her husband was dead, Feenie bent down and told Amasa to keep his eyes shut and play dead. It worked. The Indians left him and her and her mother alone. But they looted the store of almost everything. Would have got it all except a couple of squaws across the river warned them that the Mormons were coming."

Mitch had to turn away. He felt lightheaded, like he was going to throw up. He had just been there a few days ago. He had talked with Feenie. Amasa had fixed his belt. Mitch had bought some candy for the Navajo children and Feenie's little boy. And now this.

Lem gave a curt nod. "All right, Clint. You'll stay. Keep the cattle together as best you can. We'll send help as soon as possible."

The boy blanched a little but nodded.

"The rest of you, be ready to ride in ten minutes. Every man take an extra mount and enough food to get us back down. Leave the rest for Clint." Then he turned back to Hank Johnson. "Does the bishop want us at the Rincon or in Bluff?"

"At the trading post. There's a whole collection of Navajo waiting across the river, waiting to see if Amasa lives or dies. There are lots of young bucks demanding revenge."

"*They* want revenge?" Decker said hotly. "What about Feenie?"

Hank shook his head. "Atsidi is telling his people that the two of them tried to trade a gun for some jewelry but that Amasa refused to trade. When they wouldn't leave, Amasa drew his gun and shot Old Eye through the heart."

"And they believe that?" Clint Gurr cried.

"Doesn't matter much whether they do or not," Lem muttered. "When a white kills a Navajo, they start working themselves up for war."

Mitch's head came up slowly. "So who's guarding Bluff?"

Johnson frowned. "When I left it was Peter Allan and John Adams."

"What? Only two men?" He suddenly saw the face of his mother and remembered the look that came into her eyes whenever she was around Indians.

"Not much choice, Mitch. That's why the bishop wants you all down there. He's also calling in the freighters in Colorado and anyone else he can get."

Faces were flashing through his mind now. His mother. Martha. Johnny. Edie. Dan and John Perkins and a dozen other children. He grabbed his horse's reins and swung up. "Then let's get going," he said. "Lem, let's make that five minutes."

"Hold on, Mitch," Lem said. "I think we need a prayer. Will you offer it?"

"I will." He removed his hat but didn't dismount. When the others had their hats off, he bowed his head. "Oh, dear Heavenly Father, protect our families in this hour of danger. Protect Sister Barton and her family, and comfort them in their terrible tragedy." He paused for a moment. "And wilt thou give wings to the feet of our horses? In the name of our beloved Savior, Jesus Christ, amen."

Notes

Harriett Parthenia (Feenie) Hyde Barton was the first schoolteacher in San Juan County, having taught school in Montezuma Creek before the school in Bluff was started. Feenie was twenty-four years old when her husband was shot at their trading post. Amasa was thirty.

The story of the attack at the Rincon Trading Post is told here as it is found in the histories of Bluff. A few details have been left out, but what is included comes from the accounts of those who were present or arrived shortly thereafter (see *History of San Juan County*, 57–60; *Indians and Outlaws*, 86–92; *Saga*, 68).

There is a discrepancy in the sources about whether this took place in the summer of 1886 or 1887. Albert R. Lyman lists it as 1886 in one source but in 1887 in another. It is placed in 1886 for purposes of the novel, but the Barton family group sheet lists Amasa's date of death as June 16th, 1887, which likely settles the issue (see http://www.barton ancestry.com/gen/getperson.php?personID=I12425&tree=bartontree1).

Old Eye is listed by name, but no name is recorded for the young hothead who came with him.

Feenie's first child, Amasa Hyde Barton, was born in September 1885, which means he would have been about twenty-one months old at the time of the shooting. The new baby, also a boy, whom they named William Penn Barton, was born on May 18th, 1887, so he was just three weeks old when the attack occurred. Feenie was still recovering from giving birth, and this is why her mother, Angeline Hyde, was there with her.

None of the sources indicate that the note written by Feenie Barton still exists, but Albert R. Lyman quotes it verbatim, without correcting punctuation, which suggests that he had access to it, or at least a copy of it. She wrote:

> Come quick someone Amasa is shot in the head in two places and Ma and I are alone. For the sake of us do hurry. Send for Jo. A Navajo did the shooting Amasa had no gun The bullets are lodged near the surface and can be removed do come as many as can the Bishop, Platte and as many as well and do have faith.—Feenie Barton.

Jo was Joseph F. Barton, Amasa's brother and partner in the trading post. The Bishop, of course, referred to Bishop Nielson. Platte was Platte D. Lyman.

Immediately, almost all of the men at Bluff raced out to the trading post to protect Feenie, her mother, and the two children. It appears that only two men stayed back in Bluff, Peter Allan and John Adams (*Indian and Outlaws*, 92; *History of San Juan County*, 59). The women and children gathered at Bishop Nielson's home, filling up the floors inside and camping out in the yard (*Indians and Outlaws*, 92).

CHAPTER 15

June 18, 1886—Bluff City, Utah Territory

To everyone's astonishment, Amasa Barton lingered for days with two bullets in his head. The balls seemed to have lodged behind his eyes, leaving him blind, and he was paralyzed on one side of his body, but he was conscious much of that time. Every known medical effort available was used to try to nurse him through the crisis, but his wounds were too serious. At times he was aware of his surroundings and spoke with Feenie and others, but much of the time he was in a delirium or unconscious. He would speak to himself, pray, and sing songs.

To add to the horror of those days for Feenie and the others, the threat of further violence from the Navajo hung over them. Old Eye's body, which Atsidi had dumped on the south riverbank, was covered with wood and burned. The perpetrator continued to harangue the people with his accusations that Old Eye had been gunned down without warning by the wicked white man. Hordes of Navajo gathered on the rocks and cliffs directly across from the trading post, chanting and dancing and preparing for war. The young men put on war paint, shouting that Old Eye must be avenged.

Finally, one week after he was so brutally shot, Amasa Barton passed away. He was carried to Bluff along with Feenie and her children. What goods were still left after the looting were hauled back to Bluff and purchased by the San Juan Co-op Store, leaving the trading post abandoned. Amasa's funeral was held the next day in the old log schoolhouse. He was buried in the cemetery on a small hillock overlooking the town, and a grieving Feenie moved back in with her parents.

Amasa's death seemed to defuse the crisis with the Navajo. With the "guilty" person now gone, their angry gatherings dispersed. With the threat over, the Mormon men began to return to wherever they had been when the frantic call for help came. Mitch Westland, Lem Redd, and the others from Elk Mountain stayed in Bluff for the funeral but left the next day. Gwen and Edie put on brave smiles as they hugged and bade Mitch goodbye. Then both returned to their homes and privately wept.

The next day, life returned to normal—or at least, as normal as life could be in the San Juan Mission.

June 21, 1886

Gwendolyn was getting water from the well near the fort when the barking of dogs erupted. Not just one or two. It sounded like every dog in town was joining in the chorus. Before she could figure out what was causing it, she heard someone shouting her name. "Gwen! Gwen!"

She turned and then gasped. The bucket crashed to the ground, instantly soaking her dress and shoes. She wasn't aware of it. Arthur was sprinting up the street from the river. His hat was gone, and he was waving his hands wildly. But that was not what had caused her to drop the bucket. About seventy-five yards behind him, coming from the direction of the Sand Island ford, was a band of Navajo on horses. They were coming at a steady trot, kicking up a large cloud of dust. A dozen dogs ran alongside, yipping and barking furiously. Even at this distance, Gwen saw something that turned her blood to ice. Their faces were painted black and had brightly colored markings on them, and everyone carried rifles, spears, or bows and arrows.

"Run, Gwen!" Arthur shouted. "Get in the fort!"

She swung around, blood rushing to her head. She felt suddenly faint. "Martha!" she screamed. "Johnny!" She started across the open space to the cabin, which was across the compound from the fort. But her children had heard their father too. They came tearing around the house, crouching low and running hard.

"Into the fort," she screeched. "Hurry! Hurry!"

All around them screams and shouts could be heard. People were scattering in every direction. What few men there were ran for their rifles. Women and older children frantically herded the younger ones into the safety of the rock fort.

A block away, Edie Zimmer was in the back room of the co-op store, putting away the latest load of freight. She straightened and cocked her head as the faint sound of dogs barking became evident. She moved out into the store. Aunt Mary, who was clerking in the store, was standing at the window, neck craned to see up the street. Suddenly, her hand flew to her mouth. "Oh no!" she cried.

Edie felt chills shoot up and down her back and darted out to join her. Mary Nielson Jones was the wife of Kumen Jones and daughter of Bishop Nielson. To most in the town she was simply "Aunt Mary." She whirled as she heard Edie behind her. "Stay back from the window," she hissed as Edie came up.

Out the window Edie saw a street full of horsemen coming down the street toward them. She couldn't tell how many there were, for they filled the street and were kicking up a lot of dust, but she saw enough to know there could be as many as a hundred of them. And it looked like every dog in the town had come out to drive them off. But what left her dizzy with fear was the sight of them. All were men. All were armed. All had their faces painted for war, and all of them looked very, very angry.

To Edie's further horror, when the first of them reached the street in front of the co-op, they pulled their horses to a stop, turning to face the store. "Stay here," Aunt Mary hissed. "Keep the door open, but if I come diving back in here, bolt the door behind me and grab a rifle."

"Yes, Aunt Mary," Edie whispered, her head throbbing so hard she could barely hear herself. And then Aunt Mary did the unthinkable. She stepped through the door and onto the porch. With a strained smile, she lifted one hand. "*Yah-ah-tay.*"

No one moved. No one responded to her greeting. The rider on the horse closest to her stirred but said nothing. He was young, as were most of the others, and she wondered if this had been the one who actually shot Amasa, which didn't help the thumping of her heart. "Can I help you?" she said, fighting to keep her voice steady. *Show no fear.* That was one of Kumen's cardinal rules for dealing with the Indians.

"Where Big Chief? We need big talk. Very mad." He lifted his rifle and shook it at her. "Squaw, you get Big Chief now. You hear?"

"Yes," Mary said calmly. "Wait here." She turned. "Edie, go get my father."

Edie gulped. "Shall I go out the back?"

"*No!*" she hissed. "You can't show any fear. Just walk past them. Don't run, but tell Bishop Nielson what's going on. I think—I hope—Kumen is with him. If not, find him. Kumen will have to act as translator. I can understand a little of their language, but not enough to translate. Now, go."

Edie couldn't remember ever before feeling such relief as she felt when she knocked on the door of Bishop Nielson's home and his son-in-law answered. "Oh, hi, Edie," Kumen said, opening the screen. "Come on in."

"Is Bishop here?" she asked. But even as she said it, Bishop Nielson came limping out from the kitchen. He started to smile. She cut him off. "Come quick, Bishop. There's a war party of Navajo at the co-op. They want to see you."

The two men exchanged glances, and then Kumen said, "So that explains all the barking. I'll get our hats."

"Ya, but no guns," the bishop added.

Edie started at that. "They all have guns, Bishop," she blurted. "And there's about a hundred of them."

"No guns," he said again.

As Kumen came out with their hats, Edie stepped back out on the porch, holding the screen open. "Is Mary Ann all right?" Kumen asked.

"Yes. She's talking to them."

Bishop Nielson reached out and laid a hand on Edie's shoulder. "Go. Make sure everyone is in the fort. Tell the men to keep their vheapons out of sight."

"Yes, Bishop." She turned and leaped off the porch, cutting to the right so she could take a back way that would skirt the store. As she ran, she was thinking about Mitch's mother. Mitch had told her about Gwendolyn's deep, even irrational, fear of Indians, and Edie could only imagine what must be going through her mind right now.

Aunt Mary remained where she was on the porch of the store. She stared up the street toward her father's house, looking bored, while she listened to the muttering going on right beside her. She had picked up a pretty good smattering of Navajo from Kumen, so while she couldn't understand it all, she was getting enough that she wanted to bolt and run to warn her father.

From what they were saying, it was clear they had come to fight. They were going to present their demands to the Big Chief, which they knew he wouldn't accept, and then use that to whip themselves into a fury.

A cry of relief escaped her throat when she saw two figures come around the corner. She looked up. "Big Chief is coming now. You talk."

The Indians all turned and went quiet. Mary turned back, her heart feeling like it was beating in her throat. Then fear turned to surprise and surprise gave way to a warm rush of pride. Her father and husband were coming up the street at a steady but measured pace. They glanced up at the band of Indians in front of them as casually as if they had spotted a passing bird and then went on with their conversation, completely calm and unruffled. With his crippled foot, Bishop Nielson's gait was more like a roll than a walk. It made him seem all the more regal.

"Look," the young Navajo who was next to his leader said. "There is no fear in the old one's heart."

"It is the White-Haired Chief," another said with evident respect.

"Old Crooked Foot," said another. "He has the heart of a warrior."

Tears came to Aunt Mary's eyes. She had never been as proud of her father as she was right then.

"*Yah-ah-tay*, my brodders," her father said, raising his arm in greeting.

"*Yah-ah-tay*," Kumen echoed, doing the same.

There was not even a flicker of softening in the leader's stony expression. "We talk now," the leader grunted. "I am Bidzil. We come in anger. We come for justice. We—"

Kumen held up his hand and stopped the torrent of words. "The Wise Chief does not speak the *Diné* tongue, my brother," he said in Navajo. "May I translate for you?"

He grunted and nodded. Kumen turned to the bishop and spoke slowly and distinctly. Aunt Mary knew why. Though most Navajo did not speak much English, they often understood more than they let on. Kumen wanted them to see that he was translating accurately.

"This is Bidzil. His name means 'He who is strong.'"

The Indian nodded and thumped his chest once. "I am Bidzil."

"Bidzil has come for justice. They are angry."

Another torrent of Navajo. Kumen calmly translated. "One of the Mormon brothers killed one of our people, the one you called Old Eye. Blood was shed, and blood must be shed to make it right."

Bishop Nielson was nodding gravely as Kumen spoke. Then speaking directly to Bidzil, he said calmly and without rancor, "I vill speak with Bidzil and his brodders as friends. But friends do not hold their guns vhile they talk."

Mary was staring at him. He spoke calmly and yet firmly. From his tone, you would think he had asked them if they would refrain from frowning. Kumen continued translating as the bishop went on.

"Vee have no guns," the bishop said. He lifted his arms so

they could see he didn't have a pistol in his belt. Kumen did the same. "If Bidzil vants to talk, let him and his brodders get off their horses and stand their guns against the store." He motioned with his hand. "Vee vill sit in a circle as friends do."

Mary held her breath as Kumen translated. As he did, there were angry cries. One brave shook his rifle at her father and shouted, "Never!" But none of that mattered. What mattered was how Bidzil would react.

For a long moment, Bidzil sat there, looking down at her father. Then he grunted something. He swung off his horse and stepped over to the store, propping his rifle against the wall. When he did this, Bishop Nielson moved into the street and sat down in the dust, not watching to see what any of the others did. Bidzil moved over and sat down beside him.

There were more angry mutters, but one by one the Navajo began to dismount and stack their rifles against the store. A dozen or more refused to move, sitting on their horses, rifles in hand, glaring down at the Mormon chief and their own leader. It looked as though Bidzil might have a mutiny on his hands. But again her father intervened.

With almost lazy indifference, he looked up at them and said. "My people do not fight our Navajo brodders. Our captains sent us here to share the vays of peace. But if vee must fight to protect our women and our children, then vee hire our fighters. Our fighters are the blue coats who live toward the rising sun." He pointed to the east.

That got a strong reaction even before Kumen finished the translation. "No! No! Not the blue coats." Many lifted upraised hands, a sign of great alarm. Several still on their horses lowered their rifles and dismounted.

Bishop Nielson went right on. "Your Mormon brodders do

not vant to fight. Vee do not vant to call the blue coats to do our fighting. Vee vant to be at peace with the *Diné*."

When Kumen finished that, Bidzil jumped to his feet and started yelling at the ones still mounted. It came out in such a rush that Aunt Mary didn't catch much of it. But they obviously did. One by one they dismounted and put their weapons in the growing pile by the door.

They sat in that "circle of friends" for some time, Bidzil and her father talking back and forth with Kumen translating. After nearly half an hour, Bidzil nodded and got to his feet. "Thank you, my brothers," he said to the two white men sitting in the circle with him. "We shall go back and tell our people that we found not enemies but friends among the Mormons."

Bishop Nielson got to his feet and extended his hand to the young leader. "That is good. But stay vith us this night. You have come far and are tired. Vee shall kill a fat steer and put it over the fire. Vee shall get you flour and other things from the store to take back vith you. Eat and rest, and then you can return to your people on the morrow."

As Kumen translated all of that to the astonished natives, Bishop Nielson turned to his daughter. "Mary, spread the word among our sisters. It is safe to come out now. Vee are going to feast tonight. Kumen, you and a couple of the men go pick out the fattest steer you can find. Vee shall be eating vith our brothers this night."

The Zimmers and the Westlands walked slowly along, passing the campfires of the Navajo that lined the streets. Children ran out to hold their hands. Women shyly smiled at them and waved. The men bowed their heads briefly as a sign of honor.

Gwen stepped up beside Edie and nudged her with her elbow. "I guess this gives us both something to write to Mitch about, right?"

"I was just thinking that," Edie exclaimed. "This was astonishing. *Is* astonishing. I thought we were facing a bloodbath."

"So did I," Gwen said in a low voice. Then she brightened. "Platte said he's sending a man up to Elk Mountain with supplies tomorrow. Would you like to put your letter in the same envelope as mine?"

"Yes. I would like that very much." Then suddenly her countenance fell. "Do you think that's a good idea?"

"Why ever not?"

Embarrassed now, she kind of shrugged. "You know . . ."

"Ah," Gwen said after a moment. "You're worried that he might think there's a conspiracy going on between the two of us."

"Yes, exactly," Edie laughed.

Gwen slipped her arm through the younger girl's and pulled her close. "I wouldn't worry about that, my dear. I think he figured that out some time ago."

As they laughed together, a man's voice spoke behind them. "Excuse me, sisters."

They both turned. It was President Hammond, president of the stake.

"I couldn't help but overhear you. Is it your son Mitch that you are speaking about?"

Surprised, they both nodded.

"Well, I was just thinking that I needed to send him a note too. Perhaps I could impose on one of you to share some news with him."

"I'd be happy to," Edie said immediately.

"Of course," Gwen said at the same time.

"Kumen tells me that Mitch has an interest in being one of those called to the Blue Mountain Mission."

"Oh," Gwen said, "it's much more than an interest. It will break his heart if he isn't called."

"Good. That's what we're looking for." He drew in a breath. "But will you tell him that any plans for doing that this year have been taken off the table?"

Edie's head came up. "Really?"

"Yes. First there were the rumors about turning our county into a reservation for the Utes. Now we have this tension with the Navajo, which, I hope, we have resolved this day. But this is not a good time to be sending people out that far from any other settlements. So tell him we plan to send some men next spring as soon as they can get up there to get things ready. Then about this time next year, we'll start sending up the first families."

As he walked away, Gwen and Edie exchanged glances. Edie's mother stepped up beside them. "That's going to break his heart," she said.

Edie nodded solemnly. "I have mixed feelings about it too."

"You do?" Gwen asked in surprise.

"Yes." She giggled softly. "Joy and elation."

Notes

As indicated, Amasa Barton died exactly one week after being shot. He was the only Mormon in Bluff ever to be killed by Indians.

In the anger that followed the shooting at the trading post, tensions between the pioneers and the Navajo were high. A day or two after the trouble, the Mormons were suddenly alarmed to see a large, powerfully built Navajo coming toward the trading post from the south. It turned out to be a member of the Navajo Tribal Council, whose name was Tom Holiday. He said that the council had learned of the trouble and that he wanted to learn for himself what had happened. After hearing Feenie's account, which was substantiated by Cheepoots and other Utes, he said that he believed them. He promised to tell his people that what they had heard was not true and to go home. When he left and crossed the river, he spoke to the angry crowd, and soon they were dispersed. The Mormons believed the situation had been defused and sent their men back out to their various responsibilities.

So when this group of angry braves rode into Bluff, not only were the Saints stunned, but they quickly realized that should the situation turn ugly, they were in grave danger (see *Indians and Outlaws*, 92–93; *History of San Juan County*, 60).

The sources give no names of the Indians involved. One of the band that came to Bluff that day acted as the leader and spokesman for the group as they interacted with Bishop Nielson. There is also record that this group consisted mostly of young men who were spoiling for a fight.

Obviously, no sources give a full transcript of the dialogue that went on that day. However, the substantive conversation between Bishop Nielson and the leader of the band of Navajos is reported in some detail in those sources, and that was followed closely in this chapter. Also, the roles of "Aunt Mary," her husband, Kumen Jones, and her father, Bishop Jens Nielson, are accurately portrayed here (see *Indians and Outlaws*, 95–100; *History of San Juan County*, 60–61).

Albert R. Lyman, son of Platte D. Lyman, is the author of both of these works. He was born in 1880 while those first pioneers were making their way to Bluff. He was a seven-year-old boy when this encounter happened and was present that day.

CHAPTER 16

March 9, 1887—Bluff City, Utah Territory

Edie lowered the book and set it in her lap. "Mitchell?"
He cracked one eye open and sat up straight. "Yes?"
"Were you asleep?"
"No."
"Yes you were."
"All right, maybe just for a couple of seconds." Seeing her look, he moaned. "I'm sorry. I was up at four this morning trying to get everything packed." Then he straightened even more. "Wait. Did you just call me Mitchell?"
"I did."
"Uh-oh."
Her eyes narrowed dangerously. "Uh-oh? What is that supposed to mean?"
"You only call me Mitchell when I'm in trouble or it's something really serious."
"I see." She sniffed loftily and then opened the book again and pretended to read.
He reached out, took the book from her, closed it, and set it on the table. Then he turned fully to face her. "All right, what is it?"
"Nothing."
"Edie," he said, chiding her. "What is it?"

Clearly, that was all she had been waiting for. She got up, went across to the room to a large dish cabinet between two rocking chairs, and opened a drawer. Curious, Mitch started to get up.

"No. You stay there."

When she turned back, he saw that she had two packages in her hands. Both were wrapped in brown paper, and both were tied with string. One was flat and almost certainly was a book. The other was rectangular, about six inches long, but only a couple of inches wide. He gave her a quirky smile. "Aw, you got me my own copy of *Pride and Prejudice* so I don't have to keep borrowing yours all the time."

"Very funny, Westland. You're trying my patience tonight." She sat down beside him. "All right now, before you open these, you have to promise me that you will use them."

"Of course I'll use them. What are they?"

"I'm serious, Mitch. And I would appreciate it if you would be too."

"Sorry," he said contritely. "Yes, I promise to use them to the best of my ability. And also to read the book, whatever it is."

"Good." She handed him the flat package.

He untied the string and the paper came loose. It was a book, about six inches by eight inches. But strangely enough, it had no title on the cover. He opened it and then gave her a long look. All of the pages were blank.

"It's a diary, Mitch. A journal." She handed him the other box.

A moment later he was looking at a quill pen, a bottle of black ink, and six extra quills.

"Do you know how much I would love to be doing what

you're doing?" she said quietly. "Going up to a new place and creating a new settlement?" She pulled a face. "But they don't let single girls do that, so I want you to write in this every day. Describe for me what's happening, what you're doing. The challenges. The problems. The successes. Then I can share in it with you, at least to some small degree."

Mitch began to say something and was surprised that his voice suddenly caught. She had never once let on that she felt that way, and it touched him in a way he hadn't experienced before. He set the packages on the table beside them and then took both of her hands. "I will," he said simply. "I will do that for you."

"Thank you." He could tell her emotions were pretty close to the surface too. "Tell me again, who all is going?"

"The *mature* men—that's President Hammond's phrase—are Frederick Jones and Charles Walton Sr. Then there are three younger families—Alvin Decker and his wife, Emma; George Adams and his wife, whose name is . . ." He pulled a face.

"Evelyn."

"Yeah, Evelyn. And Parley and Ency Butt. Between them all I think they have ten children."

"Eleven if you count the baby Evelyn's carrying now."

"Really? I didn't know that."

"I assumed you didn't. And are you the only single man?"

"No. George has a younger brother named Fred. He's about my age. And Charles Jr. is going too. But the families aren't going with us now. You know that, right?"

"This is Bluff," she said. "We know everything about everyone."

"The families will come up in a few months, once the weather has turned."

"Do you think you'll hit snow now? Down here, the weather is quite pleasant."

"Almost guaranteed. Remember, the area around North Montezuma Creek is over 7,000 feet in elevation."

She poked him gently. "I know that too."

Then, quite abruptly, she slid closer and snuggled in against him. She slid his hand in both of hers and lifted it to touch her cheek. "Why is it that we're always saying good-bye?"

"I don't know."

"Yes, you do!" she exclaimed. "You're the one that's always leaving. Not me."

"I know, but that's just the way it is with women and men."

She pulled a face at him. "And that's your answer?"

"Yup." He glanced across the hall to the kitchen. Her father was at the table, supposedly doing his accounts, but in actuality he had dozed off. Mitch pulled her closer. "I am really going to miss you, Edie."

"When will you be home?"

"Well, you heard President Hammond. We'll come home for the winter and go back up next spring permanently."

"So, October?"

"Perhaps. More likely November."

"I like October better."

Just then Mitch heard footsteps. He looked up and saw Brother Zimmer standing at the kitchen door. "Edie?"

"Yes, Papa."

"Mitch has to leave early in the morning. I think you'd better say good-bye soon."

"Yes, Papa."

They both got up. To Mitch's surprise, her father came over and shook his hand. "Good luck, Mitch. It's an important thing you're doing."

"Thank you, sir."

He bent down and kissed Edie on the cheek. "Five minutes," he whispered.

"Yes, Papa."

Please don't stay! Please don't stay! Mitch crossed his fingers as Brother Zimmer went back into the kitchen. When he saw him bend down and blow out the kitchen lamp and then disappear into the bedroom, it was almost all he could do not to punch the air with his fist and shout aloud.

For the past two weeks, Mitch had been determined to kiss Edie before he left for the summer. He knew it was way overdue, but something about her turned him inside out every time he started to draw close. He'd start leaning in and then she'd look up at him, and that did it. He didn't understand it. He had faced down angry Indians, shot rattlesnakes, dealt with a charging bull, and broken three wild broncos. But all of that was nothing compared to this.

That morning, he had solemnly promised himself that he would not leave for the Blue Mountains without kissing her. He had renewed that vow several times through the day and thought of little else. But all day he had been fretting over how to kiss her when her parents were always hovering nearby. Now, good fortune had smiled upon him.

Glancing once more to make sure they were alone, Mitch stepped to the lamp beside the sofa and turned it down a notch so the light was softer. "I like that," she murmured. Then, as he straightened, she came over and took his hand.

Taking a deep breath, he took her in his arms, but he leaned

back a little so he could look into her eyes. That was a mistake.
A man could drown in eyes like that. So he leaned in closer. "I
am really going to miss you, Edie," he murmured.

She tried to speak but couldn't get it out. With an angry
shake of her head, she fanned her hand back and forth in front
of her face, as if that might dry the tears. "I'm not going to cry,"
she said in a fierce whisper. "I promised myself I wasn't going to
cry."

He leaned in even closer, drawing her slowly to him. For a
moment she looked startled, but then she tipped her head back
and closed her eyes.

Then it happened again. He made the mistake of keeping
his eyes open, and just as their lips were about to touch, panic
hit him like a blow. He turned his head, pulled her tightly to
him, and buried his face in her shoulder. "Oh, Edie. I don't
know if I can stand it. Promise you'll write to me."

"I will," she whispered.

Then, feeling as awkward as a newborn colt, he stepped
back and stuck out his hand. Bewildered, she just stared at it.
So he took her hand and shook it vigorously, all the while cursing himself for being such a fool. "Good-bye, Edie."

She couldn't believe it. He could see that in her eyes as he
turned and half plunged toward the door.

"Mitchell Westland!" It was a sharp bark of command.

He turned back. "Yes?"

She held his gaze for a moment and then looked away. "You
forgot your stuff."

"Oh. Yeah. Sorry." Picking up the book and the pen and
ink, he again started for the door. Again she stopped him before
he could open it. "Mitch!"

"What?" he asked, turning back to her. She took three

quick steps and stopped right in front of him. Then, face flaming, she reached up with both hands, pulled his head down, and kissed him softly on the lips.

He was stunned. "Uh . . ." He felt like his face must be glowing in the dimmed light.

"Now you know how it's done, Mitch," she stammered, averting her eyes.

"Wow!" was all he could think of to say.

"Good night." She turned him around and gave him a little push toward the door. "Please write to me." Tears sprang to her eyes and she turned away.

In a daze of wonder, he walked to the door and opened it. He stopped and turned back. Her back was to him, and he saw that her shoulders were shaking slightly as she fought back the tears. Very quietly, he set down the two packages. "Edie?"

She turned.

A silly grin spread across his face as his eyes locked on hers.

"What?" she whispered.

In three steps he was to her and had her in his arms again. "Uh . . . Could we do that again? I don't want to forget how it's done."

1887—The Blue Mountains

Sunday, March 13th, 1887. This is my first diary entry. I had planned to write every day, but I'm learning that sometimes there just isn't time at the end of the day, and so I'll have to write when I can. Sorry, Edie!

We left before dawn on Thursday. There were eight men in our party. Families will be brought up sometime in June. We have four wagons, including my own, the teams to pull them, and riding horses. We brought no cattle with us this season, thinking it wiser to get established first.

The small valley by what we call South Montezuma Creek has great promise for farming. We have taken to calling this site "Verdure," which means "green," or "greenness." It is a small but beautiful valley. This will almost certainly be the site of one of our two settlements. Yesterday we came six more miles and set up camp on North Montezuma Creek. Snow is deeper here, and the winds blow stiffly out of the northwest constantly.

Today is the Sabbath. Rested ourselves and our teams. Had a simple Sabbath service with Bishop Jones directing. We have decided to declare March 12, 1887, as the official founding day for our new settlement.

Monday, March 14th, 1887. Weather is clear but quite cold. Split up today and began exploring the water possibilities. They are very promising. The water is cold and plentiful and very sweet. We used shovels to divert the stream onto the land to help us determine where to dig the ditch that will bring water to our new town. Put in stakes dated March 12th claiming all water rights of all the streams coming off the east slopes of the Blue Mountains.

Tuesday, March 15th, 1887. Today we discovered what could be a complication. George and Charles continued exploring upstream and found stakes indicating two previous filings on the water rights. They eventually met cowboys who said they had made the filings, but they admitted they had no interest in the rights themselves but had done it in behalf of the L. C. Ranch, which is not legal, according to Charles.

This is disturbing and we must look into it. We see cattle droppings everywhere and estimate they may have as many as 2,000 head here. We have spotted riders in the distance, so they know we are here. The L. C. Ranch has been here for several years, but we believe that they have illegally taken over the best country for their own purposes without filing for title to it. We expect that they will resist any effort on our part to settle in this country.

Wednesday, April 6th, 1887. There is one dark cloud on the horizon. The foreman of the L. C. outfit came to our campsite the other day. He was quite belligerent and told us that this was their land and that we needed to move on. When we asked for some evidence that the Carlisles (owners of L. C.) had legal title to the land, he got very angry and stomped off. "You either get out or we will drive you out."

Being a prospective cattleman myself, I can see why he is angry. But it is worrisome. He seems like a decent man, but a lot of his hands are young rowdies and it's likely many have come out here to escape the eyes of the law. Some of them are reputedly wanted for murder.

We decided to consult with President Hammond, who is visiting in Mancos. Since I am familiar with that area, I will accompany Bishop Jones there in the morning.

Friday, April 15th, 1887. Our trip to Colorado proved most fruitful. President Hammond recommended that all three of us go to Durango to consult the land records and seek the advice of a lawyer. We did so and were highly gratified that after a careful search of the records, the lawyer assured us that the Carlisles' claims to the Blue Mountains are illegal. This was wonderful news and was received with much joy.

It was a long and exhausting trip, and it is good to be back. I miss Edie tremendously, even more than I expected. The thoughts of staying over here through the winter seem less and less attractive. Perhaps the next time we need someone to go down to Bluff for supplies, I shall volunteer.

Sunday, May 8th, 1887. Another Sabbath day and a chance to finally write in here again. I feel guilty about not writing more, but every day is filled with things that require immediate attention. At nightfall, I crawl into the back of my wagon and fall asleep almost the moment my head hits the pillow.

Things are progressing well. We have occasional run-ins with the L. C. hands, but it's mostly bluff and bluster and a string of profanity. I long for the day when those cattle I see spread across the countryside have my brand on them instead of theirs.

There was disturbing news from President Hammond yesterday. Congress just passed the Edmunds-Tucker Act in Washington. This is a law aimed directly at the Church and those who are living in plural marriage. It is a harsh law that will affect many of our families in Bluff. Gratefully, neither my father nor Edie's father were asked to live that law.

Among other things, President Hammond says the law will now force plural wives to testify against their husbands. All marriages will hereafter have to be performed by probate judges appointed by the president of the United States. Thus no bishop or stake president can perform a marriage, nor can there be any marriages in our temples. Anyone elected to public office must swear an oath rejecting plural marriage. The territorial militia is disbanded. And, most devastating of all, the law disincorporates the Church, which means that all Church properties, including the temples, will be seized by the U.S. government. President Hammond says that the Church plans an appeal to the Supreme Court, but he thinks that won't stop them from implementing the law immediately.

Edie's seventeenth birthday is five days away. I had hoped to go down to Bluff for supplies and to surprise her, but there is too much to do here. I left a small gift with Mama to take to her. I miss her every day.

Thursday, May 26th, 1887. A family passed through two days ago. They are moving to Moab in hopes of finding better farmland. They brought a bag of letters for us, including a letter from my family and one from Edie. What a welcome thing something as simple as a letter can be. Johnny and Martha both wrote their own small note. Mother's health is doing better than it has for years. She sees that as a fulfillment of the promise by President Smith that those who stayed in Bluff would be doubly blessed. It makes me so happy to know that she is happy.

Of course, Edie's letter filled me with joy. I was surprised to learn that she is no longer working at the store but helping Ida Nielson at the school every day now. I can tell from what she says about the children and the work that she loves it much more than she did her work in the store.

How I miss my Edie. She is a much better writer than I am and fills the pages with things that lift my heart and make me laugh. Perhaps next spring, I might ask her to be my wife. More and more, I see in her the strength and faith that I see in my mother and that I saw in Feenie Barton. She will only be eighteen then, so it would probably be best to wait until the following summer to wed. But I am sure she has many would-be suitors—though, of course, she says nothing about such things.

The other good news the passing family brought with them is that the wives and families of my other brethren will be leaving in two weeks to join their husbands and fathers up here. My brethren are rejoicing at the prospect. But that will be especially difficult for me, for when the others come, I will be the only one who is without a family here.

Notes

In March 1887, Congress passed the Edmunds-Tucker Act, which was the latest and most comprehensive attempt of the government to stop plural marriage (see http://en.wikipedia.org/wiki/Edmunds-Tucker _Act). Three months later a constitutional convention was held in Utah to try to stave off the seizure of Church property. The Church also began forming colonies in Mexico and the province of Alberta in Canada to provide safe haven from this law. Government authorities did not wait for a Supreme Court ruling but immediately began arresting and prosecuting Church members living in plural marriage. Dozens of men were arrested and hauled off to prison. Many families were left without their primary means of support.

In April 1890, the Supreme Court upheld the Edmunds-Tucker Act. Six months later, at October general conference, Wilford Woodruff issued the Manifesto that officially declared that the practice of plural marriage in the Church had stopped. Men were released from prison. Confiscated properties were returned to the Church, and formal, legal persecution stopped (see "Plural Marriage and Families in Early Utah," https://www .lds.org/topics/plural-marriage-and-families-in-early-utah?lang=eng).

CHAPTER 17

June 16, 1887—Verdure, San Juan County

Fred Adams saw them first. Mitch was working with Bishop Jones and Charles Sr. on a storage shed for the grain they hoped to harvest in the fall. They were just hoisting up the top log when Fred shouted something at them. Grunting and straining, they gave one last heave and dropped it in place. Then they turned to see what the shouting was about.

A cry of joy went up. On the south ridge that marked the beginning of Verdure, a wagon had appeared. As it pulled to a stop, another and then another pulled up alongside it.

Women and children were waving wildly and calling out. Dropping whatever they had in their hands, seven men and boys gave a whoop and took off running. They swept off their hats and waved them wildly as they ran.

Mitch sat back, took a bandanna from his back pocket, and wiped at the sweat across his forehead and his neck. He watched with a curious mixture of happiness and longing as the two groups came together. Husbands caught their wives as they leaped from the wagon seats. Brothers swept up little sisters in their arms. Older sisters raced to be the first to reach their fathers. Children danced around their parents, who were locked in a prolonged embrace.

Mitch sighed and then straightened, looking for the

sledgehammer. The top log was slightly out of alignment, but a couple of whacks with the sledge and it would be fine. He picked it up and looked back at the celebration going on up at the ridge. As he did so, something caught his eye. He lifted his arm to shade his eyes. One solitary figure stood off to the side, like him, an observer rather than a participant. The figure was somewhat silhouetted in the afternoon sun, but it was clearly a woman. She wore a bonnet and a long dress. As he looked, one arm came up and she began to wave it back and forth. Then, floating down to him on the summer air, he heard one word that made his heart leap. "Mitch!"

The sledgehammer clunked to the ground as he leaped forward, scarcely daring to believe his eyes. Then he heard it again. "Mitch Westland. You get up here, right now." He took off in a sprint.

Puffing heavily from his dash, he swept Edie into his arms, lifting her off the ground and whirling her around and around. Then he kissed her, long and hard. Men, women, and children broke into cheers and applause. Finally, Mitch pulled back and set her down.

"My, my," she managed breathlessly, her face bright red, "I see you haven't forgotten what to do."

"No siree!" And as the others looked on, he kissed her again.

It was nearly sundown before they found time to be to-gether far enough away from the others that they could talk. But now the wagons were unpacked, supper was cleaned up, and mothers were putting their children to bed. Mitch found a place on the creek bank where the grass was like a Persian carpet. As they sat down, he put his arm around her and pulled her close.

"I'm still in shock," he said. He reached up and started curling a lock of her long, dark hair around his finger. "I can't believe it."

Smiling shyly, she nodded. "I thought I might surprise you."

"Why didn't you tell me you were coming?"

"Because I wasn't sure until just a few days before we left. I have wanted to come, ever since you left. And not just for you. I think this is so exciting—being the first to start a new settlement, creating something out of nothing. But it didn't seem appropriate. A single woman coming up here is different than a single man."

"So what changed?"

"Emma Decker came and talked to me." She laughed softly. "Actually, I think your mother put her up to it. But anyway, Sister Decker wondered if I would come up for the summer and help her with the children."

"They have five, right?"

"Yes."

He nodded. "Alvin talked about them all the time. You can see how happy he is to have them here."

"No happier than Emma is to be here. So, anyway, I told my parents about her request."

"And they agreed?"

Laughing softly, she said, "This will surprise you. Mama had a lot of misgivings, but Papa said yes. Right off. He didn't even think about it."

"Then I owe him a lot," he said, taking her hands. He shook his head in wonder. "I just can't tell you how good it is to see you."

Poking him with her elbow, she said, "Oh, I thought you did a pretty good job of telling me."

He blushed. "I kind of got carried away."

She poked him again. "I wasn't complaining, Mitch." Laying her head against his shoulder, she sighed. "So, tell me about it. What is it like up here?" Then her eyes widened. "Have you been writing in your diary?"

"Yes." He frowned. "Not as much as I'd hoped, but quite a bit."

"Can I read it?"

"Um . . . Let me finish one thing first. Then you can."

"All right."

"Uh . . . Edie?"

"Yes?"

"Some of us are leaving in the morning."

She gave a low cry and reared back. "So soon?"

"Yeah. We . . . I think I told you how we started digging a ditch to bring water down to the North Montezuma Creek settlement site, but then we quit because it was going to take too long and we had to get the crops in down here first, and we also had to get some acreage fenced and—"

She cut in sweetly. "My goodness, Mitch. Take a breath." When he did so, grinning foolishly, she went on. "Yes, I remember all that."

"Well, the crops are in now, and things down here are pretty much in good order. So Parley Butt, Fred Adams, Charley Walton, and I are going up to start on the ditch again. Others will help as they can. We can't start the other settlement until we get water to it."

"How long is that going to take?"

"Probably three or four weeks."

At her look of dismay, he rushed on. "But we come back here each night. It's only six miles. We don't stay up there."

"Oh." She moved closer to him. "Then maybe I'll let you go."

June 21, 1887—Future Site of North Montezuma Creek

"Hey, Mitch! Come look."

Mitch leaned on his shovel as he turned and looked at Charley. He was standing, shovel in hand, about twenty-five yards away, right where the ditch would eventually connect with the creek. "What is it?"

"You'd better come and see."

Already guessing what it was, Mitch set the shovel down, took two steps to pick up his holster and pistol, and strapped them around his waist. Then he picked up his shovel again and started toward Charles.

"You want us to come with you?" Parley called.

"Nah. I'll go check it out."

When he joined Charley, it was exactly what he had expected. Instead of the gurgle of water over rocks, there was no sound. Instead of water rushing up to their knees, there was no more than an inch or two trickling past them.

Mitch's jaw set. "I'll be back," he called to the others.

"You sure you want to do that alone?" Parley called.

"Yeah. I don't want them thinking we're looking for a fight." Then he grinned. "But I want them to know that if that's what they want, we're ready. They'll learn to file a claim instead of just arrogantly taking whatever they want." He turned and started upstream, telling himself to hold his temper.

No surprise—no one was there. There were plenty of

hoofprints in the mud, and Mitch guessed there had been three or four men here. But they had built their dam, diverted the water into a ditch running in the direction of L. C.'s pasture-land, and then skedaddled before the Mormons realized what they were doing.

Muttering to himself, Mitch found a dry spot and sat down. He removed his boots and socks, rolled up his Levi's as much as he could, grabbed his shovel, and waded into the creek bed just below the rock and sod dam. He shoveled off the sod and then removed the rocks one by one. By the time he finished, the ice-cold water had numbed his feet and his Levi's were wet above his knees.

He got dressed again and walked back down to join his companions. By then, the creek was back to its normal flow. He gave them a brief report and they went back to work.

June 23, 1887

When the four men returned two days later, once again the ditch was empty. Muttering angrily, this time the four of them rode together upstream, rifles out and lying across their saddles. As they approached the site, they dismounted and tied their horses and then went as quietly as they could through the un-derbrush, peering through the trees for any sign of movement. There was nothing.

The dam was in the same place, only it was higher and thicker this time. There was also a cold campfire and signs that at least two cowboys had stayed overnight. With Fred and Charley nervously standing watch, Mitch and Parley waded in and tore the dam apart. Only this time, they scattered the rocks and left a terse note nailed to a tree.

To the LC Outfit. The land office in Durango has confirmed that you have no legal rights to this land or water. We have filed for those rights. Further action on your part to stop our legitimate use of this water will force us to send for a law enforcement officer to come and settle this matter.

—The Mormons

The next morning, the scene was repeated. When the men arrived the creek was a trickle. This time Bishop Jones, Charles Sr., George Adams, and Alvin Decker had come with them. The eight of them followed the creek toward the mountains, keeping alert for the possibility of an ambush. This time they caught two cowboys in the act. One was in the creek while the other carried the scattered rocks to him. Dropping the rock he was carrying, the second man gave a cry and raced for his horse.

"I wouldn't do that," Bishop Jones barked sharply.

The man pulled up and turned around. He came stalking back, his face ugly with anger. The other one, who was Mitch's age or younger, and who looked very frightened, clambered up out of the ditch and joined his partner.

"Get out of here, squatters!" the older one snarled. "We don't want no Mormons here. Get off our land!"

"Sorry," Charles said, "but we aren't the ones who are squatters. We have filed for the land and the water rights. So you go back and tell this to your foreman. We don't want to fight you. Nor are we trying to drive you out. But we *are* here to stay. And if we find that you've stolen our water one more time, we'll send a rider to Durango for a U.S. Marshall."

"We'll see about that," the man said hotly. Then he whirled to his companion. "Let's go, Spud. We're headed for the ranch house."

July 3, 1887—Verdure

When a few more days passed without hearing from or see-ing any of the L. C. boys, the little group at Verdure began to relax. Trips that had been postponed due to the tensions now were put into action. So when Sunday came, Mitch, Parley Butt, and Bishop Jones were the only men left in camp.

They had a quiet day together. Following sacrament meet-ing, the families gathered together in the shade of a large oak tree on the north side of South Montezuma Creek. The men carried over a wagon box and turned it upside down to create a table. With the heat, no one wanted a fire, so they had a cold meal of fresh vegetables from their gardens, dried venison, a cold bean soup that Mary Walton made, and Dutch oven bread pudding smothered in molasses. After the dishes were washed in the creek, the children were sent off to play and the adults sat around in the shade talking. They were right in the middle of a discussion about whether they were going to do anything to celebrate the Fourth of July the next day, when suddenly Bishop Jones sat up. "Listen," he cried, holding up one hand. He was looking to the north.

Every head turned, and instantly they heard it. It was a low, distant rumble. Edie glanced up at the sky, thinking it might be thunder. But Mitch scrambled to his feet. "It's horses. And a lot of them." Parley was up beside him. He turned to his wife. "Ency, help me get the children. Quickly!"

Mitch swung around. "Sisters, get all the children to the storage shed. Now!" Not waiting to see if they obeyed, he sprinted for his wagon. Splashing through the creek, he reached inside the wagon and grabbed his pistol belt. As he strapped it on, he saw Bishop Jones dart to their wagon. He came back out with his shotgun. Mitch turned to see that Edie and Emma Decker had the children in tow and were running for the shed they had dug into the hillside. They flung open the door. They had planned to fill it come fall, but right now it was empty. "Hurry, children! Hurry!" he called.

By the time the last of the children were inside and the mothers huddled behind the three armed men, they saw the riders come over the ridge from the north. Mitch counted quickly. Six, eight, nine. No. An even dozen. There were twelve riders. All but the lead rider had their rifles out.

"That's old Carlisle himself," Parley muttered.

Mitch knew all about the head of the L. C. Ranch but had not yet seen him in person. As their horses splashed across the creek at a canter, he saw that the man was tall and heavily built. His face was etched granite, his eyes a glacial blue, his body stiff as a ramrod. His reputation for being a tough old bird couldn't have been exaggerated too much. The others spread out in a line to his left and right. It took only a quick glance at them to see why Carlisle had to be tough. These were hardened men he employed.

"Who's in charge here?" Carlisle growled in a raspy voice.

Bishop Jones took a step forward but kept his shotgun pointed at the ground. "I am."

"You the one that put that sign up on my creek?" His accent was clipped but definitely British.

"No, I am." Mitch stepped forward, one hand resting casually on his pistol butt. Several rifles jerked downward. Mitch saw that one of them was in the hands of the kid from the creek. But with a flick of his wrist, Carlisle waved them back. Mitch went on. "It's not your creek and you know that, Mr. Carlisle. You have no title to the land or the water."

Carlisle spit a stream of brown chewing tobacco, which splattered at Mitch's feet. "Out here, sonny boy—" He sneered as his hand flashed down and came up with a pearl-handled pistol. It was pointed directly Mitch's chest. "—this is all the title we need."

Several of the women gasped behind him, and Mitch heard one of the children start to whimper. But Mitch understood that showing no fear was as important with this group as it was with the Indians. He said nothing, but his eyes never left Carlisle's.

"We've got no fight with you, Mr. Carlisle," Bishop Jones said. "There's plenty of land for the both of us, and—"

"*No!*" he roared. "You listen to me. There'll be no Mormon squatters on my land. You got that?" He turned to Mitch. "And if I see you anywhere near that ditch, it'll become your gravesite. You understand me, sonny boy?"

"You can't frighten us off, Mr. Carlisle. We are here to stay."

The ranch owner stood up in his stirrups and leaned forward, waving the pistol back and forth. But when he spoke, it was to Bishop Jones. "Let me make this perfectly clear to you. You have ten days to pack up and be gone. And that includes taking those stakes with your so-called claims on them and also taking down your fences. If you're still here after ten days, we shall annihilate you." His eyes lifted and swept across the faces of the women. "You hear that, ladies? Annihilate. Ten days, and then you will all die, and your children with you."

Jamming the pistol back in its holster, he wheeled his horse and dug his spurs in. The others wheeled in behind him, and in less than a minute, they disappeared back the way they had come.

Once the children were in bed, the adults gathered around a low campfire to discuss what had happened earlier that day. "What are we going to do, Bishop?" Mary Jones asked.

Mitch had to smile. She always called her husband "Bishop" when they were in front of others.

Bishop Jones turned and took her hand. "We can't run, Mary. We were called here by the Lord. And we knew that the cow outfits weren't going to like it."

Emma Decker spoke up. "He had eleven men with him. Do you think that's all he has?"

Parley shook his head. "They say he's got twenty or more hands. The rest were probably left with the cattle." Ency reached to take his hand but said nothing. She didn't have to. The anxiety in her eyes was there for all to see.

Edie sat next to Mitch, her arm through his. He looked at her and she smiled up at him, but she said nothing. He sensed that she was feeling like this was not her decision.

The bishop turned and looked at Mitch. "No going up to the ditch until we get this settled, Brother Mitch," he said softly.

He felt Edie's arm squeeze his for a moment, and then she leaned up and whispered in his ear, "That's right!"

"I know that, Bishop. Taunting them is not the answer."

"No, definitely not." He dropped his head and rested it in his hands, staring at the fire. "Well, there is nothing more we can do tonight. We have ten days. Let's think on it. Pray about it. Then tomorrow, we'll discuss it some more."

As he got to his feet, Edie raised her hand. "Yes, Edie?" the bishop asked.

Mitch was taken aback to see a hint of a smile on her face. "Maybe we should remind Mr. Carlisle that tomorrow is Independence Day, the day we celebrate winning freedom from oppression."

Evelyn Adams was staring at her, not sure she had heard right.

Then Edie snapped her fingers and, with an impish smile, said, "Oh, that's right. He's British. They lost that war. Maybe that's why he's so angry."

Laughing merrily, they stood and gathered in a circle. "Parley," the bishop said, "would you offer our prayer this evening?"

Note

Within a short time of their arrival on the Blue Mountains, the new settlers started clashing with the cattlemen. Water rights were a major issue. The Saints had picked a site for a settlement on North Montezuma Creek, which was directly east of the mountains. But to make that work, they had to divert water into the town site. This quickly became the flash point. For several days, the Mormons and cattlemen dammed and undammed the ditch several times. Though we don't know the exact day, a short time later Mr. Carlisle, who is said to have come from England, came to Verdure and gave the Saints the ultimatum as it is found here: "You have ten days. Then we shall annihilate you" (see *Lariats*, 86; *Saga*, 93–94; *History of San Juan County*, 61–62)

CHAPTER 18

July 4, 1887—Verdure, San Juan County, Utah Territory

When Mitch poked his head out of the wagon cover, he was startled to see Edie sitting on a stool a few feet away, obviously waiting for him.

"Happy Independence Day."

"What? Oh, yeah. That's right."

"Are you up and going or do you want me to leave you alone?"

He opened the canvas and pulled it back, revealing that he was fully dressed except for his boots. "I'm up and going. What has you up so early?"

She gave him a look that said, *Do you really have to ask?*

"Couldn't sleep?" he asked.

"Could you?"

He shook his head. "Not a lot."

"Get your boots on. I went out for a walk this morning. I want to show you something."

She led him across the creek and up the wagon road to the north ridge and then kept going for another quarter of a mile. "You walked this far?" he said after a minute. "I'm not sure that was a good idea."

"I was fine." She took his hand and pulled him to a faster walk.

226

As the trees started to thin, she stepped off the road. Ahead of them was a small rise of red earth covered with scattered cedar trees. In a moment, they came out into the open. Before them lay the grand vista of the Blue Mountain region.

"It's beautiful," he said. "A beautiful day and a beautiful view."

"Look closer."

He gave her a puzzled look. "Look closer at what?"

"Well, for a start, look out there at the La Sals."

He turned slightly. To the northeast, about forty-five miles away, were the La Sal Mountains. The highest peaks were still showing snow. In the clear morning air, they looked like you could reach out and touch them. "They're beautiful too. Probably some good cattle country up there."

She smiled, in spite of herself. Did he think of nothing else? Then she slugged him softly. "Mitch, look more closely. Pay attention to the details."

He squinted a little, and then came a soft exclamation of surprise. "Whoa! Is that smoke?"

"Yes, Mitch. I think it is."

He shaded his eyes against the morning light. There was no mistaking it. At the top of one of the snow-clad peaks there was a tiny pinpoint of golden light. As he focused on it he saw a very thin column of white, like a thin, white cloud tipped on its side. He turned and stared at her. "A signal fire?"

"Ah," she said softly, "so it wasn't just my imagination." She grabbed his arm. "Now look out there. Way out there. Just a little to the left of north. There are two red peaks."

"Yeah, those are called the Six-Shooter Peaks—one north, and on—" He jerked forward again. After what seemed like a long time, he turned and looked at her in awe. "Another one."

"Yes. Now look behind you."

He turned to face the Blue Mountains, which were just slightly north of due west from where they were standing. This time, he saw it instantly—or rather, saw them. There were two large pillars of smoke rising vertically into the sky, one near the top of Abajo Peak, which was closest to them, the other on top of Horsehead Peak.

"They are Ute signal fires," he breathed, feeling his pulse start to race. "No doubt about it."

"And what does that mean?" she said, anxiety darkening her deep eyes even more.

"It means the Utes are calling their people to battle."

The adults stood around in a circle, any thought of food forgotten as Mitch and Edie described what they had seen. "So it's true," Bishop Jones finally said.

They all turned to him. "When we were in Mancos a few weeks ago, there was news that some cowboys up on Disappointment Creek had come upon some Ute Indians and shot several of them down in cold blood, including women and children. The Indian agent had sent out a warning to the entire area that the Utes were looking for who did it and would retaliate one way or the other. Maybe they found them."

"What does that mean for us?" Evelyn Adams asked.

He turned and gave her a wan smile. "This had nothing to do with the Mormons, and the Utes know that. But that doesn't mean we shouldn't be careful. It's not a good time for a white man to be out alone, because they often don't distinguish between us and the cowboys."

That set them all to talking among themselves. After

yesterday's shocking confrontation, no matter what Bishop Jones said, the women were all pretty shaken—as were the men, though they tried not to show it as much. He watched them for a minute and then signaled Mitch and Parley to walk with him. As they moved out of earshot, he spoke in a low voice. "Brethren, what I haven't said yet is that while we were in Mancos, the sheriff told us what had happened and said that he thought some of those who were guilty of the killings had come our way, probably looking for work with Carlisle."

Parley grunted softly. "If the sheriff's heard that, there's a good chance the Utes have too."

"Exactly."

"Which means they'll be coming here. So are you saying we pack up and leave?" Mitch asked.

"No. But I am thinking that maybe I ought to head for Mancos tomorrow. I'm pretty sure President Hammond is still there. Let's get his counsel on what to do."

"Good idea," Parley said.

"I agree," Mitch nodded.

Then he glanced back and saw that the women were watching them. "If you can handle the children for a minute, I'll go tell the sisters what's going on. Then maybe later today we can sit down and make some plans."

<hr />

That idea sounded good to everyone until about eleven o'clock. Mitch and Edie were working together in the Deckers' garden, with the children gathering up the weeds and putting them in a pile. Out of the corner of his eye, Mitch saw Edie stiffen and then jerk upright. "Mitch!" she hissed. "Look!"

Mitch whirled around. Up on the south ridge, about

seventy-five yards away, a solitary figure had appeared and was shuffling slowly down the wagon road toward them.

"Is that an Indian?"

"Yes, it is, Edie. Just walk slowly, don't scare the children, but take them over to the wagons. Tell the bishop. And make sure all the children are with their mothers."

She turned. "Children, I need you to help me. Sarah, Morris. Come. I need you over at the wagons." She was glad that they hadn't seen the figure yet. As they walked back, she stepped between them and the ridge to block their view.

Mitch turned and walked over to where he had taken off his jacket and pistol belt. As he buckled it on, he saw the bishop come around his wagon. He had his shotgun, which meant he'd already seen the Indian too. But he walked as though he were going out to hunt pheasants. He joined Mitch as he reached the wagon road. "Who is that?" he whispered. "Can you tell?"

"I think it's Old Wash. A Ute. He's been down in Bluff from time to time."

Bishop Jones nodded. The man was now just thirty yards away and coming steadily. Both men were relieved to see that he carried no weapons. His face was so leathered and wrinkled he looked almost a hundred years old, but Mitch guessed he was more like forty or fifty. He was dressed in white man's clothing—a tattered pair of Levi's, a long-sleeved white dress shirt, which was heavily soiled, a dusty cowboy hat, and moccasins. He moved slowly, as if he had very little energy left, but he kept coming directly toward the two men. A moment later, Parley came out from behind his wagon, pistol on his hip as well, and hurried over to join them.

As he did so, Mitch heard Edie's voice. "Come, children.

Come stand by Mama and Aunt Edie." Which meant the children had seen him now too.

The three men didn't wait for Old Wash to cross the entire distance. They met him halfway. All three lifted their right hands, palms forward, in the traditional sign of greeting. "*Mique wush tagooven*," Bishop Jones said. "Hello, my friend."

The Ute shuffled to a stop. "You know Old Wash's name?"

"We do," the bishop said. "You are a friend to our people."

"Yes. Good friend to Mormons. I very hungry. You have food?"

Mitch opened his mouth, but the bishop spoke first. "Yes, Wash, but you must work for food. That is our way."

His eyes moved from one to the other, expressionless. Then his lips pressed together into a tight line. "No work. Long walk. Two days. Old Wash very tired."

Mitch spoke up. "To work for food is our—" The old man raised his hand and cut him off.

"Old Wash have information. Important for white brothers. You feed, I tell."

The three men exchanged glances. This was not a common ploy of the Indians.

Behind them, Ency Butt had come over to stand beside Emma and Edie and the children. "I wonder if it's about the boy," she called.

Her voice carried clearly to the three men. They turned in surprise. "What boy?" Mitch asked.

"Jack," Emma answered. "He didn't come this morning for his milk, butter, and eggs like he always does."

"Or yesterday, either," Edie added.

Mitch was nodding. Of course they knew about Jack. There was an L. C. camp just a few miles west of Verdure. Their cook

was a young lad, no more than sixteen or seventeen, named
Jack Hopkins. He would come down to Verdure on some mornings to buy fresh food for his chuck wagon. He was a shy, gentle
boy who seemed to enjoy the company of the women and children, though he barely spoke to the men. The sisters had all
taken to mothering him a little. His coming was not an every-
day thing, as far as Mitch knew.

Ency called out to Parley. "Remember, I told you on
Saturday that he didn't want to leave. He hung around much
later than usual. He said he had a bad feeling."

Evelyn Adams, who was now very heavy with child, joined
the other women. "We invited him to stay the night. There
was a thunderstorm coming and we thought maybe that was it.
But he finally said that no, he had to go back or the cowhands
would be angry with him."

Bishop Jones, thoughtful now, turned back to the Ute. "Is
this information about Jack?"

"Not know Jack."

"The young boy. The cowboy."

He nodded. "Yes, cowboy. You feed Wash, Wash tell you
about boy."

"All right," Parley said. "But you tell us first, and then you
eat."

"Yes," Bishop Jones said. "Tell us about the cowboy."

Wash hesitated, staring at the ground. "Boy dead!"

"What!" The cry of horror had come from several of the
women simultaneously.

"Find him in Devil's Canyon. He struck by lightning.
Boom! Was on ridge with—" He held both hands up to his
face, curling his fingers into two circles and putting them up to
his eyes. "How you say?"

"Binoculars?" Parley guessed. "Spy glasses?"

"Yes, glasses. Was looking for horses, I think. Find his body facedown in mud. He struck by lightning."

"Where in Devil's Canyon?" Parley demanded.

The old man didn't seem to understand.

Bishop Jones tried. "What part of Devil's Canyon?"

"Ah. Near top. Where comes out by mountains."

"Which is right near the line camp," Mitch said.

"I find him by hogan."

"You mean by his tent?" Parley asked.

"Yah. Tent. But he dead. Struck by lightning."

Ten-year-old Sarah Decker started to cry. "Is Jack dead, Mama?"

"Hush, Sarah," Edie said, pulling her close.

Parley turned to the bishop. "I'll saddle up."

"Me too," Mitch said.

The bishop grabbed his arm. "No, Mitch," he said in a low voice. "I think it's better if we stay here with the women. They're pretty spooked right now."

Mitch turned and looked back at them. All of the women and several of the older children were crying now. "All right," he said. Then to Parley, "But you watch yourself."

Parley did not return until almost sundown. By then, Ency was nearly out of her mind with worry. But he came riding in from the north shortly before five. Everyone gathered around him as he dismounted and took Ency in his arms.

Finally he stepped back, looking at the children gathered around him. "All right, children," he said, "you go play. I have to talk to your parents."

When they were gone, Parley turned to the bishop. "Hopkins is dead. But it wasn't lightning. He had been shot in the back twice."

The shock of that rippled amongst the women like they had been struck.

"Old Wash?" Emma Decker asked, her face white. "Did that old man do that? That's horrible."

Parley shrugged. "There's no way to tell. It certainly looks suspicious."

"I don't know," Bishop Jones said. "It seems odd that he would come and tell us if he was the one who did it."

"Maybe he was with another Ute, or a group of Utes. Who knows?" Mitch observed.

Parley nodded. "With all the rain, I couldn't make out many tracks or sign. But the field glasses were still there, right in front of him." He fell silent and then blew out his breath slowly. "I went to the L. C. Ranch. Nearly got shot before I could convince them I wasn't there to fight them. When I told them about the massacre in Disappointment Valley, I saw a couple men look at each other. They were really scared, so I'm guessing they were part of it. Finally, Carlisle sent some of his men back with me with a buggy. They promised to give the boy a good Christian burial." He reached up and rubbed at his forehead. "But they're real angry, too. They really liked the boy, just as we did. They're talking about going Ute hunting."

Bishop Jones shook his head. "If they do, they could set the whole country afire with war."

Suddenly, Mary Jones burst out. "Why the boy? He didn't kill anyone."

"That doesn't matter to the Utes. If the Utes think L. C.

men killed their families, then L. C. will be their target," Parley said. "That's how they see justice being done."

"And while the Utes know the Mormons were not involved," Mitch said, sobered by the thoughts going on in his head, "they believe the Mormons live in Bluff. And here we are, living right next to the L. C. outfit."

He turned to Bishop Jones. "I don't think we can wait until tomorrow to start for Mancos," he said softly. "I think we're going to need help as fast as we can get it."

The bishop nodded. "I was just thinking the same thing."

No one moved. He turned to Mitch. "Can you be ready in fifteen minutes?"

"Yes."

"Then we'll meet back here in fifteen minutes and have a prayer before we depart."

It didn't surprise Mitch to find Edie waiting for him when he came out of his wagon with his bedroll. She watched him without speaking as he tied it on the back of his saddle and checked his rifle and saddlebags.

Satisfied, he turned to her and took her in his arms. She laid her head against his chest and for almost a minute he just held her, neither of them speaking. He wondered what was going through her mind. Was she disappointed that he was going? Was she frightened to be left with only one man to guard them? Did she wish she had never come? He had so many questions, and no time to ask them.

Finally, she pulled back a little and looked up at him. Her eyes were sad but not troubled. "What are you thinking?" she asked.

"Actually, I was just wondering the same thing about you."

"Okay, I'll tell you if you tell me."

"All right. You first."

"I was thinking how glad I am that Parley is staying. Did you see Ency's eyes? She was so relieved."

He nodded. "I saw how worried she was when Parley was gone all day."

"So, what were you thinking?"

He reached up and brushed her cheeks with his fingertips. Which part should he share? He decided to take a safe route. "I was thinking how much I'm going to miss you."

Suddenly there were tears. She went up on tiptoes and kissed him. "Hurry back to me," she whispered. "I'll be anxiously waiting."

July 12, 1887—Verdure

Edie had chosen a place up on the south hillside that gave her a clear view of the wagon road on the other ridge. Whenever she was free, she came up here to watch for Mitch's return.

Today was the eighth day since Bishop Jones and Mitch had ridden away heading east. It had been nine days since Mr. Carlisle had given his dark ultimatum and eight days since Old Wash had walked in to share his news about a dead boy.

The signal fires were still burning on the mountains, but they had not seen anyone, white or Indian. Her mind wanted to worry about the danger they faced, but she refused to give in to it. There had been a lot of prayers and a day of fasting for their safety, and those had brought her some peace. What she could not get out of her mind was the realization that had hit her the day after Mitch and Bishop Jones left—the realization that the two of them were probably in much more danger than those in Verdure. If the Utes were on the warpath, two riders out alone would be easy targets. Try as she might, she couldn't shake the growing pall of dread that hung over her.

The sun was nearly behind Abajo Peak when Edie awoke with a start. Momentarily disoriented, she looked around, not sure where she was. Then her eyes focused on the children playing in the creek below, and it all came back to her. She yawned and stretched and got to her feet. And then she heard it. Or maybe felt it. Whatever it was, she knew instantly that this was what had awakened her.

She stopped and cocked her head, listening intently. Now it was unmistakable. It sent chills up and down her back. Horses. A lot of them. And they were coming from the north, from the direction of the L. C. Ranch.

"Parley! Parley!" She broke into a run, careening down the hill, waving her arms wildly.

No. It can't be. You said ten days. You said we had ten days. That's not until tomorrow.

Parley and Ency Butt came running out from behind their wagon. "Someone's coming! Get the children into the shed. Hurry."

Parley froze for a moment, cocking his head to listen too, and then he started yelling. The rumble was fast turning into a roar. This was louder than when Carlisle came. There were a lot more horses. Her face went white. Could it be Utes? Finally coming for their revenge?

She was halfway down the hill when she saw movement on the ridge above her. She pulled up. They were here. Below her it was pandemonium, women yelling at their children, children crying for their mothers. Edie skidded to a stop and watched the first horses appear on the wagon road above her. For a moment, her eyes refused to accept what they were seeing. Then with a shout of joy, she leaped into the air. They were wearing blue.

Two more horsemen appeared, then two more. They were coming in columns of two, coming down toward them at a steady trot. And each man was wearing a blue uniform.

Suddenly, a horseman shot past them. The man in the saddle was standing in the stirrups, shouting and waving his hat. His voice was the most wonderful thing she had ever heard. "Edie! Edie! We're back. We're home."

Notes

Only Bishop Jones left the settlement to go for help. When he told President Hammond of the situation in Verdure, the two men went to Fort Lewis, near Durango, and they returned with fifty soldiers. They camped at a spring just west of the current site of Monticello, which came to be known as Soldier Springs. They stayed for several months, and their presence greatly stabilized the situation with both the Utes and the L. C. outfit (see *Lariats*, 85–87; *Saga*, 94–95).

It was shortly after the arrival of the army that Evelyn Adams gave birth to a baby girl, before her husband, George, returned. This was the first white child born in the Blue Mountain Mission. Unfortunately, the little girl died the next day and was buried on a hillside at the Adams homestead (*Lariats*, 86).

CHAPTER 19

January 31, 1888—Mancos, Colorado

Tuesday, January 31st, 1888. Happy birthday to myself.

On this momentous day, I turn twenty years old. Sadly, I have no one to celebrate it with me here in Colorado, where I'm doing another freighting run. I think of my family and of Edie all the time and wish so much that I were with them. Edie keeps begging me to make this my last run.

Just a brief summary of what took place in the Blue Mountain Mission since I last wrote. After the two very serious scares with the L. C. Ranch and a Ute Indian rebellion, things settled down into a more routine existence.

We spent the summer clearing, plowing, and fencing land, digging ditches, etc. We built one log cabin and some other small buildings. We fenced more than 150 acres of rich bottomland. Our experiment with dry farming paid off handsomely.

George and Evelyn Adams brought in some wild range cows and started a dairy. It was something to watch them trying to corner the animals and get them into a stall long enough to milk them, but they started to produce milk and cheese in abundance.

Speaking of Evelyn, she was devastated with the death of her little girl last summer. But to my surprise, so was Edie. I expected her to be sad, of course, but she was almost as devastated as Evelyn was. She was inconsolable for days. I tried a couple of times to comfort her, but nothing I said seemed to help.

In early November, we placed all of our bags of grain in the log house, secured it, and then paid one of the local cowboys to guard it from thieves. What a bitter disappointment it was when Charles Walton and his boy rode up from Bluff to Verdure in December and found that most of the grain had been stolen and the cowboy was gone. A whole summer's work lost! That was a blow.

We are somewhat worried about the coming year. We are experiencing a severe drought. Cattlemen are losing their stock by the thousands, and many are selling out at a bargain price. That is part of the urgency for my freighting again. I hope to make enough money to add as many as ten more head to my herd. I will be taking them up north with me this spring as soon as the weather breaks. Not bad for a boy who at seventeen had nothing to his name.

As for Edie, I have to admit that when she first came north with the other women, even though I rejoiced to see her, I had misgivings about her being there. There were times when things got very dangerous. She was just seventeen and still a girl in some ways. Or so I thought. She proved to be far more mature than I gave her credit for. The Decker children call her Aunt Edie and absolutely adore her. That answered any questions I may have had about what kind of a mother she will be. She will be wonderful.

But it was even more than that. Though she was the youngest of the adult women, she fit right in. As I watched them interact, I saw that the other women viewed her as their equal in every way.

Being up there together for three months really did confirm to me how much I love her. But—I don't know. I guess I still have some reservations. Probably not about her so much as about whether we're ready. I just keep feeling that we need more time—time for her to grow up a little more, time for me to get better established so I can care for her.

Oh boy! What am I thinking? Why the doubts all of a sudden? I want to make this statement to myself: I want Edna Rae Zimmer to be my wife. There is no question about that in my mind. She is the woman I want to spend my life with, and eternity as well.

So with that, I am resolved to do the following:

I am going to buy a wedding ring while I'm here. Before I leave to go back up to Verdure in the spring, I am going to show her that ring and ask her if she will be my wife.

She won't be quite eighteen at that time, so maybe we can be engaged for one year and then marry on her birthday when she turns nineteen. That would be May 13th, 1889, about sixteen months from now.

Now, as I reread that, it feels mighty good.

Bluff City, Utah Territory

Tuesday, March 6th, 1888. Some very good news. At our recent stake conference, President Hammond called twenty more men to join the Blue Mountain Mission. Now we will have the manpower to really work on our settlement on the North Fork.

One note of interest. After conference, as we sat around eating, those of us who had been up north were talking with President Hammond. We kept referring to our two sites for settlements as North and South Montezuma, or sometimes Verdure for South Montezuma. President Hammond liked that name, but he didn't feel that North Montezuma was a suitable name for a settlement.

Names were bandied about, including Hammond, after President Hammond, or Antioch, which is a Biblical name. One of the younger people suggested Monticello, the name of Thomas Jefferson's plantation in Virginia. That struck a responsive chord in many of us, and President Hammond declared that henceforth, North Montezuma would be called Monticello. So now we have a name for our town—just no town yet.

Monday, March 12th, 1888. I went back this morning to try to patch things up with Edie. I think it helped, but there is still a coolness between us that hurts a little. It is completely my fault. Last night, I went over fully expecting to talk to her about getting engaged. I had hinted to her that I had something really important to talk about. In the rush of getting ready to go over, I forgot to take the ring with me. Then her parents both stayed right in the sitting room with us all night. Her father wants to know everything about the mission. I think he's a little envious. Then, as usual, he gave us five minutes to say good-bye, and I lost my nerve. I felt that rushing through it was not the best idea. She was very disappointed and a little upset, I think. Did she know what I was thinking of doing? Not sure. But I don't blame her for being frustrated. This winter has been very hard for both of us. I did not kiss her good night.

With my usual lack of finesse, I botched things badly. I leave before dawn to return to Monticello, but I plan to come back for my stock in a couple of weeks, so I hope to fix things then. I am already missing her.

Saturday, March 24th, 1888. We've been working at the town site nearly two weeks. It's been stormy and miserable all week. Not good working conditions, but we did lay out some plots for Monticello. I decided to return to Bluff tomorrow. That is good. My mind is made up. When I return home, I am going to ask Edie to marry me.

March 28, 1888—Bluff City, Utah Territory

Mitch helped Edie climb up onto the high seat of the Swing Tree and gave her a gentle push. He backed away, looking around. "I can't believe we're actually alone at last."

"You can thank me for that," she said primly.

"How so?"

"Well, first I told Papa that you and I needed some time alone to talk."

Mitch hooted. "You really did? That's wonderful. How did he take that?"

"He likes you, Mitch. He has high hopes for us, and so with a little nudge from Mama he gave his permission. He just doesn't want us home too late."

"Okay." He was watching Edie closely. Her "high hopes" comment had thrown him a little.

"I . . ." Mitch started. "I have high hopes for us too, Edie, and that's what I want to talk to you about."

"I would say that it's time."

He swallowed hard. Her tone of voice made it clear that this wasn't going to be a shoo-in. "Could we sit over here where we can talk facing each other?"

She instantly let go of the ropes and hopped down. "I would like that."

There were two short cottonwood logs that half framed the fire pit at an angle. He lifted the end of one and swung it around until they were opposite each other. Edie sat down, and Mitch took the seat across from her. It felt like the ring in his pocket weighed about a ton and a half. He resisted the temptation to pull it out and start with that. For several seconds he studied his hands, and then he finally he looked up at her. He went to open his mouth but was struck with the sight of her. The sun was down now, but the evening light was soft on her face. She was so lovely he found it hard to begin. But he knew it was time. He took a quick breath and plunged forward.

"If it's all right, Edie. I'd like to say something first. Then, if you have questions or comments, we can talk."

"All right. And after you're done, I'd like to ask you to do the same for me."

"Good." Again he hesitated. He had been going over and over this moment in his mind, rehearsing what to say. Now it all left him. He cleared his throat. "Let me begin by sharing an experience I had two years ago now. It was connected with the death of Amasa Barton out on the Rincon."

That obviously surprised her, but she only nodded. So he told her about how his belt had broken as they were leaving for Elk Mountain and how he had gone to the trading post to find a replacement. "I was so impressed with Feenie Barton," he said. "What a remarkable woman she was—out there away from everyone, with two little kids, enduring some pretty harsh living conditions. And she was not only caring for her family, but she was also helping Amasa run the store, taking inventory, ordering supplies, accounting for the money. She even dealt with the Navajo on a regular basis." He frowned. "That was a couple of days before that horrible thing took place. How she conducted herself so bravely in those circumstances is astonishing to me."

Edie was nodding. "I totally agree. She is a remarkable woman."

Mitch took another breath. *Here goes.* "Well, as I was riding back down here, I started thinking about you and me. Remember, at that point, we were just getting to know each other, and we were both still a couple of kids—you sixteen, me barely eighteen. So keep that in mind as I say what I'm going to say next."

"Okay," she said slowly.

"Well, to be honest, I started asking myself if you would turn into that kind of a woman someday."

Her eyebrows arched. "Someday?"

He shot her a look and she quickly apologized. "Sorry, go on."

"I thought I sensed that same kind of strength and faith in you, though it was too early to be sure. And—well, frankly, I started thinking about marriage. Not right away," he added hastily. "But in a few years. Like when you were at least eighteen. And that felt good. Well, two of those years have passed now. You'll be eighteen in May. I'm getting established. I'm even hoping to start on my house that I could have ready by then."

"Ready for what?"

"For us," he said in exasperation. "What did you think?"

She was watching him steadily, her eyes hooded and hard to read. Somehow he sensed that what he was saying was not getting her all warm and soft. "Go on."

How could she do that to him, even after all this time? He felt like he had on that day he'd asked to sign her dance card. So he decided to just go for it—get everything out on the table so they could talk about it.

He reached in his pocket and took out the ring but kept it cupped in his hand. Her eyes followed his movement, but he still couldn't read her expression. So he just blurted it out. "I love you, Edna Rae Zimmer. I love you so much it hurts sometimes."

She blinked quickly several times, and for a moment he thought she was going to cry. "You've never said that before."

"I know, but I'm saying it now. You're almost a woman now, and a beautiful one at that. And I love you. And I want to take care of you for the rest of your life." He opened his hand and held out the ring.

To his bewilderment, she didn't seem surprised when she saw what it was. "Will you marry me, Edie? I know we're not ready yet, but I want us to be engaged so we can start making our plans. And I was thinking that if you like, we could get married a year from this May, on your birthday. We'd have Bishop Nielson marry us and then we could go to St. George to be sealed in the temple. Or Manti. They're saying the Manti Temple will be open in a few months. Or, if you want, I'll even take you to Salt Lake so we can be married in the Endowment House and—"

She smiled and leaned forward. "It's all right to take a breath, Mitch."

Laughing, he sat back and drew in a deep breath. "Whew!"

She leaned even closer to him and stretched out her hand. "May I see it?"

"Of course." He reached over and dropped it in her hand.

She examined it for a moment. Mitch expected her to slip it on her finger to see if it fit, but she did not. When she looked up, her eyes were . . . what? Mitch searched for a word and then was startled when it came. *Sad.* Her eyes were almost sad.

"It's beautiful, Mitch."

"I thought so too. There was also an engagement ring, but . . ." He flushed a little. "But together they were pretty expensive."

"I don't need a ring to be engaged." She studied it for a moment longer and then handed it back to him.

Not sure what to say, he laughed awkwardly. "All right. It's your turn. Any questions? Comments?" There was nothing on her face as she watched him continue stammering. "A joke, maybe?"

She stood up and came around to sit down beside him. She reached out and took his hand and pulled it into both of hers. "I am deeply honored, Mitch. Do you remember the song that's in the music box you gave me?"

"Of course. 'Beautiful Dreamer.'"

"Well, that's me. Not the beautiful, but the dreamer."

He squeezed her hand. "No, Edie. You are beautiful."

She ignored that. "And I've dreamed about this moment since . . . since about the time you called me this skinny little freckle-faced kid. And now . . ."

He stared at her in disbelief. She was going to say no.

"Can I have twenty-four hours before I give you my answer?"

"Uh . . . Of course. Take whatever time you need."

"Thank you. I have some things I want to say to you and some questions as well. But I need to think about them. Will you meet me here tomorrow night? Same time?"

He forced a smile, even though he knew that it would give away the pain he was feeling. "Shall I hire Johnny and Martha to guard the tree from anyone else using it?"

A soft laugh came and went quickly, Edie's dimple showing for just a second or two. "That would be nice."

She got to her feet, and then, totally catching him off guard, she bent down and took his face in both of her hands. Tipping it up, she kissed him. She held his face for a long time, and somehow he could feel all of the love, all of the longing, all of the . . . sorrow that she was feeling. Then, without a word, she whirled and ran off into the gathering twilight.

———————————

Notes

The five families who opened up the Blue Mountain Mission in 1887 returned to Bluff for the winter. Their accomplishments are de-tailed in the sources (see *Saga*, 95).

There was a stake conference in Bluff in March of 1888 in which twenty new families were called to join the mission. It is not clear if it was at the same time that the discussion was held regarding what to call the settlement planned for North Montezuma Creek. However, by that time, President Hammond was living at Mancos. He would have come to the stake conference, and since he was present at the time when Monticello was named, it seemed logical to have both events occur at the same time (see ibid., 96).

CHAPTER 20

March 29, 1888—Bluff City, Utah Territory

Mitch came twenty minutes early. Edie was already seated on one of the logs, which were still where they had left them the night before. "Hi," he murmured before taking a seat across from her.

"How are you?"

"Well," he said, trying to keep things light, "I'm still working things out in my head."

"I'm sorry."

"No, it's not that. It's . . ." He smiled ruefully. "Somehow in my mind, when I asked you to marry me, I saw it playing out a little differently than it did."

"So did I. Up until a few days ago."

He leaned forward, clasping his hands together. "So, it's your turn, Edie. Ask what you will and I shall try to answer as honestly as I can."

"Okay. First, a simple, practical question. If I had said yes last night, would you have given me the ring to wear right then?"

"No. I . . . I wasn't thinking of it as an engagement ring. I just wanted you to see it. But I thought we'd wait until—"

"Good. I don't want to wear it unless we're married."

Unless, he thought morosely, not *until.* But he said nothing.

She sat back, and he could see she seemed to be debating what to say next. He steeled himself.

"Another question, and I need you to be totally honest with me on this, Mitch. Okay?"

"I told you I would."

"I know that my coming up with Emma Decker last June was a huge shock to you."

"It was, but I was very happy to see you."

"I know you were. And that meant a lot to me. But suppose I had asked you beforehand if you thought it was a good idea for me to come up there. What would you have said?"

"I would have counseled you against it," he said right back.

"Why?"

"Because as tempting as it would have been for me to have you up there with me, I don't think it was a place for a single young woman. We knew we could be facing some very dangerous situations—and we did. I was sick with worry for you during the time that Bishop Jones and I went for help. All I could think about was what I would do if something happened to you."

She was nodding as he finished. "Thank you. I understand. I appreciate your concern. And what if I told you that Emma Decker is with child and that she has asked me to come up again this summer? What would you say?"

Totally blindsided, he stared at her, sensing how important this question was. He was sorely tempted to soften his answer, but he had promised to be honest. "I would counsel you not to go."

"Why?"

"Because your grandmother is coming here, and—"

"No, Mitch! Tell me the truth."

"Because it could be even worse this year. Give it one more year, Edie. By next year I'll have my own ranch. There will be others around us, so there won't be as much danger."

"I understand." She sighed, and her eyes were filled with that same sadness again. "So, with that—and thank you for being honest with me—let me make two observations, and then I'll give you my answer."

He nodded, feeling a terrible hollowness in the pit of his stomach.

"This will sound like I'm being picky with words, so bear with me for a moment. Last night, after you told me that you loved me, you said, 'I want to take care of you.'"

"That's right, I do."

"You also have everything all planned out for us, Mitch. When to marry, where to marry, when to start our home. Except you didn't call it *our* home. You called it *your* home."

"But, Edie, you know it's for us."

"It may seem like a little thing, but if you had just worded that a little differently, I would have said yes." She laughed somewhat bitterly. "I would have thrown myself into your arms and shouted, 'Yes, Mitch, I will marry you. I will marry you today. I will marry you tomorrow, or a year from now, or twenty years from now.'"

Bewildered and confused, Mitch just stared at her.

"Instead of saying 'I want to take care *of* you,' I wish you had said, 'I care *for* you.' That would have made all the difference. And I would have loved it if you had said, 'I want you to help me build our new home.'"

He threw up his hands. "But I do care for you, Edie," he exploded. "And I want to take care of you, too."

"Don't say that," she snapped. "You take care of cows and

little children. It makes it sound as if you're my father or my mother. And what it says to me is that you still see me as a child, as a girl who is growing up, not as a woman who has grown up."

"Ah, Edie," he pleaded. "Don't turn me away because of a word. I'm not good with words like you are."

"It's not that at all, Mitch. Let me ask you this, then. I'll be eighteen in May. Why didn't you suggest we get married on my birthday this year? Lots of girls marry when they're eighteen."

"I . . ."

"It's because you think I'm not ready yet. And that hurts."

"I'm sorry. I didn't mean to hurt you."

"I know you didn't, and that's what hurts the most. Maybe if you were angry with me and trying to hurt me it would be easier to accept, but you're totally unaware of what you're doing when you say these things. You've got it all worked out— your life *and* mine."

He said nothing, just hunched down to ride it out.

"Don't do that," she snapped. "If you're thinking something, then say it. We need to talk this through, Mitch, not just retreat."

He shook his head. "Why? No matter what I say, you turn it against me. I can't win here, Edie. I'm safer to just keep my mouth shut."

She blinked rapidly. The anger drained from her face. "I am doing that, aren't I? I'm sorry." When he only stirred, she continued, "No, I really mean it. I didn't mean to attack you like that. It was unfair."

He watched her, encouraged by her apology, but totally lost when it came to what to say.

"It's just that I am so frustrated right now. Sometimes I want to scream."

"I'm here. Scream at me."

"No. Let me see if I can help you understand. Do you want to know why I think you talked about us getting married a year from now and not this year?"

"Yes." It felt like a lie, but saying no was hardly the right answer at this moment.

"It's not because *I'm* not ready. It's because *you're* not ready. You still have things you want to do to get your life in order." She had to look away. "And you don't want to do them *with* me. You want to do them *for* me."

She got to her feet and turned her back on him. He wanted to get up and go to her, to take her in his arms and beg for her forgiveness. But he knew it would not be welcomed.

She finally turned back around. When she spoke, he had to strain to listen. "One last question, and then I'll give you my answer."

"All right." He didn't look up at her.

"When you told me about Feenie Barton last night, you said that thinking about her got you to thinking about me. Was I old enough? Was I mature enough? Would I have the same kind of faith and courage as she did?"

His head came up. "I'm not ashamed of asking those questions, Edie. We were still getting to know each other then."

"But did you ask the same kind of questions about yourself? About Mitch Westland? Was he ready for marriage? Would he be the kind of man *I* would be looking for? Would he turn out to be a man of faith and courage? Doesn't that seem only fair?"

His head dropped. "No, I didn't. And I can see now I was wrong. I am so sorry, Edie. So sorry."

She went to him then, coming up right next to him so she could look up into his eyes. "I love you, Mitch Westland. I love you with all my heart. I can't tell you what it meant to me to finally you hear you say that you love me too. But before I can answer your question, I need you to answer one more for me."

He braced himself. "Go on."

"All right, this time it isn't a hypothetical question. Emma Decker *has* asked to go back up with them and stay through the summer. We learned last week that my grandmother will not be here until the fall, so that is not an issue. So I am asking you now. Do you think I should go?"

He was cornered and he knew it. "Of course I want you to go. You think I want to be away from you for the next six months?"

"That's not what I asked you. Do you think I *should* go?"

"I . . . It's not my decision. You don't need my permission."

"I know that, and you know that," she cried. "But again, that's not what I'm asking. *Do you think I should go?*"

Their eyes locked for several seconds. Then he shook his head.

"That's what I thought. So, with that, no, Mitch, I will not marry you. And I'm so sorry."

This time there was no kiss. With her lips trembling and her shoulders starting to shake, she turned and walked slowly away.

He watched for a moment, and then the pain was too great. He sank down on the log and buried his face in his hands.

⁂

He wasn't sure how much time had passed when he heard the rustle of sand to his left. He looked up and then leaped to his feet. "Edie?"

She took two steps closer to him, coming out of the shade

of a cottonwood tree into the moonlight. He could see that she was weeping openly now. He started for her, his heart leaping with hope, but she raised her hand, as if to block his path.

"This isn't fair to you, Mitch. It isn't fair to you in any way, but I have to ask."

"Okay."

"Last summer, when Evelyn Adams lost the baby, did you notice anything unusual in the way I reacted?"

Startled by that question, he nodded vigorously. "Yes. I noticed how deeply it affected you. Far more than the other women, though they were grieving for Evelyn too. But it was like it had been your child. In fact, I wrote about it in my journal."

That surprised her. "You did?" Then she waved that away. Wiping at the tears with the back of her hands, she went on. "As you know, I am the only child of my parents."

"Yes."

"Did you know that my mother is also the only child of her parents?"

"No. I didn't know that."

"My mother had two more children after me. One, a boy, who was stillborn. The other, a beautiful little girl, who lived two days and then died. I remember both of those births well, because I was five when the first one happened and eight when the second one occurred."

He was so shocked that he couldn't begin to find words.

"My mother," she went on, as if he weren't there, "was the third of four children."

"But . . . I thought you said she was an only child."

"She was. The only child *that lived*. Her mother had two stillborn children and one that lived not quite a week."

The reality of what she was saying was slowly dawning on him. "And you think that you might have the same problem as your—" He had to stop as the enormity of that hit him.

She looked up through her tears. "Maybe that's another reason we shouldn't marry, Mitch."

"No, Edie, I—"

She cut him off with a wave of her hand.

He sat down again, sick at heart and sick to his stomach.

"And here's another little thing you should know about me while we're baring our souls. Bishop Nielson just got word that the Supreme Court has ruled that the Edmunds-Tucker law is constitutional. Now they're saying that the Church will be forced to stop plural marriage before the year is out. Do you know how sick that makes me?"

That one came from so far out of nowhere that he just gaped at her. "You mean you'd want me to have more than one wife? I'd heard talk that it might happen, but I thought that you'd be happy about it. I would be happy about it. I don't want to love anyone but you."

"Thank you." She actually managed a fleeting smile. "That was the right thing to say." Then she took a breath. "A lot of people don't know this, but do you know why Aunt Mary Nielson Jones, Kumen's first wife, gave Kumen permission to marry May Lyman?"

He shook his head, still thoroughly baffled with where this was going. "Because he needed the permission of the first wife?"

"No. Well, that too, but that wasn't the reason. It's because they couldn't have children. They went four years, but she could never conceive a child. As you know, she's a midwife, Mitch. Who knows how many babies she's helped deliver. But never one of her own. Can you imagine how she must feel?

"Then one day she received a blessing. I don't know if Kumen gave it to her or her father, Bishop Nielson. But in that blessing she was promised that if she would consent to Kumen taking another wife, she would be blessed with a child.

"And so Kumen married May Lyman, who's had a baby about every two years. Think how that must have made Mary feel. But she trusted in the blessing and now, guess what? Aunt Mary recently announced that she is with child. Her blessing is being fulfilled."

And now Mitch understood. It hit him with such force that he sat down again on the log, putting his face in his hands. "And so you have been thinking that if you can't give me children, then a second wife could?"

"Yes," she whispered numbly. "And now it looks like I can't even do that."

He shot to his feet again. "Why didn't you tell me all of this, Edie?"

Her head came up very slowly, and in the moonlight he saw that her cheeks were wet with tears. "Because you never asked me, Mitch. Not once. You never asked."

With a cry of anguish, she whirled and stumbled away into the darkness.

The next morning, when Mitch came into the cabin for breakfast, he saw that his mother had been crying. He went to her. "What's wrong, Mother?"

Sniffing back the tears, she turned and pointed to the table. "Edie came by this morning. She left something for you."

He didn't turn around. He already knew what it was. "You keep it here, Mama," he said. He started for the door. "Mama?"

"Yes, son?"

"I'll be leaving right after breakfast."

"Where are you going?" she cried.

"To the Blue Mountains." And he went out to saddle his horse.

As the door shut behind him, Gwen went over to the table and picked up the music box. She opened the lid, and as the tiny little ballet dancer began to whirl, she listened to the first strains of "Beautiful Dreamer." She shut the lid quickly, unable to bear it. Then, as the tears started again, she whispered, "Oh, Mitch. Oh, my son."

Note

Kumen Jones and Mary Nielson, daughter of Bishop Jens Nielson, were married in the St. George Temple on December 19, 1878, just ten days before they were both called to go to San Juan with the first company of pioneers. Sometime in 1882, Mary received a blessing that promised her that if she agreed to Kumen taking a second wife, she would be blessed with her own child. Kumen and Lydia May Lyman were married on December 2, 1882, in the St. George Temple. May went on to have ten children with Kumen, all but one of whom were boys. In 1889, after eleven years of marriage, Mary finally gave birth to a son, whom they named Leonard. "Aunt Mary" outlived her son by two years. She died in 1933 at the age of 75 (see *Saga*, 314–15).

CHAPTER 21

April 3, 1888—Monticello, San Juan County, Utah Territory

As Mitch unloaded cedar poles from the Walton sleigh he kept one eye on the northern sky. From this vantage point, he could normally see as far out as The Needles and North and South Six-Shooter Peaks. But now a wall of gray blotted everything across the landscape. And to his left, the tops of the Blue Mountains had disappeared and he could actually see the gray descending as if it were sliding down the snow-covered slopes.

"Steady, boys," he called to his team. "I'm as anxious to get out of here as you are."

With an elevation at the base of slightly over 7,000 feet and with three peaks over 11,000 feet, the Blue Mountains could take a serious spring storm and twist it into something really dangerous. And this one felt like one of those.

By the time Mitch got under way again, the first snowflakes were swirling around him, and the wind had picked up by ten or fifteen miles per hour. With a flick of the reins, he urged the big bays into a steady trot. "There's hay at the barn, boys. Take her home."

The team sensed that they were at the turnoff before Mitch saw it. When they started to slow, Mitch raised his head and

shook the snow off the hood of his jacket. "Good boys," he
called. "Sharp eyes. We'll be home in about twenty minutes
now."

But as they started to make the turn, Mitch suddenly jerked
up and grabbed the reins. "Whoa!" They pulled to a stop, their
breath making explosions of mist as they snorted and stomped
their feet. Mitch looked around. Were they where he thought
they were? There was no sense looking for major landmarks.
Visibility was now down to less than twenty yards. But he had
the distinct feeling that something was wrong. He pulled himself up, shielding his eyes from the snow with one hand. No,
this was the junction. He was positive of that.

Keep going straight.

He peered to the south. He could see nothing. It wasn't a
voice or anything, but the feeling was very strong. *Keep going
straight.*

"Not a good idea," he muttered. Going straight would not
get them home. He was not going to keep on going south. He
picked up the reins and slipped them between the fingers of his
gloves. Then he stopped.

Go south.

As he wondered what was going on, he suddenly remembered that night up on Elk Mountain with Moenkopi Mike. A
situation that could have turned deadly had been completely
altered when Kumen Jones had suddenly had the feeling to offer Mike a slice of bread covered with molasses. That was how
he had described it when Mitch asked him about it later. A
feeling. Like he was experiencing right now.

With a sigh, he wheeled the horses back around and turned
them south again. There was a problem with feelings, though.
You were always having feelings of one kind or another. How

did you know when it wasn't just you being your worrisome self?

Go south. Keep going straight.

"All right," he muttered. "I'm going. I'm going."

He told himself he would go two miles. If nothing was wrong, then he would turn back. But when those two miles were covered, the feeling was stronger than ever. So he went two more miles. And another feeling started pressing in on him. The snow up here was almost two feet deep, and the team was laboring to keep the sleigh moving. They were a strong team, but they had already brought down two loads of cedar poles that day. If they got too exhausted, Mitch could end up being the one with a very serious problem.

He reined up and sat there for a minute, debating with himself as he stared out into the swirling snow. It wasn't yet five o'clock, but it was nearly dark. It would be an easy thing to get lost in a whiteout like this. This was crazy. No one would be out here on a night like this.

One more mile.

"Okay," he grumbled. "But that's it. Then I'm turning around, no matter what."

Not even two minutes later one of the bays suddenly whinnied and jerked his head up. Mitch pulled the team to a stop. He threw off the blanket covering his legs and stood up in the sleigh. "What is it, boy? What did you hear?"

He pulled back the earflap of his hat and turned it away from the wind.

"Help!"

It was so faint, Mitch nearly missed it. He swung his head back and forth, looking for the source of the sound. Now the other horse was snorting and blowing. There was definitely something out there. Leaping out of the sleigh, Mitch ran and grabbed their heads. "Easy, boys. Easy."

"Help! Help us! Please!" He was astonished. It sounded like a woman's voice.

And then, as a gust of wind whipped the snow away for just an instant, he gasped. There were figures up ahead. Human figures! "What?" he gasped.

He grabbed the reins and tied them to a nearby cedar tree and then lumbered forward, pushing his way through the deep snow. In a moment they came into a view. Three figures, huddled together. No, four! One of them was holding a child.

Thrusting the snow aside with powerful strides, he ran to them, stunned speechless. What he found shocked him even more. As he came up, the tallest woman pulled the scarf away from her face. A gasp was torn from his throat. "Evelyn? Evelyn Adams?"

The second figure pulled her scarf away and waved a hand weakly. She croaked something, but Mitch couldn't understand what she said. But he recognized Leona Walton.

Evelyn dropped to her knees as Mitch took the child from her. "Oh, Lord," she sobbed. "We're saved. We're saved." Her head dropped on her chest. "Thank you! Thank you."

Mitch reached down, took her elbow, and lifted her up. "Come," he said. "Let's get you in the sleigh." As she started to follow him, the third woman pulled back her scarf, knocking two inches of snow from the top of her head and revealing long, dark hair.

As Mitch went rigid as a cedar post, Edna Rae Zimmer stepped forward, shivering violently. And yet she managed a tiny smile. "Is that really you, Mitch? Or are you an angel from heaven come to take us home?"

Fortunately, the Waltons always kept extra blankets and quilts beneath the seat of the sleigh. Unfortunately, the seat itself only held two people. Mitch started barking directions as soon as they returned to the sleigh. "Evelyn, Nean is in bad shape. It looks like her core temperature has really dropped. I'm going to put her in the corner right behind me. Then you and Leona huddle in against her. We'll wrap you up good in quilts."

They nodded, too exhausted for words.

He looked at Edie. "We can put you in the other corner. Up on the seat with me is the coldest place because it catches the wind. But you could ride up there if—"

"I'll ride with you," she said, hugging herself and stomping her feet.

"Good." He took three-year-old Cornelia, or Nean, as everyone called her, wrapped her in a quilt, and lifted her over the side of the sleigh. She moaned softly as he placed her carefully in the corner. When the two women were in place around her he wrapped them up tightly in three quilts. "I'm guessing we're about thirty minutes from home. Will you be all right?"

There was one quick nod.

He was so dumbfounded, he was still trying to take it all in. "What were you doing out here on foot? Does George know you're coming?"

She shook her head. When she spoke, her teeth were chattering so badly he could barely understand her. "It . . . it . . . it . . . was sup . . . supposed . . . to be . . . to be . . . a . . . a . . . sur . . . sur . . . sur . . ."

"A surprise," Edie finished for her. She caught Mitch's eye and shook her head. "I'll explain later," she murmured

Mitch helped Edie up and got her wrapped in a thick quilt and then swung up himself and took the reins. "Gee-up," he shouted, pulling on the reins and turning the sleigh around in a wide arc. He looked back over his shoulder. "The snow will cushion the ride somewhat, but I'm going to let the team have their head, so it may get a little bumpy."

"We're all right," Leona said. "The faster the better." Then she buried her face into the quilt.

Mitch started to speak several times, but each time he looked over at Edie, who was wrapped in a quilt from head to toe, with only a small slit for her eyes, he changed his mind. He was still shocked almost beyond words at what he had found, but he was remembering their last time together and held his tongue.

Finally, after about fifteen minutes, she pulled the quilt away from her face and half turned in her seat. "Evelyn decided that she wanted to surprise George and come up early," she began, speaking in a low voice.

Mitch leaned closer so he could hear her over the sound of the horses and the whistling wind.

"Leona thought that was a great idea too. She's coming up to cook for the men. The weather was perfect in Bluff. It was eighty-five degrees and the skies were clear for as far as we could see. It was like summer had arrived."

But Bluff is 3,000 feet lower than we are here. Didn't anyone think of that? But again he bit his tongue and just nodded.

"The Deckers aren't leaving for another couple of weeks," she went on, "so when Evelyn asked me if I wanted to join them, I thought, 'Why not?'" Her head lifted and her eyes met and held his. There was a touch of defiance in them. "I didn't come for you, Mitch. Emma's having a hard time with the baby. She needs me."

He held up a hand in protest. "I didn't say anything, Edie."

"I know. I know." She brushed one mittened hand across her brow. "I'm sorry. I'm not myself. This was such a terrifying experience. We were sure we were all dead and wouldn't be found until summer."

He reached out and touched her hand for a moment. "It's all right, Edie. Tell me what happened."

She turned and stared at the snow swirling around them, blotting out everything but the horses. "Everything was fine for the first two days. We crossed White Mesa with no problems. It was a little cloudy by the time we reached Recapture Creek, but the temperature was mild and there was no snow."

"I'll bet that changed about the time you reached Alkali."

"Exactly. We could see the sky darkening and knew there was a storm coming. We pushed the horses as hard as we could, but it caught us about halfway to the top." Her voice was hushed and tight with pain. "It was horrible. Suddenly we were in snow almost two feet deep. And then the blizzard hit. The higher we went, the deeper it got. Pretty soon it was up to the bellies of the horses, and they eventually stopped. It was too much for them. They couldn't go any farther."

She stopped and turned away, staring out into the gathering darkness. Her voice had a faraway, ethereal quality to it. "Nothing we could do would make them go any farther." She looked up at him. "And that's when I thought we were going to die. And that's when we really started to pray. I mean, we *really* started to pray."

"Did you know how close you were to Verdure by that point?"

"Not for sure. I've only been across this road twice, and with all that snow it was hard to know where we were." When she looked up at him, her eyes were swimming with tears. "How did you know where we were?"

"I didn't. But finish your story first. So when the horses refused to go any farther, you got out and walked?"

"Not exactly. Not at first. We unhitched the team and took the stronger one." She turned around and glanced back at the other passengers. "I think they may be asleep," she whispered.

"Good. Especially for Nean."

"Anyway, we took turns. One of us would ride the horse for a while, holding Nean on our lap, while the other two walked alongside. Fortunately, the horse seemed to know where we were going."

She stopped and started picking nervously at the balls of snow on her mittens.

"We walked for what seemed like hours until . . ." Her voice caught. "The horse just gave up. It gave this horrible shudder and then lay down and refused to move."

She buried her face in her hands and began to silently shake. Mitch laid a hand on her shoulder. "It's all right, Edie. You don't have to talk about it now."

She wiped at her nose with the back of her mitten, sniffing back the tears. "I want to." A long pause. "I need to."

She looked up at him. "That's when I lost all hope. I thought . . ." A sob was torn from her throat. "I thought, 'It's over. And what if no one ever finds us?' I thought of Mama and Papa and how awful that would be for them. I thought of Oma, of never seeing her again, either."

She looked up him as tears ran down her cheeks. He was weeping with her now. "And I thought of you." She had to stop again. He put his arm around her and pulled her in tight against him. "And I cried to God, 'Please, Heavenly Father. Please let me see Mitch again so that our last time together will not be his memory of me.'"

She slid closer and leaned her head against him. "It was no more than five or six minutes after that cry of anguish that we heard horses coming. Can you imagine how we felt at that moment? I was dizzy with joy. Delirious, almost."

She took his hand and intertwined her fingers with his. "And then I heard your voice." She couldn't go on. She just squeezed his hand so hard that it hurt. He squeezed it back.

"At first I couldn't believe it. Wouldn't believe it. And then, there you were." Turning her head, she buried it against him. "How did you know?" she whispered. "How ever did you know where to find us? No one even knew we were coming."

"Someone knew." And so, in a quiet voice filled with emotion, he told her about his feelings.

They drove in silence for a long time. They had come back to the junction with the road that led to Verdure. The wind had died down a little, but the snow was thickening. He kept glancing at Edie. Her head was on his shoulder and her eyes were closed. He could see her body slowly relaxing, her emotions calming. There was so much he was longing to say, but he made himself wait.

As the team turned again, he squeezed her hand. "About ten minutes now."

She nodded.

He took a deep breath, and then another. He opened his mouth to speak but then changed his mind. Watching him closely, she sat up straighter. But she too chose not to speak. And then came another impression. It wasn't as strong as the one to go south. But it didn't need to be. He transferred the reins from his right hand to his left and then removed his right glove and fished in his pocket.

Curious, she sat back a little to give him more room. When he pulled his hand out, he had something clenched in his fist. He held it out in front of her and then slowly opened his fingers.

She stared at it for several seconds before finally looking up at him. Her eyes were wide and luminous. "You keep it in your pocket?" she exclaimed in wonder.

"I do. All the time. It helps me remember how stupid I was. What a *dummkopf* I was."

He closed his fist again while he wrapped the reins around the seat handle. He removed his other glove and dropped it in his lap. Then he took the ring between the thumb and forefinger of his right hand. He held it out for her to see.

"Miss Edna Rae Zimmer. I have been thinking about you and your grandmother."

"Oma Zimmer?" she exclaimed in surprise. She had not expected a man holding a ring out at her to bring up her grandmother. "What about her?"

"I've been thinking about her patriarchal blessing."

Edie was clearly taken aback by this unexpected line of conversation. "What about it?"

"No offense intended, but I was thinking that if we leave it up to you to teach our children German, it's not going to work. You don't speak it often enough to make a difference."

Her eyes were almost glowing in the darkness. "Our children?"

"Yes. So, I think when we build *our* new ranch house"— he emphasized the possessive pronoun—"we need to put in an extra room for Oma Zimmer. She can live with us and make sure our children help to fulfill her blessing."

"Stop!" Edie breathed, half laughing and half crying as she slipped the glove off her left hand. "Will you let me catch my breath for a moment?"

"No." Mitch took her hand and moved the ring near the tip of her ring finger.

"Edna Rae Zimmer, if I solemnly promise to spend my life caring about you, loving you, worshipping you, working with you, cherishing you, counseling with you, would you consent to be my wife?"

"Yes!" she cried in exultation. She took off her mitten and stuck out her left hand, and he slipped the ring on her finger. "Yes! Yes! Yes!" She reached up and pulled his head down and kissed him with joyous abandon.

He kissed her back and then finally pulled away. He was grinning like a little kid. "That went better this time," he said with a straight face. "Don't you think?"

Notes

In the spring of 1888, Evelyn Adams decided to surprise her husband by driving herself from Bluff to Verdure, a distance of forty-five miles. Feeling adventurous and encouraged by the near-summer temperatures in Bluff, she decided not to wait for the others. She took her daughter Cornelia, who was three, and brought along Leona Walton (later Nielson), who was going up to cook for the men (see *History of San Juan County*, 66). They set off in a single wagon.

Aside from the season, it was a difficult journey even for experienced travelers. The road was in some places nearly impassable even in dry weather. A rainstorm could turn long stretches into a quagmire. And they were traveling alone through Indian country. But one has to remember that Evelyn had never seen the Blue Mountain region in winter. She had joined her husband, George H. Adams, and the other four families in June of 1886, and they had returned to Bluff in October or November of that same year.

The details of their harrowing experience and their struggle for survival are accurately portrayed here. The rescue was somewhat different, however. A cowhand from the L. C. Ranch named Frank Taylor was driving home in a light sleigh with a load of oats when he came upon the two women and the child. He threw off the oats and took them safely to Verdure (see *Saga*, 98–99; *Lariats*, 87–88).

Nevertheless, the settlers saw this remarkable occurrence as an example of divine intervention. In the first place, at that time in that area of San Juan County, the total population of whites would have been somewhere around fifty, and they were scattered over hundreds of square miles. That means the traffic on any given road at any given time would have been sparse at best, nonexistent at worst.

Second, the storms of the Blue Mountains had such a fearsome reputation that there are accounts of how even the hardiest of men would hole up inside to avoid being out in them.

Third, if the snow was up to the horses' bellies, those women had to have been pushing through snow that reached to mid-thigh. They also had to be soaking wet from the waist down—and all of this while they carried a three-year-old child.

Fourth, these women were not near any settlement when they first stopped. How they even managed to stay on the road is a wonder. So to have someone just happen to come along in the middle of a blizzard and pass by exactly where they were at that time seems more than remarkable.

Years later, Evelyn's husband, George, would say of this experience: "Their surprise was a complete success, although they had taken their lives into their own hands to bring it about" (*Lariats*, 88).

Cornelia, or Nean, who was three at the time, later helped author *Saga of the San Juan*, an important source for this novel.

NOTE TO READERS

As I mentioned in the preface, I have decided to extend the story of Mitch Westland and Edna Rae Zimmer beyond this book. I am excited to continue, through them, the story of the early San Juan pioneers who spread out from Bluff to establish new settlements and stabilize a difficult and isolated part of the western United States. Thanks to them, their descendants no longer had to fulfill the role of "buffers," "shock absorbers," and "lightning rods." Those pioneers also left their descendants an incredible legacy of faith, courage, determination, and that most remarkable of qualities—what Bishop Jens Nielson called "stick-a-ty-tootie." It was a marvelous gift for the rising generations.

In continuing this story, however, I'm going to try something I've never done before. I'm going to take the characters from one series and introduce them into a new series. I hope my reasons for doing so will become obvious as readers see how two families from rural southern Utah—the Westlands and the Zimmers—merge with one another and then eventually cross paths with a family in southern Germany.

Only the Brave is a sequel to *The Undaunted*, but that series ends here. However, Mitch and Edie will continue their story in volume two of my new series, Fire and Steel. The first volume in that series, *A Generation Rising*, is available now. It introduces the family of Hans and Inga Eckhardt, who live in Bavaria in southern Germany. In the second volume, we will come to learn how the Westlands' and the Eckhardts' lives will become forever intertwined.

BIBLIOGRAPHY

Blankenagel, Norma Palmer. "Portrait of our Past: A History of the Monticello Utah Stake of The Church of Jesus Christ of Latter-day Saints." Unpublished manuscript, 1988.

Hafen, LeRoy R., and Ann W. Hafen. *Handcarts to Zion: The Story of a Unique Western Migration, 1856–1860.* Lincoln: University of Nebraska Press, 1960.

Jenson, Andrew, ed. *Latter-day Saint Biographical Encyclopedia: A Compilation of Biographical Sketches of Prominent Men and Women in The Church of Jesus Christ of Latter-day Saints.* 4 vols. Salt Lake City: Andrew Jenson History Company, 1901.

Lyman, Albert R. *History of San Juan County 1879–1917.* Privately printed, 1919.

Lyman, Albert R. *Indians and Outlaws: Settling of the San Juan Frontier.* Salt Lake City: Bookcraft, 1962.

Miller, David E. *Hole in the Rock: An Epic in the Colonization of the Great American West.* Salt Lake City: University of Utah Press, 1966.

Perkins, Cornelia Adams, Marian Gardner Nielson,, and Lenora Butt Jones. *Saga of the San Juan.* San Juan County Daughters of Utah Pioneers, 1968.

Young, Norma Perkins. *Anchored Lariats on the San Juan Frontier.* Provo, UT: Community Press, 1985.

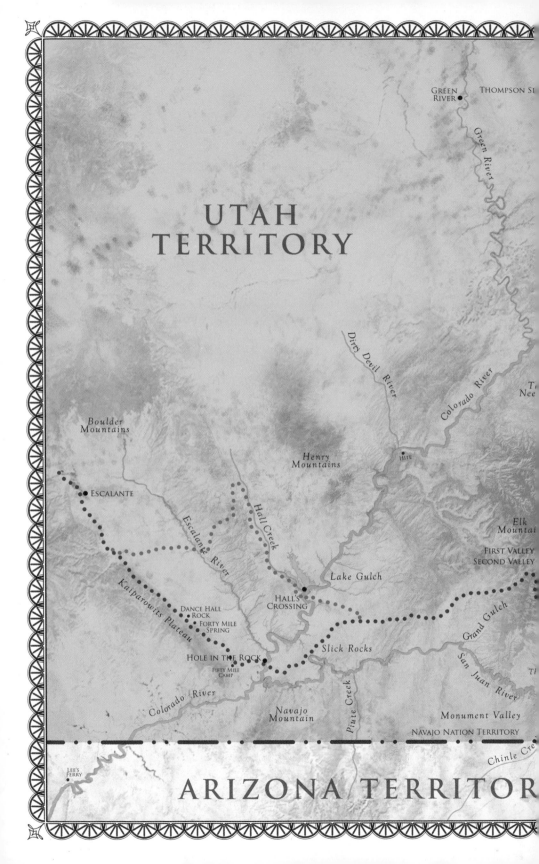